I0586948

Guitars & Cadillacs

From the SoundMaster Romance Series

Sabine Keevil

Please leave a review

Playlist for the music from Guitars & Cadillacs
https://open.spotify.com/playlist/71ymCTx5YJP
zroWBg4gWHF?si=6ba9447454a64aa7

A Thinking Dog Publishing Book
www.thinkingdogpublishing.com

Early Reviews - Guitars & Cadillacs

Thatscountry.com

"I read the first couple of pages, fully intending to put the book down and review it when I had more time. Needless to say, I read the whole book that day (I'm a fast reader) and I'm looking forward to the next book in the series. Guitars and Cadillacs is about a Country superstar and a radio announcer who meet on the worst of terms and chronicles how building a relationship with a public icon isn't the easiest thing to do, especially when the parties concerned have skeletons in their closet." -Marti Clayton ThatsCountry.com

Country Weekly

Guitars & Cadillacs is the entertaining story of the fire and fury stirred up by the relationship between Reanne (Parker) and fictional country superstar Colton Wright...Offering surprise twists, intrigue and mystery...Keep turning the pages to see what happens next in the well-paced plot. Pat Mandia Country Weekly, the world's #1 Selling Country Music Magazine

Publisher's Note: This is a work of fiction. Names, characters, places, incidents and dialogues are products of the author's imagination or are used fictitiously, and any resemblance to actual events or persons, living or dead, or locales is entirely coincidental.

GUITARS & CADILLACS
Published by Thinking Dog Publishing, a division of
2214098 Ontario Ltd.
Oakville, Ontario, Canada

Copyright © Sabine Keevil 2002
ISBN, Standard ed.: 978-0-9878580-4-7

FOREVER LOVE, by Deanna Bryant, Liz Hengber, Sunny Russ
© 1998 WB Music Corp. (ASCAP), Glen Nikki Music (ASCAP),
Warner-Tamerlane Publishing Corp. (BMI) & Missoula Music
(BMI)
All Rights o/b/o Glen Nikki Music administered by WB Music Corp.
All Rights o/b/o Missoula Music administered by Warner-
Tamerlane Publishing Corp.
All Rights Reserved   Used by Permission
WARNER BROS. PUBLICATIONS U.S. INC., Miami, FL. 33014

Published in Canada

ALL RIGHTS RESERVED
No part of this publication may be reproduced, stored in a retrieval system, or transmitted, in any form or by any means—electronic, mechanical, photocopying, recording, or otherwise—without prior written permission.

For information:
THINKING DOG PUBLSIHING
info@thinkingdogpublishing.com

CHAPTER ONE

"COL-TON, COL-TON"

Fifty thousand voices screaming—the sound was almost deafening, even backstage. Only a few minutes now and they would give him the signal to step out in front of the fully packed arena.

Oblivious to the security people by his side and the backstage personnel hurrying by, feeling completely alone, he stood in the chilly, barren corridor leading to the stage, waiting for his cue to go on.

It was hard to tell who was more anxious to see the stage lights come up, the crowd, waiting to see him, or Colton himself, waiting to get out there and just let 'er rip'. As always just before a big concert, he was nervous and tight-lipped. These last few minutes were the worst, waiting to just get out there and start singing.

Nervously he paced the small expanse of the corridor, irritating his security guards in their identical red and black satin shirts, black Stetson hats and black cowboy boots. Unfortunately they had become a necessity of late, what with the threats he sometimes got—some serious, some just from wild fans who wanted a piece of anything that was his. He rubbed his hands up and down the legs of his jeans and studied his reflection in the shiny glass of a display case on the wall.

His stage outfit was relatively simple, having been worked at and refined by so many image consultants and now, finally, getting back to the same type of clothes he had been wearing since he first stepped onto a stage, Levis so tight it was hard to even stand up in them, a rhinestone studded, black tuxedo jacket, and the ubiquitous Stetson and boots. Of the hats, he had several in reserve as he had a habit of throwing them into the crowd at various points during his act.

They had come to see him, Colton, *Mr. Right,* Wright. *Mr. Right* to the ladies who comprised about eighty percent of his fans and who became dreamy eyed over his pictures all around the country. One day it had gone beyond the music, and Colton Wright had become an image, the mysterious stranger of so many dreams, epitomized by a smoldering stare out of a glossy eight by ten.

The crew exited the stage and Colton readied himself. He could still hear the cheers. "Col-ton, Col-ton, Col-ton", and smiled to himself, adjusted his hat and put himself silently into that mental space that said, *Showtime.*

"Showtime," he said out loud, gave his lead guitarist a high five and stepped onto the platform that would lift him through a cloud of smoke onto the stage. His opening special effects were as legendary as he was, and often copied. For a kid who had started with one beat up Sunburst guitar and a used amp, he had come a long way, now employing an army of special effects technicians and stage designers.

The lights went down and the voice of his road manager echoed over the cheers of the crowd. "Ladies and gentlemen, would you welcome to the stage, straight out of Nashville, Tennessee…SoundMaster recording artist…our very own…Mr. Colton Wriiiight!"

The stage platform came up, the smoke billowed and the noise hit him like a tornado at full gale force, fifty thousand fans on their feet, screaming.

"Helloooooo Nashville! How y'all doing tonight?"

The cheers became deafening.

"I thought I'd come down here, do a few songs from my new album, if that's all right. Let's see how y'all like it."

He slung his guitar in front of him, pointed a finger at his band and leapt right into it.

> "I know I'm just a simple man,
> Don't use a lot of fancy words.
> But when the day's work is done,
> I come alive at the Honky Tonk.
> My truck, my boots, my Stetson hat,
> Everything I ever had,
> My Honky Tonk Hardware, my Honky Tonk Hardware."

The beat of the drums made the floor vibrate. He raised his hands and began clapping in huge sweeping gestures. "Hey!" he screamed, and on the next turn fifty thousand people in the audience had picked up the rhythm and clapped right along with him.

"Hey!" they screamed right back at him. Frank on electric guitar and Tony on fiddle fell into the rhythm of the song.

"Hey!" By this time he owned them. A sea of fifty thousand faces, every man and woman on their feet.

This was what they had come for and he would give them everything he had. He owned them for this night, for the next few hours.

"Col-ton, Col-ton, Col-ton!" They screamed his name. He reached out as if he could touch each and every one of them. The melody, the rhythm started taking over his heart and soul, his entire self now, he lived every note and he wanted them to feel the same way. He stepped to the edge of the stage spreading his arms wide. They were singing right along with him by now. Arms reached out, clutched at his boots, his legs, just to touch a part of him, of the legend. He reached down to grasp reaching hands, eliciting more screams, more excitement.

Oh yeah, this was it, they were his now, he'd make them forget their worries and their lives for a few hours and let the music take them away as it took him in a rush of rhythm and drumbeats and breathless guitar riffs.

With a final "Hey!" he reached high for the bank of spotlights above him and gave himself over to the power of his songs pulling along an audience of fifty thousand. They stood on the chairs for the fast, rocking numbers, they danced in the aisles, they pulled out their Bic lighters and illuminated the arena for his slow ballads, and the more they got into his songs, into his music, the more Colton came alive on that stage. And they sang along, swaying and waving, beating him to the words of his own songs sometimes. They knew them by heart—just as well as he did.

And just when they thought there was nothing new he could come up with, he would throw in stunts that got crazier by the minute. He covered the stage, dancing from one end to the other, never standing still for longer than a few seconds, dancing, running and jumping like the devil himself. There was very little choreography, he let the energy flow from the audience to him and back to the audience again. He shot cannons of confetti at the crowd and stood in circles of fire and smoke. He climbed the rigging, sang sitting in the rafters and running down the aisles in the midst of his fans.

There was nothing he couldn't do and nowhere he couldn't go tonight. He felt like a king on that stage holding a court of thousands. When he was singing, when he had a crowd screaming at him, he was invincible, he could do anything, be anything, he was no longer just a man, just a singer, he reigned supreme, he was indestructible. The *Feeling*—yes the *Feeling* had come back into him tonight.

The more the crowd was into it the more it made anything he was doing feel right. Few of his stunts were planned, set up. He just went out there and winged it—felt it, did whatever came to mind, to the point that sometimes he got in the way of his own band, or waded out into the audience if that's what felt right just about then. His security people called it a nightmare, but anyone who had ever attended a Colton Wright concert came away believing they had seen a once in a lifetime event. And most assuredly they had.

"And we are live in $3 - 2 - 1$..."

The 'on air' light above her head turned red and Reanne moved closer to the microphone and smiled at it. She always did that, certain that her attitude would come through over the airwaves.

"And welcome back to KSOM Radio, you're with Reanne Parker and the Early Morning Show. And what a morning it is, 78 degrees outside our studio windows and the sun is just a-smiling down on us. So let's start the day out on the right foot. I've got a great lineup of songs here. Give me a call if there's something special you'd like to hear, if you want to say hi to someone or if you just want to talk to us. Here we go, let's get the day off to a good start with Garth Brooks!"

Carefully she hit the button on her console that would bring the music up—it wouldn't do to get that one wrong, again—and turned the swinging microphone away. Yet another switch activated the intercom.

"Where on earth is Jack?" she asked of her sound engineer. "Seems to me my dear co-host is leaving pretty much everything to me...again".

Alan gave her an exaggerated shrug from behind the soundproofed glass of the engineering booth. "Jack's never been a guy to get up before the sun darlin'. How he ever ended up with the early morning gig is beyond me. You got three minutes of music left—notes are on your desk."

Reanne thumbed the headphones back into place and sorted through the notes for this morning's show. Weather, traffic, business news, more traffic, more weather, that was all she had...b o r i n g.

How was she supposed to put together a show out of this—without the aid of a co-host, or even a listener calling with a dedication, a joke...anything. Right about now even a lame joke would do, at least give her something to talk about at six a.m. on a Wednesday morning without putting folks to sleep. How about a nice little crime somewhere she could mention, at least a misdemeanor. In all her years of listening to radio, it had never occurred to her to pay attention to the content, the flow of the show and, even now, under Jack's careful tutelage there were moments when she just hit a wall. When she was stuck for something to say or do that would keep her listeners from touching that dial. And keeping those listeners, that's what it was all about. She was just hoping and praying she would not lose too many before she acquired Jack's casual ease at the microphone. 'You either sink or swim,' was one of his favorite lines. Unfortunately, right now she was in serious need of a life preserver.

"Come on Jack," she muttered under her breath, eyes on the digital clock on the wall. For all his faults Jack had this ability to make even traffic sound entertaining if he wanted to. In his opinion, however, his hours were at best flexible. And KSOM could not afford to even threaten to fire him. He was one of Nashville's most popular DJs. As the story went, when Jack had switched from his old station to KSOM he brought most of his listeners with him. Because of that the old station had changed their format to hard rock. Well, that was his version of the story anyway and, all things considered, Reanne could count herself fortunate to be training under him, especially with her own checkered career history. KSOM and Jack Daniels were a plum job assignment, but...

I am grateful for this job, she repeated like a mantra to try and stop her mind from going back onto that particular train of thought. It was useless and painful to worry about the things that might have been. *I am grateful for this job, and things are looking up*.

After her disastrous attempt to make it as a performer in the music business—*Stop it! Stop it, stop feeling sorry for yourself!*

But the thought didn't stop and it didn't stop the feeling that it should be her record being announced next, that she should be preparing for an interview with some hapless radio DJ...if she hadn't blown her one big chance at a live performance...

Alan caught her eye with a hand signal. *Coming up on traffic time and weather in five...*

The seat beside Reanne exploded with movement as Jack slid into it.

"Well a top o' the morning to you Nashville, it's 6:05 in the a.m. and this is Jack Daniels telling you where you're going to be stuck in traffic this morning, and you will be stuck, if you aren't already. Grab the cell phones folks, call in late cause it's a doozie out there. One of our typical Nashville mornings that is. Hey, what can you do. Sit back, relax, listen to us. More on this and the local weather when we come back with Jack and Reanne in the morning."

Effortlessly his stubby fingers flew over the buttons keying up a commercial break. Reanne felt a momentary stab of envy. His apparent ease on air, confidence and assurance around the most sophisticated equipment, anywhere really, almost to the point of arrogance...perhaps if she could stick it out with this job for a while, perhaps then she could have a portion of that. And just a portion would make her grateful.

"Mornin' Doll," he drawled, grinning and raising a quick eyebrow at the misery in her face. "Anythin' happen before I got here?"

She flicked a finger at their notes, scattering them towards him. "Nothing worth mentioning in here, unless you can get some more mileage out of the fact that Colton Wright is in town, and I talked that single fact to death yesterday. Any more to the rumors that he might do an interview with us?"

"Ah, *Mr. Right*, the dream of thousands of ladies, he's in town again as of yesterday, isn't he? His nationwide tour is finished. Well, if we do get him for an interview, get ready. That'll be one of your finest moments yet. You can draw the charm right out of him. He'll just absolutely adore you my dear Reanne."

"Me? Interview Colton Wright? Surely you jest kind sir. Jack I couldn't do nearly as good a job as you. I still screw up the buttons around here if I don't concentrate every second. Naw, I'd prefer to just watch while you do something brilliant."

"Hello…, this is *Mr. Right* we're talking about. There's no way I can do it, Babe! A guy talking to Mr. Sexy? The country music gods would have my scalp. Honey you'll be fabulous. Anyway, you'll have plenty of time to practice before then, if we do get one. And if you get totally stuck, drop a hint or two on how you used to be a singer and the story that goes with that, you'll have him eating out of your hand."

Reanne winced. In a weak moment she had told Jack a few bits and pieces of her singer/songwriter past. Not enough for him to piece the whole story together—but enough for him to know that there was more to it than she had let on.

"Yeah right Jack. I never even got close to his level. He's a Superstar times ten. Three platinum albums, fifteen singles that went to number one, not a single concert in the last two years that wasn't sold out within hours of going on sale…Colton Wright would see me as an amateur, Jack, a bad one at that."

Jack just waved his hand. "You're my student, you'll not only do well, you'll glow. Now…" He put down his coffee cup and pulled up the microphone, the discussion was over, it was as if he had a switch on him somewhere, he could go from chatting with you to 'on-air' in two seconds flat.

"Well set the UV index to bust folks, its going to be hot hot hot all day. Mind you, not as hot as it is here in the studio with Jack and his puuuurty lil' assistant Reanne…"

"Don't listen to him people, he's overdone the donuts this morning."

"Woo-ho and the sassy little mouth she's got on her. Well Reanne my dear what do you think of the stories that are circulating now that *Mr. Right*, Colton Wright, is back here in town this week. Does that give you some wonderful dreams?"

"Well, Jack they say he's one of the most talented country singers of our time and he certainly has a string of number one records to prove it, but as a woman I've got to tell you one thing—there is no one in this business who wears a pair of tight blue jeans quite like Colton Wright. He is dee-licious. Mm-hm."

"I am so hurt Reanne, that you would pick a pretty boy like *Mr. Right* over good ol' Jack—my heart is breaking."

"Well Jack, you'll get over it all two hundred pounds of you. But until you do, here is the Man himself, *Mr. Right* and his latest single *It's Always Been You.*"

Jack keyed up the next music segment and pushed his microphone away.

"Ya see, you can do it if you put your mind to it. Now hold the fort here, will you. I'll be in Rod's office in conference for a while."

Rod Steele was their station manager and, somehow, Reanne suspected Jack was giving him an update on how she, the newcomer, was doing. From the way he acted Jack was happy with how she had settled in and there was nothing she had to worry about. Her performance reviews kept getting better as time wore on. It was really her own inner critic she had to silence, especially in the dark moments, when she was alone and allowed herself to think about such things. That was when she wondered and worried, when she asked herself if she was truly happy with this new career, if she had found something she truly loved, '*Your soul's work*' as Oprah would call it. The thing with radio was, you didn't really get an immediate feedback from your public. Yeah, if your ratings are telling you you're losing listeners, then something is wrong. Or if a disproportionate number of people are calling in and calling you distinctly unflattering names, then you know you have to do something. Until then, peer review or the sometimes jaded opinions of your friends are really all you had to go on.

Reanne sighed and tried to remember which one of the buttons in front of her would cue up the commercial track and not a loud whistle, a dog bark or a giant explosion, all of which she had set off by mistake at various times. In every case Jack, and probably a large number of listeners too, had been laughing until their eyes watered but Reanne had not been amused.

"Give yourself a break," Jack would say. "You haven't been here all that long." Which was true even if it didn't help much. A few months ago, when she was desperately looking for a job, any job, she had applied as a receptionist with KSOM. Jack had by chance been in the lobby when she dropped off her resume.

"Hey you've got a beautiful voice, did you ever think about being on radio?" he had asked and to this day he wouldn't admit to whether it was a pick-up line or the truth. And that, as they say, was that. How a career was born. Things had just kind of worked out without any major participation on her part, and now here she was, the on-air co-host of the 'Jack and Reanne in the Morning' show.

I am grateful, she thought. Grateful not to be washing dishes or cleaning floors or any of the other menial job she had been ready to tackle to keep the rent money coming in. This thing had all of sudden turned into a career but she still wasn't too sure if it was truly the one she wanted. A year ago she would have said no, the only career she was interested in was one that involved her standing on a stage entertaining large audiences. Now, however...

Nevertheless, no matter how things turned out, she was determined to do the best job she could, while trying to figure out if her dreams of being a singer belonged on the shelf permanently.

Working the morning show had its own problems if you were single. A lot of folks preferred it because it meant you were home by maybe two in the afternoon with lots of time to spend with your family and friends. To Reanne it meant she was home by maybe two in the afternoon with too much time on her hands to think. She didn't know that many people in Nashville yet, none of them close enough to be called friends. Calling home was out of the question for its own set of reasons, and so Reanne had taken to long solitary walks. She learned to navigate Nashville on foot in a hurry, always listening to loud music through her ear buds.

It was late that night when a bout of insomnia drove her out of her apartment again and into the streets. Jack's hints at a solo interview with Colton Wright and his unshakable belief in her abilities had brought up the old doubts again. Thoughts of her messed up career in music and her odd rise to where she was now in the radio business, and they had not left her alone all day. And, really, it was mostly the memories that haunted her, memories and thoughts of what could have been, might have been, if she just had been a tiny bit more courageous. Mostly, her thoughts seemed to start with, *if I had only*. Once that train of thought got a hold of her, it usually would not let go. There was nothing to do but grab a coat and her music, and head out for a long, exhausting walk, in the hopes of tiring herself out so much that she would come back to the apartment, slip into bed and fall asleep.

Since she had come to Nashville ten months ago she really hadn't made many new friends, whatever acquaintances she had made in the music business had disappeared in a hurry after the 'big disaster,' as if she was carrying something contagious and they might catch it if they hung around her. The radio business didn't really lend itself to making lots of friends either, mostly it was you and a microphone and what you hoped were large numbers of listeners glued to their radios in rapt attention. No, as a place for a social life it sucked. There was Jack of course, he seemed to have formed an odd attachment to her as if at his age he had finally realized that he would never have a daughter and he had taken her under his wing. Or, perhaps more simply, they were just two lonely people.

Reanne headed through Riverfront Park and down the familiar road to the Cumberland River. During the day this area would have been humming with people. Sightseers enjoying the park or taking one of the riverboat cruises and locals who liked to take their lunch on one of the benches scattered throughout.

Riverfront Park was a good spot to get lost in during the day, just follow the crowds. But now, at night, the paths were deserted, locals and visitors alike having decamped to the more popular nightclubs and bars of downtown Nashville. Reanne wasn't really afraid of walking alone at night, she had done it many times and the thought of her own safety had never crossed her mind.

Slowly she kept turning up the volume on her phone to keep the loneliness at bay. It didn't truly matter what was playing, anything fast with a beat to it would do and she just kept turning it up hoping it would drown out her own racing mind and the press of memories. Memories, doubts and, sometimes, tears.

Sometimes, like tonight, she would walk so far, so fast, she would lose track of her immediate surroundings and she would have to stop and check for major landmarks before turning and finding her way back again. Oh yeah, you could get lost in this city, easily, but the one thing you couldn't do was outrun your past, lose some of the sad memories along the track, they had a way of sticking with you.

Still, like a barely healed wound that one can't resist picking at, she let her mind return to the very same thought almost every day. *If only—If only...* She clung to those ifs in her life hoping that one day she would be able to take out the memories of that very best, very wonderful but very short moment of her life and enjoy them without feeling the pain. That glorious moment when all her hopes and dreams for the future, her deepest and fondest wishes seemed to have come true...for one instant, only to be snatched away again almost immediately.

Reanne picked up her pace; trying to walk away from the memory...faster, faster, follow the beat. The road down to the river followed a hill, winding and curving to the bottom, where it followed the riverbank. From the top of the hill she could see the dark band of the river winding away. Here and there reflected streetlights glittered on the surface, as if someone had spilled a bag of diamonds there. Diamonds. *"Diamond West,"* Reanne said quietly as if tasting her erstwhile stage name on her lips. Diamond West—that was me, she thought, for about thirty seconds—and then....

Don't think about it, don't think Unfortunately her stubborn mind refused the silent command.

Up ahead a piece of orange construction fencing surrounded a hole, most likely one of the city's many notorious potholes being worked on.

Reanne, with her music leaving her oblivious to her surroundings and half of her mind persistently gnawing on one single subject while the other half tried to ignore that same thought, turned to pass the fence on the left. She didn't hear the car coming up behind her, never realized that she was in any danger...until it was too late.

Chapter Two

Two hours earlier.

"For the last time...mind your own business," Colton Wright growled, pointing the microphone at his friend Mike who was casually leaning over his keyboard. "Let's call it a day for this rehearsal, I can't concentrate on the music with all this going on."

He replaced the microphone in its stand, suspiciously eyeing Mike who wiped some imaginary speck of dust off the gleaming keys of his synthesizer and remained silent, one eyebrow raised. Mike had the good sense to keep quiet, knowing that he was the one who had brought up *The Subject* and as such he would take the shit for distracting Colton, but certain things needed saying and this was one of them.

Colton glared back, waiting for him to say something else and, when nothing was forthcoming, started to busy himself with the miles of cable needing to be rolled up and put away.

"All right, all right," he said finally. "I know you mean well Mike, but I wish you and Ken would just stay out of my personal life. Stop trying to fix me up with some bimbo for the sake of a few tabloid pictures and the great '*Colton Wright Image*'. I'm getting a bit tired of the whole Big Stud, *Mr. Right* thing anyway. I wish we'd never invented it, no matter how good it's been for sales."

"It's not like that Cole, what we're trying to do…"

"What you're trying to do is keep alive this image you've created for me, but it's not working for me any more, can't I get that through your heads? Ken?"

Ken shrugged. "On a personal level, sure Cole. Maybe I'd also feel a little uncomfortable having all those women swooning over me," turning quickly and glaring when he heard a snorting noise from Mike's direction. "I said maybe, but as your manager, I have to tell you that what you call, *this image thing,* has made you a star. It's making you obscene amounts of money. You know that an awful lot of your fans are women. They like to idolize you and think of you as *Mr. Right.* There are thousands of ladies' bedrooms and exercise rooms around the world with your picture on the wall. Have you checked your website lately? They're in love with you, and as long as they are, they'll keep buying your albums."

"I'd rather they bought the albums because they liked our music. The image, the clothes, the pictures—it's all part of the delivery—of our music and of my ideas, I understand all that. Look, Ken, I don't insist on shooting myself in the foot, keep the myth alive if you have to, all I'm saying is, don't make me date any more brainless blondes for the sake of a photo op."

"But what...?"

"No more actresses either, no more super models, no more beauty queens, capisce? Other than that, I don't care what you do. That's why I hired you, to manage, now go manage; manage to get me out of all these set up dates.

You should have been there last night, hours of boredom that made raking leaves seem like a thrill ride— no more."

He carefully laid the roll of cable he'd been mangling through his hands down on the floor and stared at it for a moment. "I've got to go. If nobody needs me anymore—I'm out of here. I've got to air out my head. Last night's date fiasco made my brain go numb. For all of our sakes, I hope *Star Insight* got some good pictures."

He jammed a battered Stetson onto his head and swung his denim jacket over his shoulder. "You know where to find me if you need me," stomping out of the rehearsal studio.

"Ain't it hard to be one of Americas most eligible bachelors," Mike quipped.

"You know," Ken said to no one in particular as the soundproof door swung shut behind Colton, "There goes what thousands of women's dreams are made of. Sometimes even I don't get him. I would've thought ten years after the divorce would be long enough for him to snap out of it, but you get anyone of the female persuasion close to him, he clams up tighter 'n a walnut."

The rest of the band members were quietly busying themselves with equipment. An answer was neither required nor recommended. Mike had been with Colton's band from the very early days and Ken had been his manager longer than that. They could allow themselves liberties that would have gotten the others into a heap of trouble. Like, for example, asking how last night's dates went, one of the many Ken was in the habit of setting up with beautiful and eligible ladies. Colton would usually go along for the sake of the publicity but asking how it went, well that was considered, *The Subject* and, depending on how the night had actually gone, could get you yelled at, laughed at or a simple eye rolling. Colton was never in a good mood the day after, that much was certain.

Mike finally raised his trademark eyebrow and replied. "For you ten years might be long enough maybe, for me—sure. But Colton—his first wife tore out his heart and left it for buzzard bait. That whole *Mr. Right* myth we built around him—it attracts women by the score, no doubt. But maybe by now even we should have learned that it's not going to work. There is no way, and I mean absolutely no way, that he will ever let anyone near his heart again, not even a little. That boy has learned his lesson good."

"It's not like I'm selling him into slavery, you know. If I leave him to his own devices he's going to sit in that studio of his days on end, writing songs." Ken usually prided himself as an excellent judge of the female character and to have struck out again at trying to find the right one for his client and friend bothered him more than he was willing to admit.

"And then we'd have hundreds of Colton Wright songs. The bad thing about that being…"

"Mike…!"

"Alright, alright, I guess I'm wrong then."

Out in the parking lot Colton threw his denim jacket and guitar case into the back seat and walked around the car, his pride and joy, a 1961 red and white Cadillac Fleetwood. This car, more than anything, reminded him of his early days in the music business, the innocence, the enthusiasm. He remembered the day he had walked into the dealership on Fifth Ave, a fistful of cash in his pocket, intending to purchase the classic Cadillac he had been eyeing through the windows for months. It was the kind of car he thought his father might have driven and he bought it the day he signed his first recording contract. A signal to himself, with perhaps a little nod to his father, that he had finally made it, that he was on the way and that great and wonderful things were headed his way.

Since then he had spent many an hour driving around aimlessly, asking himself how he had got this lucky, why he got to be the star and the next guy didn't. Was it any kind of magic he possessed? Ultimately, and secretly, he'd had to admit it to himself that the answer had very little to do with his own brilliance and greatness. He'd been in the right place at the right time, with the right team around him, and he had just enough talent to be able to capitalize on that twist of fate.

The habit of driving around in the old caddy when he had to work something out in his mind had stuck with him, though. He'd get into the car and remember how it had all started, how it had felt at the beginning. Some of the best ideas for his songs had been jotted down on the ragged notepad he kept on the passenger seat for that purpose, in handwriting barely legible because he was going so fast as he wrote it. There was always a guitar in the backseat and he had developed a knack for ignoring the passersby who stared at the guy parked by the side of the road strumming a particular chord mix on a guitar memorizing it for later.

Today felt like a driving around day. He slid into the driver's seat and turned the key, listening to the old caddy respond with a satisfying roar. The radio was tuned to a country station and he fiddled with it until loud rock blasted at him from the new eight speaker system he'd had installed, the loudspeakers cleverly hidden in the old wood grain paneling. If today was for driving around then it also required good old rock & roll.

He listened to country when he wanted to compare his songwriting to that of others, or find out what was new, he listened to classical music when he was composing so as not to contaminate his own sound, and he listened to rock when he was aimlessly driving around in his car.

He steered the powerful car out of the parking lot and down the hill toward River road, watching the accelerator needle climbing steadily. Colton enjoyed the feel of the powerful engine at his command, its power barely contained as he steered onto the tight winding turns of River Road. And still he was accelerating, spending his anger, his impotent fury. Her face seemed to be taunting him from the highway signs or in the reflection of the streetlights in puddles on the road.

Oh yes, he was still angry at the woman who had shown him a hundred new ways to be cruel, only to turn away when someone else, someone more exciting, captured her interest, and ten years hadn't even started to dim that anger. Something was sure to remind him of it every day. He was also angry at the manager who had created the *Mr. Right* image the public currently snapped up like so many gold coins, ensuring that he couldn't even go out into public anymore without being mobbed by scores of crazed women. Any one of them would sell her soul if he so much as crooked his little finger at her. They had crowned him the new King of Country Music.

Mr. Right—*Right For You*—was one of Ken's slogans in their promotions. The record label was deliriously happy with the image and its results, after all, sex sold. And yet the image they had created, the face they were presenting to the public, could not be further from the truth. Colton considered himself an intensely private person. He would rather have root canal without the aid of an anesthetic than give an interview or talk about his private life.

These days he opened and read his fan mail only on rare occasions, another one of the joys of a successful music career, but the letters from his female fans that referred to his sexy strut, his seductive moves, his mesmerizing stare…he was quickly embarrassed at best, shocked and dismayed at worst, by what some of them offered to do for and to him. He realized that they didn't know the real Colton, that they were writing to the image his agent had created, but still the letters bothered him. None of them could see past the surface, to the broken heart, the shattered confidence and yes—the wounded pride—and that was just the way he liked it. Some things should be worked out alone, in the privacy of a classic car.

If his fans knew the real Colton, he figured, their idol, *Mr. Right,* would topple very quickly. So amongst all his other talents he had developed the art of acting, acting as if he really was the *Mr. Right* they expected. How ironic, that the one man who probably received on average a dozen proposals every week, by mail, email and in person, had vowed a long time ago to keep his heart in a safe place under lock and key and to never, never, ever let anyone near it again.

He had his music. How often had he heard other musicians refer to their music as their mistress, their lover?

He had his music and his audiences and they would always be there for him, love him, and never let him down.

All of this had happened such a long time ago. By now, he had expected some of the hurt to fade, perhaps to meet someone who could make him forget, but every time he dated someone, every time Ken or one of the guys in the band set him up with someone, he could see that they expected a date with *Mr. Right*. Colton Wright, the real Colton Wright, the one who worried and wondered, the one who said the wrong thing sometimes, or did something decidedly unglamorous—he simply would not do. He would disappoint those who caught a glimpse of him and so, while *Mr. Right* gathered the accolades and cheers, Colton Wright drove around in his Caddy, driving his anger, his disappointment, and her, out of his mind.

Colton unwound as the car shifted smoothly through the gears, the thump of the music, the growl of the engine finally soothing some of his jangled nerves and letting him pull a thin and uneasy film of peace over the heartache, sure to be pierced again.

He was well out of the city now, and left and right of the River Road the towering pines threw dark shadows as behind him the skyline softened slowly. Realizing just how far he had come, Colton pulled over to the side, watching Nashville prepare for the coming night. In any of a dozen clubs tonight his songs would be requested and played countless times. Autographed keepsakes he gave away to some of the larger clubs as a way of promotion would be traded for top dollar and the story of his success would be traded behind hands in hushed voices. Country music was the very life blood of Nashville and so were the stories of the lives that were inevitably linked to that music.

There were as many stories of how he came to be *Mr. Right* as there were ambitious, creative folks in Nashville. The truth was far more simple and definitely much less interesting.

He had made and written music for as long as he could remember. He had pictures of himself carrying a guitar when he was a small boy, barely as tall as the instrument itself. His childhood had not been an easy one and music had become his way of communicating early on. He never knew his father, and his mother had spent most of her waking hours at one of her three jobs trying to provide for herself and her three children. She was always proud of him, no matter what he did. His perfectionism, his constant desire to be the best at whatever he was involved in, he traced back to her. She had given him all she could, mostly an unconditional love and security, and the knowledge that no matter what happened, he would always be loved, and that made him want to be the best in every area of his life.

Colton had done okay in school. Higher education, though, didn't hold a lure for him as soon as he figured out that his guitar was more than an instrument, his music more than songs. He found that there were things he could not put into words that came easily in a song, there were emotions and moments in life he could capture and preserve perfectly there. From that start it had been a straight line to singing in some of the night clubs around town, sometimes getting up in the middle of the night to play after last call, because he wasn't yet old enough to be in a licensed establishment. And still his mother was there for him, driving him to his various gigs, waiting around until he finished his last set to drive him home again. Then after school he found work as a busboy in a hotel in town and, sometimes, when it wasn't too busy the owner would let him play for the late night crowd.

Colton had played a lot of the popular stuff, Elvis, the Beatles, the Stones, Jimmy Buffett, whatever struck his fancy and seemed popular with the crowd. Sometimes he would try to sneak one of his own songs in and he would catch hell for it because they didn't seem to be what the patrons wanted to hear. A few years later he hooked up with a few guys in the same position as he was. They were all musicians and they kept on meeting at the dingy places they all played. Pooling their talents they formed a band, called themselves the *Blonde Strangers* and actually started to make a meager living out of playing the clubs late at night.

Colton knew he wanted more, he wanted to write and play his own songs, and he wanted the people to recognize him. There was a power he gained from an audience that was having a good time, that was in tune with him and the band. Performing was almost intoxicating to him. The more the people enjoyed it, the more he got out of it too. He started playing to the crowds, finding out what they would most go for that night, and giving it to them. His stage antics grew bolder and bolder, running around on the stage, throwing his hat into the crowd, getting the audience to sing and scream with him on a particular song—he knew this was what he was born for.

A few years later he finally made the decision to move to Nashville. Not for any other reason than that Nashville and country music seemed to be more open to new artists than rock and pop. Someone in an audience had told him that one night, and to this day he didn't know if they knew what they were talking about or not, but a week later he had packed everything he owned into a battered Chevrolet and set out for Nashville.

He arrived broke, tired and dirty, and got turned down for every job he applied for in his first week. Just when he was ready to sleep one more day in his car then quit and go home, he landed a job as a dishwasher in a dingy little hole in the wall by night, and then another selling shoes during the day.

He felt he had arrived.

Bit by bit he started picking up gigs in tiny little clubs and holes-in-the wall and again there was the power jolt he got from performing in front of a live audience. It was like a fix to him, nothing could compare to it. He gave the audiences what they wanted and they gave him the applause he needed in return. It was recognition, it was appreciation, it was his life, his proof that even a shy guy from the backwaters of Ohio could make it.

And he loved the feeling of coming together with the crowd, when he could pull them along and stir up feelings in them. His reviews were getting better and better and suddenly people started to come to see him specifically.

There are literally thousands of hopefuls coming to Nashville every year, hoping for their big break, hoping against hope that one night one record producer or manager will sit in the audience and discover them. Only a very rare handful ever makes it further than this.

Colton realized that a lot of hard work went into a truly stellar career and he was willing to do it, to follow all the necessary steps one by one. He revived the *Blonde Strangers* and made them all stick to a regular practice schedule. He realized that they needed an agent if they were going to get anywhere with the record companies so he hooked up with Ken Taylor, a young fellow who was trying to make a name for himself, just as Colton was. He wasn't famous and he didn't have all the connections someone more established would have, but he could afford him. They spent a lot of hard earned money and time on an excellent demo tape, which they both carried wherever they went. Whenever he wasn't working, he and his agent made the rounds of record producers and major label heads begging for a chance to audition. Their basic reception was always the same, 'Don't call us, we'll call you.'

Again Colton was almost ready to give up, to go home and admit defeat but, a few months earlier, fate had put a young record label executive in his way on the # 5 highway at a red light. He had almost rear-ended Colton's Chevrolet, and only quick thinking on Cole's part prevented an accident. A few months later that same young man was promoted to head of the Acquisition and Repertoire department for the record label and, when a new demo tape landed on his desk, he remembered the young kid with the quick mind and lightning reaction. He hesitated as he was about to toss it into the trash pile. Something made him stop, made him want to give the kid another chance. He decided to go see Cole perform live again and, the next morning, made that fateful phone call that would start Cole's rise to stardom.

Colton had retold that story many times and he always maintained his career had happened entirely *by accident*. From then on it had been hard work, tenacity and an unshaken belief in giving the audiences what they wanted. His first album barely registered on the charts, his second did all right, but by the time he was ready to bring out his third album, the initial production was close to sold out in the first week of release. His rise to fame had been almost magical, and if it hadn't been for Amber...

Amber, even her name made his heart clench. She was what dreams were made of...a young girl he had met on one of his first dishwashing jobs. They were two kids stuck in miserable jobs waiting for their dreams to come true. While he was waiting for his big break as a singer she was waiting for hers as an actress. They had hit it off right away, two starving artists in the same situation feeding on each other's dreams, and it was only a short matter of time before they started living together. Always they promised that whoever got their big break first would pull the other one along with them.

After he signed his first recording contract, Colton arrived home with a huge bunch of flowers and an engagement ring. Two weeks later they got married, and for a time they looked like the fairy tale couple. In the weeks and months that followed Colton worked like a mule to prove the record label hadn't been wrong to place their trust in him. Amber said she was happy for him but he could never shake the feeling that she resented the fact that he had made it first. He had a suspicion something was wrong but he ignored it, hoping it would go away.

Amber knew how much he depended on the approval of his fans, his recording company, his manager—that was why he wrote his music. She knew that was what he lived for, as an actress she lived for the same thing, didn't she? So how could she resent the very foundation of their life's' work?

He got her a few jobs as a backup singer, to tide her over, give her some confidence, but after a while she turned him down, it wasn't 'her thing' Amber was a wonderful actress though, she played the part of the wife, allaying everyone's worries and suspicions, biding her time until she found something one day that would give her a leg up in the film industry.

One night Colton arrived home unexpectedly to pick up the lyrics for a song he had written, and found her sleeping with the producer of a major TV Soap Opera. He begged and pleaded for an explanation, he wanted to understand, but Amber only shrugged, the man had something to offer that she wanted. She had left that night.

Here and there he saw her picture in the tabloids. She had made it big on that soap opera: it was what she had always wanted, but that day, when she walked out, trading him in for a guy with a TV role for her, she had taken his heart with her, and he had never forgiven her for it. A year later he quietly filed for divorce, made Ken handle everything, and tried to forget the whole thing had ever happened. Had he ever even been in love with her? He figured he must have been, or the pain wouldn't be so great. Since that day he had never trusted another woman.

Cole realized by the stiffness in his legs just how long he had been standing there. What had made him think of Amber now? He tried to keep her out of his thoughts as much as possible. Oh yes, the 'dates' Ken, and his friends, Tony and Mike, always tried to set up for him. Those three believed that Colton Wright had everything in his life except a major romantic love story. They had created this image of Country Music's most eligible bachelor and arranged these dates to support the myth. And it was working. The majority of his fans were women and they adored *Mr. Right*. *Mr. Right* was right for all of them, he'd just never met anyone who came even close to being right for him.

Anyway, that was all water under the bridge now. He had effectively had put a stop to the set up dates and, if his image and record sales suffered, so be it, he'd already made enough money to buy Miami. His sixth album was ready for release and the sales would show the true fans. Those who found a measure of joy and comfort in his music, just as he did. And perhaps he should find a way to get closer to those true fans.

It was time to head back to the studio, make up with Ken and Mike and discuss plans they had for a radio station give away and contest. He folded his tall frame back into the Cadillac and started back toward the city. His mood was better now, although he knew he was still driving too fast...old habits and all that. The caddy had somehow become a symbol of him moving through life, and the rush he found from driving it fast showed no signs of abating. Smoothly he pulled around a curve and suddenly spotted a piece of orange construction fencing surrounding a pothole. About time they started fixing some of the streets around here, a guy could lose a car the size of this caddy in some of the potholes he had seen. He swerved to get around it and never noticed the dark clad figure stepping out from behind the fence at the very same moment.

Colton yanked the steering wheel around and braked. Hadn't he just remembered another near miss accident many years ago? He braked violently, finally got the heavy Cadillac stopped and jumped out instantly. Where had the pedestrian gone? He fought the sinking feeling in his stomach, scanning the roadway behind him, seeing nothing.

Reanne had stepped out from behind the fence to get around it, when a powerful set of headlights caught her in its beam. She hadn't heard anything over the din of her headphones and was more surprised than anything to see the big vehicle pass so close. The rush of air almost drew her hat off. She stepped back to avoid getting hit and got her foot tangled in the construction fencing. Arms windmilling wildly she fought to keep her balance and, as the taillights of the car rushed on, she pitched head first into the mud beside her.

She was covered in mud and furious as a cat when she finally untangled herself from the fencing, the dirt and the bits and pieces of broken asphalt. Her headphones were gone, probably lost forever. Her phone had a huge crack in it where it had struck the pavement and her new coat was looking decidedly worse for wear. She fully expected the careless driver to have taken off, but when she saw him walking towards her, she got ready to give him a huge piece of her mind, a piece he would not like at all.

"Are you all right?" a male voice called out to her. She could not really see him too well, as his face was mostly in the dark shadows and he was wearing a huge Stetson, pulled down low over his face.

"All right? All right???" her temper had her shrieking at the man. "What the heck were you thinking , barreling down this road in the middle of the night without looking. What did you think this was, NASCAR? Well the Speedway is that way, buddy and while you're at it, get a drivers license."

Colton, having got over his initial shock and worry was just glad she was alright and, apparently, unharmed, even though the lady was shaking her fists at him. Her red hair was sticking up from her head like a mop; there was mud all over her, and a faint scratch going down one cheek. In her fury she cut an almost amusing figure.

"Well your tongue and temper seem to have escaped serious injury," he said, trying to defuse the situation with a little humor. After all, nothing serious seemed to have happened. He would offer to have her clothes dry cleaned, her head phones replaced, maybe buy her a drink, and the whole thing would be forgotten. As long as she didn't go to the tabloids with a, '*Mr. Right* almost ran me down' story, everything should be fine.

"Why...I can't believe you're laughing at me, if you hadn't been driving like a madman..."

"Madman? Now hold on for just a second, if you'd been paying attention to the traffic instead of your head phones nothing would have happened, you know."

"Oh how very macho, blame it all on me why don't you. You know what, just get out of here, leave me alone, and take off, before I call the cops!" Suddenly she became all too aware that she was standing on a deserted street arguing with a stranger in the middle of the night.

"Not until I'm sure you're all right."

"I am, see!" Reanne waved her arms and legs. "Everything's still working, so you can take a hike...now."

"Come on," Colton took her lightly by the arm. "The least I can do is give you a ride into town, we're miles from anywhere."

"Let go of me, let go you, you...lunatic," Reanne screeched swatting at him ineffectively. Colton pulled his hand back as fast as he could. This situation was getting swiftly out of hand, and he had better not get involved into anything that might end up in the papers.

"Hey, I didn't mean any harm. All I was offering was a ride into town, honest."

Reanne looked up, a little shaken over the near miss, a little embarrassed over her outburst. She looked into the brightest blue eyes she had ever seen, a fine boned sensitive face showing nothing but concern. He thumbed his Stetson back from where it was riding low on his forehead and that simple movement sent a tremble up her spine. This stranger was powerfully built, long legs encased in the tightest fitting jeans she had ever seen, a loose white shirt carelessly untucked...he looked more like a romantic hero from a western movie than a dangerous night stalker, and—yet again—her temper and vivid imagination seemed to be getting her into trouble.

"Never...never mind", she stuttered suddenly tongue tied and awkward. "I'm used to walking, I do it every night as a matter of fact." Why was she telling him any of this? The fact that he was incredibly good looking only reminded her of the fact that she must look an awful fright. Never one to be called a classic beauty she tended to become frazzled quickly. With her hair in a state of constant disarray, her skin prone to blush deeply and quickly, an unkind soul had once compared her to a plump red scarecrow. At this point that description was probably sadly accurate. Why couldn't one meet incredibly good looking men while dressed in a long evening gown and made up to the nines? There ought to be a law...

"Come on, let me at least give you a ride," her handsome friend repeated and even his voice, she noticed, had a beautiful quality, like dark soft velvet. "I feel bad for not paying attention."

"Just forget it," she stuttered. "It's really nothing," she stuffed what remained of her phone in her pocket. "So long, I hope I don't see you again." She started to walk away down the footpath that led parallel to the street, quickly, lest her pounding heart gave her away.

Colton watched her walk away so fast you could almost call it running, but by the time he had reached his car, started it up again and turned around, she had disappeared into a side street and he felt it would be uncalled for to track her down. That would be crossing the line. He shook his head, this wasn't really the effect he usually had on women, come to think of it this one had looked at him without the ubiquitous "Oh my gosh, aren't you *Mr. Right*?" squeal. He readjusted his hat, although it didn't need adjusting, and shook his head again. The girl had completely shaken him out of his earlier depressed mood and shaken him up in the process, perhaps more than he cared to admit. He had known scores of women, all beautiful, all ready and willing to be and to do whatever he wanted, they were slick, polished, beautiful and perfect—

but none of them had ever spoken to him in that manner. 'Madman', indeed.

It was actually quite possible that he had not met a woman like her in a very long time. He employed an army of guards to keep the scores of admirers who fancied themselves in love with him from getting too close at his concerts. He had a staff of five reading their letters and emails, weeding out the complete weirdoes, those were kept well away from him, and he never really had a chance to meet someone in a street, at a mall, without his fame interfering.

The latest case in point, the famous setup dates he was currently fighting. Whenever his image spin-doctors set up a date with the newest hot supermodel to get his name linked with hers, he had to sit through those terminally monotone, scripted dates. There was nothing natural about them. Other guys thought of this as a dream come true, but Colton usually worked on his latest song lyrics in his head, keeping a small portion of his brain attended to the date, saying 'yes' and 'no' at the appropriate moments. It had been a long time since someone, anyone, had intrigued him such. Not since Amber anyway, and right now he would not let his thoughts return to the subject of Amber. Most certainly no woman had ever called him a madman.

He was driving slower now, back toward the city, still thinking of the mysterious girl out walking late at night, alone on a deserted road. Too bad he hadn't thought to ask her name, something about her had been most intriguing. On the other hand, with fame like his and a complete security team at constant standby there were ways for a guy to find out a girl's phone number, if he really wanted to.

"Good morning Nashville! This is Reanne Parker on the 'Jack and Reanne in the Morning' show. Well we have got a hot, hot…hot show coming up for you today, so sit tight, don't go anywhere and don't you dare move that dial. Keep it right here on KSOM Hot Country, and I've got Tim McGraw coming right at you."

Confidently she hit the switches that would bring up '35 minutes of continuous music', all programmed earlier, and turned to Jack, grinning like a proud puppy performing her latest trick. Today nothing would go wrong!

"So tell me the big news," she asked. "*Mr. Right* himself is coming in for an interview tomorrow morning? As in Wednesday? The whole building is buzzing, all the girls are primped and primed and everyone is carrying a Sharpie around for the autographs. Have you laid out the show yet? What's happening, when?"

"Whoa, slowdown a bit Reanne. Yeah he'll be here tomorrow. Don't know when he's going to show up though, darlin'. His promo department gave me 'sometime between 9 and 11.'"

"Well, at least we have a date," Reanne said sarcastically. "So what are we supposed to do, sit on our hands and wait for the big cheese?"

"Stars, darlin', stars. What we have here is nothing compared to the stunts some of the others pull. I have seen things—well never mind. Believe me, once you've been here in Nashville for a while you'll find their hats aren't the only things that are huge—egos are right up there too."

He opened a folder in front of him and Reanne was amazed that for once he was meticulously organized. "Now here's a list of topics that Colton Wright definitely considers taboo, so you're going to..."

"What? He's trying to tell us what to ask him, why doesn't he write the interview for us while he's at it?"

"Par for the course, Reanne. More like he's telling us what not to ask, because you won't get an answer and you definitely won't get another interview. You don't want to piss these guys off, you know. Now this being your first live interview, pay attention, I'm trying to show you the ropes here. His main goal is to promote his new album, right? So that's one area where you'll be able to get a lot of mileage. I've never met the man in person, but if he's like a lot of other stars, appeal to his ego, his vanity, he'll want to look good. If he has his guitar with him, and he will, ask him to play a tune, beg and plead, make the listeners think he's doing us a favor, he'll eat that up. You follow me so far?"

"Right along", Reanne said. "Pander to his macho side and we'll be fine."

"Oh, don't be like that! I told you I've never met the guy. I'm just drawing conclusions from other stars I've met. He's one of the biggest ones around, so to answer your unasked question, yes he does get away with everything, because he can. Now I'm planning to stay in the background with this interview. Colton Wright in his *Mr. Right* persona plays best to women, you know that. He oozes charm, he dresses sexy, the mysterious smile, the songs—he definitely plays at his best to women, so you'll get a far better rapport and interview with him than I would. But you have to cater to him—have to, no options, don't ask anything that won't make him look fantastic, brilliant, wonderful or all of the above. He's doing us a favor by being here."

"We're the ones playing his records, that should matter. Without radio he wouldn't be a star, you know."

"It matters, yes it does, in the beginning, but he's reached a level of fame where he can dictate to us the format of the interview, and we'll play right along. Do you know how many people we'll have tuning in tomorrow, all day, on the mere suspicion that he'll be on at some point?"

"Sure, sure, but I just...resent it...maybe...I don't know."

"It's natural, you hear the word interview, you think you get to do some sort of journalistic thing—but that's not the way it works on live radio. Colton is here to promote his album, we're giving him that promotion, at the same time the mere hint that he's visiting our station probably almost doubles our numbers, understand now?"

"Yeah, okay, I get it, sorry I'm such a rookie at this."

"That's okay, Reanne, this is your first interview, you haven't been in radio that long. It's a game and you just have to learn how to play it. Just remember, make him look good, give him lots of chances to promote his album and provide a foil—if you will—for the famous *Mr. Right* charm, and you'll do just fine."

Reanne picked up the sheet of fax paper in front of her. "Right On Communications—catchy name. Let's see what we don't want to talk about. Girlfriends, Love Life, Private Life, well...that certainly cuts out a lot doesn't it?"

She shuffled through the papers one more time, her forehead creased in an intense frown.

"Okay," she finally said to Jack, "I want to do this properly, tell me what to ask."

And for the next few hours, she listened to Jack take apart and explain the dynamics of her upcoming first interview, piece by piece.

Chapter Three

Colton and Ken sat in Cole's office going over the KSOM radio proposal.

"I'm still not so sure about this give away idea," Ken said. "I don't mind you spending time with the fans, matter of fact I think it'd be good for your image again, but are you sure we can fit them into the video the way it's set up?"

"Yeah, I think so Ken. We'll just go with it, no prompting no scripting, the way we used to do them before production companies and actors. Remember those days? I want to—no, I need to—get in touch with the fans again, the real fans, the ones who listen to my music because they get something out of it. That's the reason I want to do it this way Ken. I don't know when it happened, but somewhere around our second platinum album we stopped doing this for the sake of the music, and that's not right. Performing, that's always been my thing. Being up on that stage, hearing them scream—there's nothing like it. I don't want to end up 'doing music' strictly as a business."

"Cole, I know you love the crowds, but we've got to be concerned with your safety too. You know the types of sickos that are out there? Have you looked at some of the emails lately?"

"I think you're overreacting a bit, it's always been safe so far."

"You don't know that. Now you shouldn't be taking risks like this. Please…"

"Ken, enough. We'll be at a resort in Honolulu, a relatively contained environment, a limited number of fans, I'm sure security will always be with me. I won't go off and do anything stupid. I want to do this. Get the security guys in there even tighter if you want to, but let me do the one thing that means something to me in this business. Let me show the fans a good time."

Ken shrugged and took a few steps to his 'trophy wall.' With his forefinger he wiped an imaginary speck of dust from Colton's first platinum record in its silver frame on the wall.

"From the very beginning, I never could tell you anything where the fans or performing was concerned, could I Cole? It was always about the show for you. The moment those lights go on and you step out in front of that crowd, that's when it all happens for you isn't it?"

"I can't describe it for you Ken, but after all these years as my manager, you know that as well as anyone."

"I've always known you had no head for the business side of things, that's why I became your manager. And it's an arrangement that's done remarkably well for both of us. Cole, in all these years we've worked together we've been friends as well as partners. I want to do what's best for you for your career."

"Ken if it stops being fun, I'm going to walk away from it, but those people spend their time and their money to go see Colton Wright, to buy his albums. Maybe I feel I owe them something, beyond even the shows and the CDs. I owe them something more than a pretty face on a glossy eight by ten."

Ken lifted his hands in surrender. "Okay, let's do it. Just as long as you let me get enough security in there, we have a tight plan and we stick to it. We go in on a weekend, let everybody get to know each other. Maybe three days to shoot the video, a few more days to relax, sight-see, and then it's off back home."

"I've invited the radio station guys along for a direct broadcast."

"KSOM? You have an interview scheduled tomorrow morning, with...," he shuffled some notes on the table. "Jack and Reanne on the morning show."

"That's right, I'm planning to present it to them tomorrow, just before the interview."

"Smart move Cole, don't make me worry you'll be firing your manager any time soon."

"No such luck."

"All right then, let's get this baby off the ground. I've sent the standard promotion package over, things you don't like to be asked on air and such. That should keep the interview within reason."

"Its not reason I'm worried about. I just don't like the focus away from the music and on me, that's all. As a matter of fact, I'd like to discuss this whole image thing with you as soon as possible. I think we're going to make some changes in that area."

"Oh?"

"Don't 'oh' me Ken, you know exactly what I'm talking about. I'd like to get the focus back onto the music, on the fans on performing—and this giveaway is one step towards that."

"I won't kid you, I don't like it, but I get the feeling this has been bothering you for a while."

"I feel like there's two of me. The guy who just likes to run around on stage, sing and have a great time, raise some hell—and the other guy who's this sexy super star. The guy with the image, the one who charms all the women—to tell you the truth Ken, sometimes it's getting hard to get remember which one is which."

"All right, we'll see what we can do without ruining your career, okay?"

"You won't ruin anything Ken, my fans will still be my fans."

"Okay, okay, we'll deal with this later. Back to your radio interview. These people have their standard interview points. I think they might want to do a trivia game of sorts to pick the winners of the contest, so be prepared for that. Are you thinking of taking your guitar, do a little live set?"

"I'd like to, the stations go for that pretty much. And, since KSOM was the first station to play my songs, it would be a nice gesture."

"Hmm, maybe you can do a little nostalgia thing, play your first hit, *Always You*. They'll probably want a few minutes after the interview to tape same sound bites, 'this is Colton Wright and you're with KSOM' that type of thing, you're ok with that?"

"Just fine."

"All right then," Ken walked to the door and opened it. "That's it, you're on your own with the radio station types, so if you're ok with everything I have to run. I'll be over at SoundMaster checking on the progress of the new album so I won't be available for a while. You'll be all right?"

"Ken, I'm going home, work on some songs. As for tomorrow, it's just a radio interview, I've done a thousand of them. I'll be fine."

"Our position on the charts right now is a little precarious, Cole, there's a lot of competition. A lot of younger performers are coming out with awfully good material. Your strength is live shows, so this new album has to hit, and it has to hit hard. As for the contest and the interview, remember we want to get as much publicity mileage as we can out of this, okay?"

"The publicity is your business, Ken, as long as you let me do this, you can milk it for all it's worth. It'll be fun. I'm sure everything will be smooth as silk"

Little did he know that in all of his 35 years he had never been so wrong.

The red light above the door to Studio Five was still on, so Rod checked with the show's engineer first, then stepped into the broadcast room.

"Okay guys, new planning session, right now," he said with his usual exuberant, take-charge attitude. A huge grin split his face from side to side and that usually meant good news. "I have news from Colton Wright's management company that's going to change a few things."

Moments later they were seated in Rod's cavernous office, one of the few in the entire KSOM building that actually had any window, let alone three of them. His picture windows looked out at the bustling city of Nashville below them. Right there in the heart of Music Row was where country music lived. Here record deals were made, futures created and destroyed. It lay like a living thing below them. Reanne had been in this room only once, a few months ago when Rod had hired her and, even then, the view of the city and the various record label headquarters had taken her breath away.

She hadn't really got a good look at the office itself, she'd been too nervous to look around then. Everything was done in soothing tones of cool blue, paired with plenty of natural stone and shining chrome. One corner was taken up entirely by an L-shaped powder blue leather couch, which is where Rod asked them to sit.

Directly ahead of Reanne the wall was covered with autographed pictures of all the country music stars who had passed through this office, on their way to do an interview or to promote a record or to get the station, one way or another, to play their new song on air. Reanne's eyes passed by such greats as Patsy Cline, George Jones, Reba McEntire and, at the far end of a row, Garth Brooks. Slightly awed by the presence of such talent and fame Reanne tried to find a picture of *Mr. Right* but without getting up and walking to the far wall she was out of luck. She had seen the usual promotion shots and tabloid pictures but hadn't paid much attention at the time. He was said to be the best looking performer in country music. All the girls at the radio station were half in love with him. Carol in reception had some of his promotional shots in her cubicle. Most of them with the infamous and mysterious smile in a James Dean like pose with a guitar against a European sport car, his hat pulled down very low.

"Now then," Rod brought three dark green folders to the table each one of them emblazoned with a silver 'CW'—the Colton Wright logo.

"This is huge and it's exclusive to KSOM," Rod said, picking up a folder and tapping it on the glass in front of him. "I have here a chance for ten of our listeners to win a trip to Hawaii. All expenses paid, to attend and participate in the taping of Mr. Wright's newest music video."

"Wow," Jack and Reanne said at the same time. "When did this come in?"

"Just today, together with the interview package. Here's a list of sponsoring companies for the trip, conditions, etc. etc. The main thing is you must work this into this morning's show. What they want to do is have some sort of a trivia contest, make sure the 'true fans' win. I gather they've been working on this since the last single came out, *Paradise Found*, or some such thing about paradise. Hence the tropical location. They film in Honolulu, use our listeners as extras, get a little promotion out of it, the sponsors are happy, we're picking up listeners—everybody's getting a good deal."

"Wow, I don't know what to say. I knew we were getting a big deal with the interview but this..."

"Well hold on Jack, because it's about to get better. They want us do a live broadcast every morning from Honolulu while they're down there."

"What?" Reanne had been silent so far, stunned by the publicity machine that seemed to surround Colton Wright. "Somebody from this station gets to go with them?"

"That's right, two extra tickets for the two of you. We're getting in touch with a radio station from down there right now, you'll be getting a remote transmission booth right on the premises. Somewhere in the hotel's lobby or courtyard. Somewhere where you'll be highly visible.

We'll be doing the music feeds and the advertising and such from here. Every five minutes or so we'll cut live to you, you'll give us lots of background, local weather, sound bites from the winners, Colton if you can get him, then you read the Nashville weather and traffic just as a contrast. Our listeners will go crazy over it. And that's still not all."

"How can there be any more? What else does the guy do, adopt us?"

"Just about Jack, just about. We'll install web cams all over the pool area and the spot where your broadcast booth will be as well as the video site. Then we'll simulcast the whole thing on our website and on Wright's website. Every now and then, randomly, one of you will do a live chat on line. Since our listeners never know when or who it'll be, they'll keep on tuning in. It's cutting edge technology. Reality show on the internet and on radio. As far as I know, no one has ever done anything like this. The publicity value should be great."

"I'm speechless," Jack said. "Speechless and a little suspicious, after years of trying to avoid the limelight, why is Wright doing this now, all of a sudden? What's he getting out of it?"

"I don't know Jack, I really don't know. There are rumors that Colton Wright has withdrawn from his fans a bit too much. He, who used to say that his fans are everything to him, doesn't do a lot of publicity any more or even leave the house without security. He's become somewhat of a recluse."

"I don't blame him, Rod, guy like him? He must bring out the crazies."

"I guess that's the price he pays for being a superstar, anyway he's decided to get closer to his fans. Up close and personal so to speak. These video and live web casts are a great opportunity. He gets together with his fans but he controls the environment. Perfect. He got his start in Nashville, this station was the first one to give him an interview I gather—not that I was around back then—but he remembered, and so we get to be the lucky ones. Reanne, you've been quiet, this is going to be a huge opportunity for you, what do you think?"

"I think it's wonderful, a great opportunity. I'm just wondering…well, I'm wondering whether or not I'm experienced enough at this point to take on a responsibility like this. I also don't want to step on anyone's toes here at the station. Maybe Jack should take one of the more experienced DJs, someone who's been here longer. Don't forget I've only been doing this for a very short while."

"Jack?"

"Nonsense! You're a natural on air. True, you lack some experience, but I've been coaching and watching you for the last while. You bring something new to this station, something fresh. I don't know what to call it, but if we want to bring country music to a younger audience we have to start by using younger DJs, you know what I mean. It's even more important if we're doing the whole thing on the internet. You know I don't know a web cast from a fishing cast. And anyway, you're only a year or two younger than Colton Wright. To him I'm an old geezer, he'll relate to you, I told you that earlier."

"Earlier?" Rod asked. "You talked about the interview already, made plans?"

"I've asked Reanne to do the interview solo Rod. He's a charmer, he fascinates women and he reacts to them, I think Reanne will get ten times more out of him than I would. "

"I think you're right," Rod stood up and motioned both of them to do the same. "I have another meeting. You two have the green light for this morning's show. Set up the interview Reanne, give it some thought, check your questions against his list, we can't afford to alienate him. Then get your trivia questions together, make it interesting but not too tough. Maybe you can take qualifiers and another day Colton comes back and draws the winners. See if you can get him to go for it, we could get another live appearance out of him. I'd love to get a sound bite of his new song too, if you can get him there."

"I'll try. Even though the single isn't out yet and I remember the hoopla when someone got a hold of his last one a week ahead of the release date."

"Ah, I remember that, it was probably a publicity stunt," Rod said and waved his hand in the air. "But I like the idea of being the first station to play the single. Now, let me check with accounting and run some numbers on our remote broadcast. By the time you've done your interview, we should have a preliminary plan. You two go and write down any and all of your ideas. I want there to be a huge brainstorming session tomorrow. And you Reanne, I mean it, I think I want you to step a little more in the foreground, you have the right persona for the job. No offense, Jack."

"None taken, Rod. We'll get back to you with some outlines."

Out in the hallway, by themselves again, Reanne's knees almost buckled. An on-location broadcast, possibly her own show in the future, it was almost too much to comprehend right now. Could she have finally broken the streak of bad luck that started when she stepped out onto the stage at the Sweetwater Auditorium?

"Yes!" she said, and gave Jack a high five. "This could be my big break, Jack. I don't believe it. I take back everything I said about Colton Wright earlier. Yes, I am finally getting a break."

"You better believe it kid, you better believe it."

The next morning saw Reanne pacing the floor in the tiny broadcast room of studio five, which was in itself quite an accomplishment, because studio five was one of the smallest at KSOM.

"Where is he Alan?" she asked of her unflappable broadcast engineer. "I know he asked me to do the interview by myself, but today of all days, he could have been on time, just for the moral support. And for some questions maybe. He's doing this on purpose I know he is. I'm probably supposed to learn something here!"

Rod Steele stepped into the room, instantly crowding it with his girth if not his presence. "Where's Jack…not here yet?"

"No, and I'm going nuts, I know I agreed to do the interview solo, but Rod…"

"Relax. Colton Wright is going to be here soon. I suggest you concentrate on your interview script, take a deep breath and get ready. With or without Jack, you're flying solo today. I'm sure you'll do fine."

"I don't know Rod, I just don't know!"

"Easy Reanne, easy."

In the background Alan cued up the live morning show from studio six, temporarily hosted by another young newcomer by the name of Marilynn Matters. Reanne hadn't yet found out if the silly name was real or a figment of someone's overactive imagination, but Marilynn had a bubbly personality that went over well on air. She had a regular slot in the KSOM show lineup and, until Colton Wright showed up, she was doing the morning show to give Reanne a chance to get ready before the interview. Right now Reanne would give anything to be sitting in the studio doing the show, anything to keep her mind occupied.

"Good morning Nashville! This is Marilyn Matters, in for Jack and Reanne, and I have some things here that really matter! I know you're all anxiously awaiting the arrival of Colton Wright and, as of the latest update, he's on his way. I know the girls here are all excited and waiting. Call me if you have a question you always wanted to ask him, or if you want to hear a song, or even if you just want to say hi, call me! This is Marilyn Matters and here we go!"

Reanne resumed her pacing. "She's so bubbly she should be in a toothpaste commercial," she mumbled aloud.

"Ouch, Reanne, I didn't know you had a catty side as well."

"And that name, is that for real, *Marilyn Matters*, I mean who ever heard of something like that?" she continued as if Rod had not even spoken.

"Reanne, I know the waiting is a little enervating, especially with Jack not being here, but if he didn't think you could do this interview—believe me, you would not be here

"Yes I know, but that doesn't seem to help right now."

"Just relax and…"

At that moment there was a knock on the door. "Oh my God, he's here," Reanne said. "I don't remember what to say, oh, Rod what if I make a complete fool out of myself? Don't open that door!"

Of course Rod stood to open the door. "Relax, you'll be okay, just relax and it'll all come back to you in a minute!"

"Don't…" But the door swung wide open and Reanne caught a glimpse of tight, black denim jeans and a huge Stetson around Rod's big frame as he went to admit their visitor and make introductions. There were no security guards…somehow she had expected security guards. Maybe he had left them downstairs, and what about a driver? Did country music stars drive themselves?

"Mr. Wright, welcome to KSOM. We are quite glad to have you here. Let me introduce you to the lady who will be conducting the on air interview. Mr. Colton Wright—Reanne Parker. Reanne—Mr. Wright."

Reanne's gaze traveled from a pair of well worn cowboy boots over the ubiquitous tight, black jeans, halted for a moment on the huge metal studs sewn all down the side seams, past a loose fringed leather jacket and simple white shirt. This guy was going all country. The huge Stetson almost obscured his face until he thumbed it back a little and she finally caught a look at his face.

They stared at each other for a second then, almost in unison, two voices shouted.

"You!!"

Chapter Four

"Errr—you two know each other?" This much was obvious but still Rod glanced from one to the other, confused. This was not starting out as planned at all. The two of them were staring at each other like prizefighters in the ring and the situation needed defusing immediately.

"This jerk almost ran me down with his car a couple of nights ago, when he was going a hundred miles an hour down the River Road."

Rod almost had a fit hearing Reanne call his star a 'jerk'.

"Your little lady here tried to throw herself in front of my car and if you had heard her talk, *Lady* is the last thing you would call her."

"I did no such thing, it was you…"

"Yes, yes…now," Rod tried to calm them both down and to avoid Colton Wright walking out, if possible.

"If you're uncomfortable doing this interview together maybe I can make alternate arrangements, let me just check…"

"No," Reanne almost shouted. Only yesterday she had told Jack this could be her big break. She would be damned if she'd let a snooty super star ruin this one chance she had to advance her career, just because he liked to drive too fast. Oh no, not this time.

"No, Rod, I'm a professional, I can handle it. After all, it was just an accident, wasn't it Mr. Wright?" Sweetly she added, "I'm sorry if I didn't recognize you that day, after all it was pretty dark on that road, and the hat and all."

There Mr. Ladies-man Wright, chew on that for a while, she thought. This lady has enough class for the both of us. But to her dismay a huge grin appeared on his finely chiseled face. Did he think this was funny?

"No need to apologize for an accident Miss...Parker was it? Certainly we can do the interview, since I assume you've already done a lot of preparation for it?"

"Fine, let's go," she said brusquely and headed through the open door toward the empty studio which had been set up for the interview. As she passed Colton Wright he leaned close to her ear and whispered, "I admire spunk, you know!"

The—the jerk, she thought. She seemed to be running out of descriptions for him. The nerve, *I admire spunk,* ha! She would give him spunk, lots of it, and one of the finest interviews he had ever seen in his sorry life—jerk! Still, he was an exceptionally good-looking jerk. Now where had that thought come from? She watched him as he picked up his guitar case—no real question where the thought had come from, he made a great sight in his trademark, skintight pants. Watching him bend down for the guitar made her legs feel a little wobbly. How did one sit down in those jeans? That had to hurt! The thought made her chuckle quietly, but still, Colton Wright heard her.

"Something funny?" he asked.

Yes, I was just wondering how you managed to get into those pants of yours, do you have to have help? she thought and bit back another chuckle. "No, nothing, just getting into the groove for the interview, it does come through on the radio if you're in a good mood, you know."

That met with a raised eyebrow and a "Does it now?" but no further comment.

Rod hung like a nervous chicken around the fringes of the whole scene. He knew there was something going on but he couldn't put his finger on exactly what it was. It involved an accident and their halfhearted apologies, this much he understood. Still, having the star and his DJ have a go at each other made him a little nervous of the outcome. He didn't really want them to sit in a tiny little room locked up alone together. Reanne seemed to have recovered and lost all her nervousness, now she was just mad.

"You're right, Rod, this will go just fine, why don't you go see Marylyn and tell her we're ready to go in about five minutes. Sir," she turned to Wright, "if you want to get comfortable in the studio, I'll get our notes, we can go over them for a second before we start. Just to avoid any, shall we say…further surprises."?

He shrugged, "Fine with me. In here?"

The moment they were alone together Reanne found his bluster was gone, replaced by an extreme stiff politeness that made him look almost shy. He sat down beside her, fidgeting with the fringes of his jacket and read her notes. Reanne watched him out of the corner of her eye. He read and refused to look up or meet her eye. Why the sudden show of reticence? Of course it must be her imagination, who had ever heard of a shy super star?

So what was his game all of a sudden? Did he want to make her nervous? No such luck, he was not going to spoil her once-in-a-lifetime chance at this interview and the rewards it could bring for her. Still, what could he have to gain from acting the introverted, retiring eccentric? Finally she gave up guessing.

"Well?" she asked, and Colton looked up from the notes he had been studying.

"Fine," he said. "Fine, nothing here raises any red flags." And, after a moment, "listen, you really didn't give me a chance the other day to apologize for scaring you. You were off so quickly, still I believe we're fortunate that nothing serious happened, so shall we let bygones be bygones?"

Darn, a real apology. He was taking all the anger right out of her sails. And she had counted on that anger to make for a real juicy interview, now she was stuck with her lukewarm notes! Nevertheless…

"Sure," she said, "I probably shouldn't have been walking by myself on a dark road with headphones on. So do you think we can get past this and on with the show now? Your public awaits."

The last was supposed to come out sounding sarcastic, but as she heard herself she realized she only sounded bitchy. He rested his chin on his right hand and gave her a brilliant smile that made his face light up and his blue eyes sparkle.

"Ready when you are Miss Parker."

Oh darn him again for rolling the charm out now, just when she had no use for it! Jack had warned her about this—no he had told her to capitalize on it.

"Here we go!"

"Welcome back everyone to KSOM, after that long commercial break. This is Reanne Parker and I would like to introduce everyone's favorite Country Music Star and the winner of the Artist of the Year for the last five years running—Mr. Colton Wright, also known as *Mr. Right* to all our lady listeners. Good morning Colton."

"Thank you Reanne, and to all the folks at KSOM for having me this morning, and of course a big thank you to all the listeners and fans out there for your patience with my arrival."

"Well Colton, we've been taking questions from our listeners all morning, and we hope to get to a lot of them over the course of this show. But first of all tell us about your new album *Right Beside You,* due out next week, I believe."

"*Right Beside You* is a project I've been working on for quite some time now. It, of all my previous albums, is perhaps the one that took the longest to produce. It's rather experimental in places, in that I've let my song writing go down a few different musical paths, exploring styles with my new studio band that I hadn't previously. So in many ways it will be quite an experience for our fans."

"So it's not a typical Colton Wright album then?"

"Insofar as I'm not really sure what a 'typical' CW album would actually be like, if such a thing exists. We reinvent and project ourselves really with each new collection of songs, inasmuch as all my songs represent the collective experiences I'm having and have had at the time of writing them. But, having said that, this new album is really different from anything we've done before, and from anything that's out on the country music market at this time."

Heavens, any more ten dollar words and the guy would start being called the human dictionary. Hello, short snappy answers, something the listeners can follow so they'll stay with us. They said Colton Wright didn't like doing interviews, and perhaps his tendency to a certain wordiness could be the reason. Reanne laughed silently wondering how many folks had told him to 'keep it short'.

"Well let's get to some of the audience questions right now. Darla from Nashville wants to know which of your songs is your favorite."

"Oh my, any answer I might give really begs to be contradicted. So I'm just going to say, whichever I'm singing at the time."

"And how long have you been playing the guitar?"

"As long as I can remember. There isn't really a time that I can think of when I didn't express myself with a guitar or some type of instrument. So in many ways it's really more than an instrument to me, as my songs are more than just songs, but my way of communicating with the world, of getting across the feeling of a particular moment."

Well you're sure not doing it with words buddy, Reanne thought, a girl needs to make notes just to follow along. And then it struck her, of course, his guitar and his music was his way of communicating, that wasn't just a phrase with him. He could sing things he could probably never get out in words. Funny how he had become this famous without ever being called on that. But really, it was hell on wheels to get an interview with him, especially these days, and in the early stages of his fame he had probably stuck as close to the script as he possibly could. Time to use this to her advantage.

"Colton Wright ladies, the man of music, of country music, so before we go any further, let's listen to a few tracks. When we come back we'll take a few more audience questions. Here's one of my favorites, *Always You.*

Reanne keyed up the advertising track and the music, then took a deep breath. Being alone with Colton Wright in this studio was making her nervous. She pretended to shuffle through her notes while Colton remained silent. Finally she looked up, directly into those deep, blue eyes. Why did he have to have that look that went right through her and made the small hairs at the back her neck stand up? And was that a smirk that lifted the corners of his mouth? He was laughing at her. The devil was laughing at her!

Quickly she looked down at her papers again so he wouldn't see the quick flash of anger in her eyes. "Well I think maybe we should have a look at those ques…" She stopped in mid sentence, startled. His hand was on hers, blue eyes still locked on her own.

"Do I make you nervous Miss Parker?" he asked in that seductive drawl of his that managed to send another shiver down her spine.

It was just embarrassment at not having recognized him on the road the other day, for having yelled at him like that. Sure, that's what was making her blush so furiously right now that she could feel the color creeping up her face, unable to concentrate on one thought long enough to think it through to the end. It couldn't be nerves.

"Certainly not!" she said and snatched her hand back as if burned. "I must admit that I am kind of new at this job and you're the first star I've gotten to interview, you see, and I'm trying not to…not to screw up and not to…"

"Not to babble Miss Parker?"

"I do not babble!" she shot back, furiously. He was amused, amused! He was definitely smirking now! And still, through all her anger, she couldn't overlook how that smile lit up his entire face. It made him look like a mischievous boy of about ten.

"Touché" Mr. Wright" she finally said, "and I guess that would be part of your repertoire, throwing women off balance?"

The smile disappeared immediately from his face. "Don't believe everything you hear Miss Parker." And now it was his turn to shuffle through the papers in front of them. "With regards to the interview questions, I trust you have thoroughly reviewed the material my management company provided you with."

"I did."

"Now then, as for the contest, I quite like the idea of the quiz show type setup, however, I believe time constraints were cited in that case…so we…" he looked through his notes again as if to search for the rest of his sentence. "We decided to take the first ten callers to correctly identify all ten songs on the new CD. I've brought a few pieces of CW merchandise; you can always use your trivia questions to give those away."

Reanne was momentarily shocked, just like a light switch had been thrown. The charming *Mr. Right* was gone and instead this dry-as-straw businessman had appeared. What had happened to the charismatic singer, the charmer, the handsome, debonair heartthrob with a guitar? That's what some of the women's magazines Reanne read were calling him, but it certainly didn't apply to the guy sitting beside her. Apparently there was another side to Colton Wright, one he didn't show readily. He squeezed the bridge of his nose with his thumb and forefinger and closed his eyes for a second, focusing. Then that switch was thrown again, the famous coy smile was back on his face—*Mr. Right* had returned.

Reanne took a few audience questions, which Colton answered in his usual charming manner. He got the callers to laugh, he gave funny and witty answers and Reanne was truly confused, he could change colors like a chameleon, but right now she was too happy that her interview was on the right track again to worry about Colton Wright's changing attitudes. She gently steered him back to the topic of his new album with some lighthearted banter before running a few more minutes of advertising. They both seemed to be watching the clock on the wall, only a few more minutes. Reanne took another deep breath.

"And we are back here on KSOM with Colton Wright. Colton, your new album is due out in stores a week from today, you called it experimental and different. Can you tell us a little more about what we can expect?"

"Reanne, as I said, this album has been a real experiment for me. After the success of my first albums, like *Colton Wright* and *Right In Your Eyes,* I felt I had proved myself as an artist and I could afford to take a slightly different approach this time around. I wanted to show the fans a different side."

"Different in what way?"

"In that I've allowed other styles of music, other than country music as such, to influence and inspire me to create a number of very non traditional songs while still staying true to the roots and the intents of country music."

"Like using those Hawaiian slack key guitar players on *Paradise Found?*"

"Exactly. That song was really inspired on a recent trip to Honolulu. I was there on a quasi vacation when I heard these slack key guitar players, and immediately thought that there had to be a way to incorporate that sound into one of my songs. It's not a sound that has been used in country music previously, although I found it blends beautifully with some of the material that we were—ah—working on at the time."

"Colton, let's listen to a few bars of *Paradise Found*, and then I know you have some extremely good news and a big surprise for all our listeners, so stay tuned or you'll miss the chance of a life time. This is Reanne Parker, and you're listening to Colton Wright live in our studios."

Reanne looked over to the engineer's booth. Through the soundproof window Alan gave her a thumbs up and she keyed up the music track. Colton Wright's album was, of course, top secret and, as such, not available even for KSOM for an important interview such as this one, but CW management had made a few samples available, sound bites if you will, to be played during the interview. Colton had brought them with him in a sealed package and delivered them directly to the sound engineer. This time around he was taking no chances with material from his album being available ahead of time. Now she heard the soft, lilting strains of the Hawaiian guitars and then the seductive sound of Colton Wright's voice.

"When I look into your eyes,
I see my private paradise.
When I take you by the hand
You take me to another land.
Your magic makes my world go round,
You are my paradise found."

She was stunned by the soft and dreamy ballad about a love that built its own paradise. The slack key guitars put her into vacation mood almost immediately and Colton's rich baritone managed to wrap itself around her like soft velvet. It was the kind of song that drew you in right away. Reanne could almost see the picture he created with words and sounds: A couple who created their own reality, away from everyday worries and sorrows, creating and living in their own paradise. So much so that she almost missed the end of the sound bite. There was a second or two of dead air, but most likely everyone thought it was for effect.

"Colton, that was absolutely amazing. I was out on the beach there for a minute or so."

"Thank you," he smiled as if the listeners out there could both see and hear him "That's what I was trying to do with this song, create a feeling of the moment. I'm glad you liked it. Now, perhaps this is a good time to thank all my fans who've been buying our albums and coming to our shows. Thank you all, you've allowed me and the band to make a living at what we would otherwise be doing for free."

"Thank you Colton, it's been our pleasure. Now before we all burn up with curiosity I understand you have a special surprise for all your Nashville fans as well. Why don't you tell us about it."

"That's right Reanne, we decided to shoot the video for *Paradise* in Honolulu, seeing as the song was inspired there. So we thought, why should we have all the fun, why not take ten of your listeners along with us. They'll get a week long vacation in Hawaii, a starring role in our new video and one thousand dollars in spending money each."

"Right on Colton."

"Now that sounds like my next album title, do you know something I don't?"

"Maybe I could be on to something. And thank you again, you're certainly most generous. Now before all of you rush to the phones, right after this next song Colton will pose a question to you. You can call us here in the studio with the answer, but be prepared and be fast, because the ten first correct callers will be the lucky winners of the trips. Our number here at the studio is 555-KSOM, write that down and stand by. The excitement starts right after this next song, from one of Colton's earlier albums."

She leaned back in her chair and sighed. The tension of the interview was starting to wear on her. After this she would probably go home, collapse in her bed and deal with whatever fallout there was tomorrow morning. Yes, that was the deal, just go home after this, and maybe even come in late tomorrow. Jack could deal with the morning broadcast for once.

"Are we actually going to be answering calls in here?" Colton asked.

"Not really, we have a switchboard doing that for us, somehow or other they can tell who the first ten callers are. To tell you the truth I've never got into the technicalities. Too many buttons and switches for me. But I think we should talk to as many as possible to let the excitement build a little for the other listeners."

"Fair enough. Are you ok? You look tremendously tired."

"Probably because I am, but thank you for the concern. I'll just be glad when we finish this interview, no offense but it's hard work, believe it or not."

"Having to do a bunch of these every month believe me, I know. Take a few more audience questions, why don't you, that's less strenuous on you. If you'd like I could play a few songs live for you."

As if you hadn't planned this from the beginning, Reanne thought, but out loud she said "How kind of you, Mr. Wright."

"Is that a bit of sarcasm I detect there?"

"Sorry, but…"

"But you think it's a shameless bit of self promotion. Well look at it this way, I get the promotion, your radio station gets the ratings, somehow I think we both win."

The song was starting to wind down and Reanne sat up straighter in her chair. "And we're back! Its 12:45 now, outside our studio windows it's 75 degrees and the sun is shining beautifully. Our forecast for the next few days…all right all right, I know that's not what you want to hear. You're all standing by for our Colton Wright vacation giveaway. So without further ado, here is the man of the hour, Colton himself to pose the question."

"Thank you. Now I know you're all anxiously awaiting the release of my new album, but of course, the papers have already written a lot about it. So this one is for all you quick listeners and fans out there. What are the twelve songs on my new CD?"

The lights on their switchboard started lighting up like a Christmas tree. The girls in reception must be going crazy. Rod paged them on the intercom. "Colton could you take two or three calls from the winning callers. It'll make it more interesting."

He spoke to the first three callers, getting past their squeals of 'Oh my gosh I can't believe I won, I can't believe I'm speaking to you'. He was actually quite gracious, Reanne thought. He was said to be quite close to his fans but somehow she always assumed he would hold himself aloof like other super stars. But right now he was quite relaxed, animated and charming.

Finally he asked, "Reanne, I have a question for you."

"Go ahead."

"Well, I brought this little ole' guitar with me, and it's really just kind of sitting there in the corner. Do you think anyone would mind if I maybe—you know—played a song or two?"

"No Colton, I don't think anyone would mind. What did you have in mind?"

Colton played a couple of songs, chatted a little more with callers and soon, all too soon, the interview was over. Reanne pulled her headphones off and sighed. "Whew, that was one hell of a show. Thank you, you've been absolutely great."

Colton beside her was doing the same thing, carefully replacing the headphones on the control table in front of him. With the world shut out beyond those powerful headphones they had almost felt like they were in a space of their own and returning to reality always brought a moment of awkwardness, as if one had to own up to everything one had said on air.

Colton stood up and stretched the kinks out of his back, which was no mean feat in the tiny, cramped broadcast studio. "Well, you're right," he said, "That was one heck of a show we did." He looked at Reanne, "What?"

Since he had stood up, stretching his long, lean frame she had been staring open mouthed at him. His worn and faded jeans with the strategically placed rips and tears fit like a second skin, the chambray shirt he wore was casually open at the neck and draped softly over his broad shoulders. Sometime during the show he had slipped out of his jacket and it made a fringed puddle on the floor behind him. Now, as he bent down to retrieve it, Reanne got another good look at those legs. When he first came in, she had been far too nervous and angry to notice how good-looking he really was. Her mouth had gone dry and she couldn't even form the snappy response she wanted to give him.

That smile was back again too and, together with those sparkling blue eyes and those laugh lines around his mouth, it gave him a look of intense mischief. He was looking around for his battered, white Stetson hat, which had had to go in deference to the headset. He had to be aware of what his every movement in the tiny space was doing.

Finally he located the hat, forked his fingers quickly though the shoulder length blonde hair—wouldn't a woman kill for hair like that—and put the hat back into place. Too bad, Reanne thought, for there it overshadowed that finely chiseled face, the strong chin and small nose that on a smaller man would have been called abjectly pretty. But there was nothing diminutive about Colton Wright He was altogether too strongly male there in the tiny studio with her. The wide hat brim almost covered his eyes so that he never really seemed to look at a person directly, but Reanne had seen those eyes and the depth in them. A look one could drown in if…

"Well?"

Embarrassed, she realized that she was still staring and had been doing so ever since the end of the interview. And that she had entirely missed what he had said. "Excuse me," she said as nonchalantly as she could. "My mind was elsewhere for a moment, what did you say?"

His smile widened, if at all possible. "I said, that's it. Someone from my management company will be by to discuss all the details with regards to the vacation, etcetera. But if you need any more information you can always call my manager, Ken."

He had gathered all his belongings, including the snow white and gold guitar and was ready to leave the studio.

"Wait!"

Chapter Five

"Wait," she called out much too loudly, almost shouting. Suddenly she didn't want to let him leave. If he left this room where they had spent the last two hours, she would never see him again. *See him again?* A ridiculous notion, the man had hundreds of beautiful women throwing themselves at his feet. Reanne Parker was no more than a cog in the machinery that was Colton Wright and Colton Wright Merchandising. She knew that, but then they had just shared two hours of closeness, something she didn't want to let go of just yet.

"Wait," she said again. "I...I'd like to apologize. You must have thought me a real bitch the other night on the street, I'm sorry, really."

"Forget it Miss Parker, the incident never happened, okay?"

Again his hand was on the door handle and he bent to pick up the guitar case.

"No...I mean, would you let me make it up to you?"

"What did you have in mind?"

"Maybe you'd let me buy you a cup of coffee?"

An awkward silence spread between them, Colton standing by the door, handle in hand, and Reanne still sitting in her chair by the broadcast console. What have I done, she thought, wondering what on earth had possessed her to ask Colton Wright out for coffee. Colton Wright for heavens sake! Had her mind taken a leave of absence? He was giving her a look as if to ask if she was for real. Any moment now he would say *Lady I get better offers at four o clock in the morning on the road.* Any moment now he would walk out and, though he had belonged to her here in this studio, once past the door he would become Colton Wright, super star again and she would still be Reanne nobody.

Indeed Colton was tempted to just say *Thank you very much* and be on his way. He didn't usually linger after these types of interviews. Talking privately, one on one about himself and his music tired him and, though he had to psych himself up for it, he preferred to disappear quickly after. It was better to just finish and leave so he could devote the afternoon to his main passion, songwriting. There was so little time in his day that he quite literally had to wrestle the hours from his schedule to do the things he really wanted to do.

He mustered the little redhead from head to toe, trying to figure her and her sudden invitation for coffee out. Maybe it was the wild head of red curls or the lively, green eyes that made him pause, maybe it was a kind of innocence that he hadn't recently encountered, or perhaps it was the way she had called him a jerk out on River Road. He didn't know but something about her intrigued him. He was more used to brash and forward women who knew exactly what they wanted and who rarely had any problems letting him know. Sometimes it bordered on the embarrassing. He should probably say something polite and non-committal and be on his way.

This little elfin, however, looked fragile, and everything about her said, *I'm not really sure about this, please don't hurt me,* and somehow he sensed that this insecurity could hurt her easily, perhaps already had. If he turned her down she'd be crushed, he didn't really need that on his conscience. Still, who knows what could happen if he went with her. Better to turn and walk away and go back to the business of being the *Mr. Right* of country music. Damn that nickname of his. Well, she would get over it.

"Any chance there's a quiet spot around where we wouldn't get mobbed?" he heard himself say. Now where had that come from, that was all wrong, he was going to turn her down politely and spend the rest of the afternoon in his studio. He was about to correct himself when he saw the smile spread over her petite features. Almost as if she had been honored with a huge reward of one type or another. It would be cruel to turn back now he reasoned, anyway what would it hurt to spend another hour with her. He'd be gone and it would mean something to her. Just an hour he promised himself, just an hour to make her happy, give her something to paste into her memory album and then back to the office after that. Funny how an afternoon of songwriting had all of a sudden turned into an afternoon of doing paperwork at the office.

"I know just the place," she beamed, "Merielle's around the corner. It's quiet, it's private and the chocolate cake is out of this world!"

"Did you say chocolate cake? Lead on, my lady. Where there is chocolate thou shalt find joy."

She looked at him, as if expecting him to place the quote.

"Colton Wright, circa 1999," he said, and held the door with a smile. "And I've never met a chocolate I didn't like."

Ten minutes later they were comfortably seated in one of Merielle's cozy little booths awaiting their coffee and cakes. With a little exaggeration Merielle's could be called a hole in the wall, but it catered mostly to the harried workers of the office buildings in the block and nobody really complained. The prices were low, the coffee plentiful and good and, if Merielle could be persuaded to bake, her chocolate cake that truly didn't last very long. Today they were lucky. The lunch crowd locusts hadn't managed to eradicate all the cake yet. True to expectation, no one had bothered them yet, although they did gather a few curious looks. Colton had taken his hat off, and without it he was just another one of Nashville's tall blond guys escorting a lively little redhead. Reanne could appreciate his wish for privacy but there was a part of her that wanted to stand up and shout, hey look at me, I'm with Colton Wright!

"I can't tell you what a find a place like this is," he said. "By all means, I love my fans and I go out of my way to show my appreciation, but last week someone asked for an autograph in the men's room at JoJo's for crying out loud."

JoJo's was a rather upscale steakhouse in downtown Nashville. "The men's room?" Reanne giggled, "I gather you were otherwise…occupied. That would be so embarrassing. My God, what did you do, autograph toilet paper?"

"Tell me about it! I've autographed some strange things. Usually I try to remind myself that it means something to the fan, so I try to comply when I can, but there are boundaries."

"What's the strangest thing you've ever been asked to autograph?"

"You don't want to know."

"I do, come on!"

"You mean beside the pieces of women's undergarments I've been handed on stage?"

"No."

"Yes, and money, and clothing, and once some guy handed me a small painting he had done, why he wanted me to autograph it I don't know, but he went away happy. Then there was the girl who wanted me to autograph her arm."

"And?"

"And she tells me to be careful because she's going to have it tattooed after the show…but her boyfriend was with her so I guess that's okay."

"It sounds so amazing."

"Reanne…when you're not famous, it sounds like the most awesome thing in the world. When you are, all you want is to go to the Walmart without being recognized."

"Walmart?"

"Walmart. I'm serious. I do it for the live performances, for the shows, for the fans. If it weren't for that relationship I have with my fans, I would've got out of this business a long time ago. I love the fans. To see the crowds when they're excited, screaming, when they really get into the show…there's nothing like it. Really, it's like a fix for me, you know."

The waitress brought their coffee and cake and an awkward little silence ensued. Reanne was toying with her fork and Colton busied himself stirring his coffee. He didn't know why he was sharing this part of himself with her, except, that for once, he felt totally relaxed around someone, that he wasn't playing a part or pretending. Reanne had a way about her that put him at ease, made him feel like they could sit here all afternoon just chatting away.

"Listen…" they both said at the same time, and burst out laughing.

"As long as we're both listening, ladies first."

"Colton, I wanted to apologize again for the other night. I know I said that already, but I still feel like a fool. I was startled by your car and I'm sure I acted like a witch!"

"Maybe a little," he cocked his head, smiling.

"I'm truly sorry." Reanne blushed.

"Well I'm sure it complemented my acting like an absolute jerk, so in my book we're just about even. What say we forget all about it and stop apologizing to each other? I'm just glad we didn't end up in some local newspaper."

"Country superstar runs down local radio DJ, I forgot, celebrity can do that to you."

"How about local radio DJ jumps in front of country superstar…all for an autograph."

They both burst out laughing, followed by another awkward silence. They had said what needed to be said, and nobody wanted to take the next step.

"I feel a little strange sitting here with you, like this," Reanne finally admitted.

"Why?"

"Well, Mr. Wright…"

"Colton."

"Colton, you are a superstar and I—well I'm just me, this is a little overwhelming, you know."

"Only because you started thinking about it. Don't let it get to you. To me it's actually kind of fun not to be a star all the time. Right now I'd like to be just ordinary Cole who works in one of those buildings out there," he nodded his head toward the window. "And we're on our lunch hour and sitting here bitching about our boss. And in about ten minutes we have to be back punching that clock."

"You're not serious."

"I am too. I play these little games of pretend. You know, everybody thinks being a celebrity is so cool all the time. And it is, most of the time. It's just that sometimes I'd just like to be Cole. Just Cole, whose every word and deed is not going to end up in the paper or—forgive me—on the radio. It can get a little much every now and then."

"Well Colton, I'd be only too glad to help you out," Reanne smiled. "You don't act the way one usually thinks famous people should act."

"And just how is that? Snobby?"

"No, more…I can't find the right word now…regal maybe"

"Regal? Regal?" Colton laughed. "That's rich, Reanne, regal I must write that one down. You're talking to a kid from Trout Creek, Ohio who likes to sing and dance and act wild at times, show people a good time. You know, some days I wake up and I can't believe I'm getting paid to do this, but I am, and that makes me a star? I've wondered about that many times."

"About performing?"

"Performing, singing, songwriting—don't tell my record label, but I think I would be doing what I do for free if I didn't have a recording contract. It's what I do, it's my life. It's the fans who decided to all of a sudden make a star out of me, just for doing what I love. I've never felt personally responsible for being on top. There were times when I couldn't have paid people to listen to me…today they do. Now, tomorrow, they may discover someone else and Colton *Mr. Right* Wright will be gone, who knows, but until then I intend to ride this thing as long and as hard as it will go and when it's over I don't know what I'll do but I'll still be playing my guitar while I do it."

"You're lucky, you found something that makes you happy. I know precious few people who get such a charge out of their job. Precious few people get out of bed in the morning knowing they'll be doing exactly what they like to do all day long."

"Well, I don't know about all day long. There's a lot of other stuff that comes with being a recording artist. I still have to go to work, you know, even do paperwork—yuck! And then I go out at night, go and perform. It's made this total vampire out of me; I seem to be up at all hours of the night. Which is probably why I've never heard your show, sorry, I'm sleeping then. But come on, radio has got to be a pretty exciting job too, at least I imagine it would be, and you're good at it."

"How do you know if you've never heard the show?"

"You did a fantastic job at the interview. I don't mind telling you I don't normally interview very well, Reanne. You made the whole experience…well, pleasant."

"Thanks, that was my first interview."

"No kidding, beginners luck. So if it's not radio then tell me, what is it that you've always wanted to do, there must be something."

Oh he got to the heart of things. What did the man have, x-ray vision, second sight? The very question Reanne had been trying to avoid, circumnavigate, obfuscate—he went straight ahead and asked it. Oh damn Colton Wright. Now what? On the one hand there was a lot of pain connected with her singer/songwriter past. Pain that best lay buried and forgotten. On the other, perhaps talking about it would eventually heal it, if she found the right person to talk to.

Colton and his stardom had made her feel things again that she thought long forgotten. Thoughts and feelings were floating to the top, but somehow she felt comfortable with him. If she closed her eyes the Colton Wright sitting across from her was more like a close friend. A buddy who happened to be into music as well, the Cole he had mentioned, the one who worked in the building over there and was on his lunch hour just now. Yet the man who sat there with his legs crossed and his chin in his hands sold out every concert he gave and his last albums had gone double and triple platinum.

"See what I mean?" he said.

"What? See what?"

"*Mr. Right*! For a minute we were sitting here chatting like a couple of friends and then all of a sudden you remember that I'm the famous *Mr. Right* and bam…conversation over."

"It's hard not to remember Colton, but I can't help it…it does make a difference."

"Try harder. Now where were we? I know, dreams, what did you want to be when you grew up?"

"Oh…I don't know…"

"Go ahead, I promise…I won't laugh!"

"Promise, promise, triple promise?"

"Reanne, you're scaring me, what are we talking about, famous lady bank robbers?"

"Okay, here goes…I…I…I wanted to be a singer."

"No way?"

"I did. I made it as far as singing in the church choir, writing a few songs, hooking up with a band…"

"And?"

Reanne had to smile. Colton's face was animated, completely absorbed in her story. Gone was the mysterious smile from the promo shots. He seemed…normal. He could be a friend, he could be the guy next door. His blue eyes sparkled and a mischievous grin lit up his face.

"Well, don't leave me hanging! What happened?"

Reanne drew a pattern on the tablecloth with her finger, trying to work around what had to come next. Somehow her voice managed its way around the lump in her throat.

"Nothing, nothing happened. I flopped. The first time out in front of an audience I completely flopped. I got one look at the people, the lights and I couldn't get a single word out. My voice was totally gone, I couldn't even apologize for not going on. Nothing, like I was completely frozen. So I ran off the stage and out of the building and I've never been back. So when you talk about audiences, about performing live—I can't help but be a little envious."

"Wow! I would have never guessed, though this town is full of country singer wannabe's."

Reanne shook her head. "No reason you should have, it didn't exactly make the news. Do you know, you're the first person I've ever told this story to?"

"Well, I'm honored, I'm sure, but what about your family?"

"Not in so many words. My parents think I'm still working on my career and one day they'll just figure I couldn't make it, and they'll be right."

"Reanne," Colton reached over the table and took her hand. "I can't even imagine a moment like that. It must have been the absolute worst moment of your life. And to carry it around by yourself…why?"

"It was…yeah, kind of. Success was always a huge thing in my family. You either made it big or you didn't make it at all, you know. Coming home a semi…failure, well let's just say it wouldn't go over too well. But you know, this is embarrassing. Here I told you this sob story and you're…"

"For the rest of the day I'm just Cole, let's just agree on that, ok?"

"Oh? You're taking a vacation."

"You know what, that's not a bad idea at all. A vacation from *Mr. Right*. Let him get along without me for a while, after all, he is a famous star."

"You're not serious."

"I am too. I don't get to goof off a lot. Now what would you like to do today."

"Me? You're asking me? Cole I have no idea. I mean who...what...where? You act like I'm the specialist in ego vacations. This is pretty confusing."

"Only because you are confusing it my dear Reanne, oh no you don't get out of this one that fast. The vacation was your idea and you're coming with me, unless of course there's something you'd rather be doing."

He shot her such a hurt-puppy look that Reanne had to smile again. If this whole situation had not been so absurd she would have laughed out loud. This type of thing just did not happen to people like her. Here she was sitting in a dingy coffee shop with Colton Wright, the mega star and not only did he turn out to be one of the nicest guys, he was inviting her to come play hooky with him. The entire image she had of him, the larger than life star with the attitude, the empty-headed hunk dripping blondes...none of it held true. Who knew he was really incredibly charming and sweet. Sweet! That was just not a word one applied to Colton Wright. It was just too much to get her mind around at the moment.

She took a moment to call in to the station for her messages, and stood in the ladies room for a moment, putting her forehead against the cool glass of the mirror. The cold hard impression of the mirror reminded her that this was indeed real. She straightened up, looking at her image in the mirror. She was sitting in a coffee shop with Colton Wright! Unbelievable. She took another moment freshening up and went back to the dining room. He was chatting with their waitress flashing his incredible charm and apparently leaving her a huge tip.

"You know," she was telling him, "I could have sworn you were Colton Wright. You look just like him. You're sure you're not?"

Colton winked at her. "Absolutely sure. I get this all the time, maybe I should get a job as his stunt double, do you think?"

"Oh, now you're joshing me, you look sort of like him but from up close I can tell you're not. Thanks for the tip."

Reanne shook her head, but it was hard to argue with that grin and that charm

"Well, then?" he asked Reanne. "Ready? Let's go play."

Outside the sun was slowly going down, preparing the city for a long, lazy evening. Reanne couldn't believe they had spent the entire afternoon at Merielle's chatting. They headed for a close by parking lot, Colton lost in thought as he waited for a traffic light, and Reanne watching him. The low-slung Stetson almost obscured his eyes—here and there she could see just a quick flash of brilliant blue. Strands of blonde hair curled over his collar; just inviting her to take off that hat and run her fingers …

Reanne shook her head to clear it. Where had that thought come from? That particular thought and the dozens like it that had been flitting through her mind ever since she met him. They were getting along this afternoon but there was absolutely no indication he was even interested in anything more. Colton Wright the star was literally surrounded by beautiful women. The local paper had run a full page spread of him and his 'entourage' at the country music awards recently. What had that caption been again? 'Cowboy and the Angels'? It had been hard to tell just which one of the beautiful ladies had been his date for the night, but it was a sure bet she was a gorgeous actress or model. 'Cowboy and the Angels'—it almost sounded like one of those romance novels Reanne liked to devour in her spare time. Briefly she thought of asking him about it, but thought better of it. Better to enjoy the few hours of fantasy he was offering, an afternoon with Cole Wright, something to remember and treasure, in real life she would never have a chance at him.

"All right, ready to play hooky," she finally said. "Only I haven't as much experience as you think, you may have to take the lead here, seeing as you're the creative type. If you don't mind, that is."

"Chicken." Colton said and cocked his head to one side. "Always the responsible one, are you? Never late for work, always prepared properly. You know, I bet you keep a couple of maps in your car, along with your day timer and your list for the day."

"There's nothing wrong with being organized," Reanne said stiffly. She was about to continue, but Cole's grin stopped her. He was smiling again, from one ear to the other. Would she ever get used to his particular brand of humor?

"What's so funny?" she asked.

"You. You are. You get so excited. I bet you there's a wild, electrifying side in you somewhere. You just buried it after your bad experience on the stage. I think I'm going to help you touch that side."

"Now, how would you know that?"

Colton stepped closer and lifted a strand of her hair. "Red hair," he said, "I've never met a boring redhead before. And the fact that you have no problem cussing out strangers on a dark, deserted street."

"Oh that, I thought you had forgiven me for that."

"Forgiven yes, forgotten no. Go with that impulse. Set the wild spirit free, let it soar." He glided his hands through the air in mock seriousness and balanced on the curb.

"And what are you? Air traffic control?"

"You see, there it is, that was funny." He leaned closer to her "Brainy and funny, now that's a lethal combination," he whispered in her ear and Reanne felt a little shiver go down her spine from his warm breath on her ear and his softly spoken words. He could have asked her to walk into traffic right there such was the spell he had her under. Surely Colton Wright had magic of some sorts.

They finally reached the parking lot and Colton headed straight for an old Cadillac, its fins gleaming, simulated jet exhaust ports polished, metal grillwork buffed so it almost glittered in the setting sun.

"Oh, my gosh," Reanne said. Is that yours? That's what almost got me run over the other night? I never noticed. I love these old cars. I've always wanted to ride in one."

She dashed over to the white Caddy and ran her hand along the long tailfin.

"They don't make them like this anymore—that's a cliché but it's true."

Colton unlocked the passenger door. "My Lady," he said, bowing, "Your caddy awaits."

Reanne gingerly sat in the car and touched the cream colored leather and wood grain panels almost reverently.

"I'm sorry if I'm gushing. I don't know why I have such a thing for these old cars. I just love them. How long have you had this beauty?"

"I could bore you with miles and engine details and such, and a true aficionado probably would. Suffice it to say that it was the first thing I bought for myself after I signed my first recording contract. It was the one thing I had always wanted if I ever made it big. Now…"

He started the engine and watched her eyes light up at the satisfying purr. "Where to my lady?"

Reanne chewed her lower lip for a moment. "I guess you wouldn't have any maps in your car?" which earned her a dirty look. "Just for a drive along the road is fine, unless you would rather do something in the city, but…"

"But you would rather not get out of the car for a while, am I right? Anyway, if we go into the city we'd just get mobbed for autographs. That's the one drawback about driving a flashy car like this, you do stand out. We're supposed to be goofing off, remember."

"There is that," Reanne mumbled, and settled back into the leather seat. His remark about autographs had reminded her again that she was driving around town with one of the biggest celebrities in country music. Things like that just didn't happen. This was a once in a lifetime occasion…right?

Colton threaded the huge automobile into traffic expertly and headed south toward the River Road. Despite his concern about someone recognizing the car, they hardly raised an eyebrow in the passersby. Nashville's traffic was simply too busy and too grid locked for anyone to be paying attention to anything but their own situation.

"I've spent a lot of time driving around that area myself," he said after a while, remembering her remark about walking a lot here. She didn't answer and he thought if her solitary walks were anything like his own drives around town, then he knew what she was talking about. He watched her out of the corner of his eye. She looked like a little pixie sitting there with her round face, red hair and pert, upturned nose. There was roundness about everything about her, not quite in keeping with current fashion sense, that kept her features from being sharp. Colton had little use for the fashion of straight lines and sharp angles. Just like his music, everything had to flow softly rather than hitting you hard.

He had to smile at the dreamy look on her face and wondered what, or perhaps whom, she was thinking about. Something about her kept him intrigued, something that wasn't looks or fame, or a fabulous career. It came to him all of a sudden: She made no demands on him or his fame. She was merely happy to accept what he had to give for now and to enjoy it. There was no question what being with him could do for her image. The only thing that existed right now was this moment and the two of them. That was a new and quite pleasant feeling for Colton. Being with her didn't involve living up to an expectation, they were just simply partners out for the ride.

Reanne, meanwhile, stared unseeingly at the landscape passing by her car window frantically searching her mind for something to say, anything. Times like these she felt an old social ineptness creeping up on her. She used to practice for situations like this, but her standard conversation opener *so what kind of music do you like?* would have been silly, not to mention pointless. Colton thought it should be so easy to forget about his stardom, but he didn't have to start a conversation with himself, did he now?

"How long have you lived in Nashville?" she finally asked.

"Going on ten years now. I figured if I was going to go anywhere in country music this is where I would find out." Ten years since he had signed his first recording contract, ten years since he met Amber, ten years of being totally devoted to music and nothing else. But he didn't want to think about that again, not here and not now. "How about yourself?"

"Six months maybe, didn't take me long to find out I wasn't going anywhere, after that first disaster. I lucked into that radio job via Jack. If I hadn't found that, I would have had to crawl back home with my tail between my legs. As it stands, I have yet to figure out what to do next."

"So where's home?"

"Atlanta, would you believe?"

"Ah, a true southern belle. And you don't miss it at all?'

"Sometimes, but I kind of figured I wasn't going home until I had made something of myself, you know what I mean?"

"Oddly enough, I do. The first time I went back to Trout Creek the town threw me this huge party. Absolutely everyone was there. It was like I was their claim to fame, like I had made something out of all of us, because I made it big. It would be like disappointing them if you didn't make it, wouldn't it."

Reanne swallowed, gnawed at her lower lip. There was nothing really to be said, hearing all her thoughts spoken out loud, laid out in the open by Colton.

"Listen," he said. "Have you ever tried the stage again since?"

"Of course not!" It came out fast, almost horrified. "After what happened? I don't' think I could ever, ever…no not really!"

"It could have been a one time thing, you know." Colton mused, "Something that happened only the first time because you were nervous and whatnot. I was lucky, I took to the crowds, it's something that feels natural, something I don't even think about. Fame and celebrity, on the other hand, I'm not so comfortable with. It's odd really, being famous allows me to do what I do and make a very good living at it but still, when I'm not performing, I rather enjoy my solitude. Until I get up on that stage, that is. Then that's my whole world."

He paused for a moment concentrating on the road ahead. "It's different for everyone, but I was more thinking if you tried with someone else, a duet, maybe even backup vocals, something where you're not alone out in front of a crowd, that might get you back into performing."

She shook her head slowly. "I don't even want to think about it. If I can't give one hundred percent right out I don't even want to try." Her hands pleated and unpleated the fabric of her denim skirt nervously. "I just don't want to try and fail again."

"Listen," Colton said, his hand covering hers to still the nervous movement. "I won't give you the old spiel about winners never quitting and quitters never winning, you've heard all that, probably told yourself a hundred times. You know that there's absolutely nothing wrong with taking it slow. If it's worth doing you'll get there eventually."

Blue eyes met green and a spark flashed. There was no mistaking the double meaning in his words. Reanne sat in the deep leather chair frozen. Every nerve ending in her body was concentrated in her hands under his. She could feel the warmth and softness of his fingers and the tiny little calluses at their tips. Probably from the steel strings on his guitar a stray thought from somewhere reasoned. Somehow that tiny little sensation was so powerful and so personal, it almost overwhelmed her. Eventually he had to break eye contact and concentrate on the road ahead of them again. Minutes went by and they were both silent, each unraveling the web of their own thoughts.

Reanne let her head fall back onto the headrest and closed her eyes. I have nothing to offer you Colton Wright, she thought, we're from two completely different worlds. Why am I here with you? If this is an afternoon of diversion you could have had more fun somewhere else. With someone else perhaps, anyone else. This was Colton Wright after all, there had to be someone special in his life.

It took her by surprise how bereft she felt when he took his hand off hers to turn on the radio. He fiddled with the station dial for a moment until he found KSOM, Marilyn Matters' afternoon show. Reanne listened to Marylyn's cheerful bubblyness for a while, cringing, and Colton once again read her thoughts.

"She's too sweet," he said, "like too much candy, it hurts your teeth after a while." He was about to change stations when they played a Reba McEntire song. "Oh, leave it", Reanne said. "I love that song."

He reached over again and turned the sound up.

"Sing for me." he said simply.

"What?"

"Sing for me. I want to hear your voice, I want to see what you can do."

"But…"

"No buts, just sing, before the song is over."

Reanne concentrated on the song for a moment and then fell in with Reba.

> "Forever Love,
> I promise you,
> Some day we'll be together,
> Forever love.
> I won't give up, no matter what,
> I'll be waiting for you
> Forever love."

She closed her eyes and let the song she had practiced a dozen times take her away, the emotion and depth of the words and melody took on their own life, their own command. Suddenly she was back home singing for the critical ears of her parents and siblings. As always she turned in her seat and focused the song on one person— Colton. She had been taught to focus her songs on one person in the audience but suddenly she was singing this song to Colton, for him, about him.

> "Love is the road to our destiny,
> Nothing can change what is meant to be,
> Forever love."

The car, the road, the landscape, everything just fell away, disappeared, as she became one with the song, promised the love of her life to be there—forever. The words and melody of the song wove a magic spell that captured them both and held them together in a place that knew neither time nor space.

> "Forever love, I promise you."

The song ended and KSOM went on to another, but inside the white Cadillac time had stopped.

Neither dared say anything for fear of shattering the feeling. Reanne realized that at one point he had pulled over and stopped the car on the shoulder of the road. Too much emotion, too many memories, not enough room. She couldn't sit here with Colton's eyes on her like this, couldn't stand remembering her singing, the song, the lyrics. Reanne opened the car door and scrambled out as fast as she could, walking, almost running down the road. That song, just singing that one song had stirred up a cauldron of emotions that had lain dormant for a long time.

A desire to let her voice soar and climb, to capture passion in a note, a single note and to give it to an audience. Singing to Cole, seeing him react the way he did— everything she knew she could never have was all wrapped into one package. Why had she ever agreed to sing for him? She should have known it would bring back the past, a past she could never have. And now Colton was probably laughing at her, amused that she should ever have wanted to be a singer.

"Wait, Reanne, wait!"

Colton stepped out of the car, catching up easily with his long strides. "Wait!" Finally he caught her, grabbed her shoulder and spun her around to face him. He looked into her eyes for a long moment and caught a tear on her cheek with his forefinger.

"I'm sorry, I'm really sorry, Reanne, I didn't know it would be this painful for you. I wouldn't have…"

There was no help for it. Having him apologize the to her the way he did after everything that had happened only made the tears worse. As she threw her head back they ran down her face unchecked, and even her hands wouldn't stop them. It was like the first time, mourning the end of all of her dreams.

"It's ok Let it all out. It's ok" He drew her into a comforting embrace and rested his chin on her head. "It's ok, little one, it's ok."

When his hands started to gently massage the space between her shoulders she looked up into his concerned face.

"Cole, it's not your fault. It was just the memories coming back. All I ever wanted to do was sing, I never thought about the audiences that much, I just wanted to use my voice, I guess I blocked out the thought that I would have to be in front of a crowd some day and then, when I failed…well I thought I would never sing again, I promised myself I would never be tempted again, and now…"

"And now I made you do the thing that hurt you the most."

"No, Cole, it's not your fault. It's just that I thought I…could just forget, you know, but I can't. Not really."

"No, not if it's something you really want to do. Your life will always gravitate back to it one way or another. You'll try to forget it, or do something else and it will work—for a while. And then something happens and—boom—it all comes back to you. There's nothing you can do about that. It's just fate, or destiny or something like that."

"But I can't, you know I can't, I'm just…"

She never got any farther, as suddenly his mouth claimed hers in a tender kiss. Gentle at first, and then more insistent, deepening, claiming her and erasing every sensation except that of his soft lips on hers and his hands tangling in her long hair. Finally his tongue, teasing and playful, found its mate and they joined in a dance that was as ancient as time and yet new and untried every time.

Somewhere in the back of her mind an echo played: *Forever Love – I promise you*, but did it play for Colton and her? *Someday we'll be together,* then there was no thought and no reason any more, only feeling and love.

When he released her she swayed on her feet for a moment. She felt like she had just stepped off a fast moving roller coaster. Two fingers went to her lips where just a moment ago she had tasted Cole. "We…I…"

"Ssshhh," he said. "Don't say a thing. Just come back to the car, we're kind of out in the open here."

He took her hand and led her back, opening the car door for her and helping her in.

Automatically she fastened her seat belt, trying to order her mind with simple, familiar tasks, but the jumble of her thoughts refused to unravel. When he sat beside her again she reached out and tried to say something but he didn't give her a chance.

"If I had known that song would stir up such memories for you, I sure wouldn't have asked you to sing it," he said, concern in his voice. "I hope you know this. I just wanted to hear you sing."

Never mind the song, what about the kiss, what about what had just happened between them. Reanne cocked her head and searched his concerned face for any trace of the gentle moment they had shared. Could it be I was the only one there? She wondered. Come on, something did just happen between us, didn't it.

"Are you ok now?"

All right, if that was the way he wanted to play it. "Yes, fine, don't apologize. It was all just a bit much. All the memories coming back at once. Everything I had been trying to forget. Gosh…I'm a little embarrassed now. I hope you don't think me crazy or something…"

The rest of the sentence drifted off as the engine growled to life and they were driving down the road once more. The landscape passed by her window again, flying faster and faster as Colton sped up the car and Reanne tried to get a handle on her confused emotions and thoughts.

"Your voice," Colton said, "is unbelievable. You have true passion. What you need is a coach, someone to ease you into performing. It sounds like you threw yourself into it initially without really planning it out. You just weren't ready. I think if you prepared differently…"

"Since then, I'd rather not think about it at all. That one time was hard enough for me. It was just so different from what I had imagined, and nothing like auditioning. It was like it was me against the crowd. Not like the magic you seem to have with an audience."

"I'm lucky I guess. The bigger the crowds, the better for me. There's an energy I get from them, when they get into the music. Now for you, you might be better one on one, but that doesn't mean you can't learn to perform in front of an audience. Don't fight it, don't think of it as you versus them, try to tap into their energy, their…"

"Learn it, maybe, be okay, maybe too, but Colton, no matter what you tell me I don't think I could ever have that same kind of rapport with an audience that you do. It's just something you have or you don't."

"Who says you don't? You might just have to learn to relax into it. And anyway…" the mischievous little smile was back again. "Not everybody gets to be as good as me, you know"

"You know, on the radio there may be a crowd out there, but I don't see them. It's like I'm just talking to one person, to a good friend at the other end of that microphone. They're there but I don't see their eyes, their faces."

"See this hat? Why do you think I wear it all the way over my eyes sometimes? It blocks out everything, I can look down and just see my hands on the guitar. And then, when the moment passes, I shove it back and I look out at everything again."

"I wish I could do that, but I can't."

"But you can learn. You see, give me an auditorium full of people and I'm in my element under those lights. One-on-one on the other hand…forget it. I sound like a blithering idiot. Remember the interview today? I bet you there were at least two or three times where you thought 'what is the idiot talking about?'"

"Well…."

"Well, yes, you see. Leave it up to me, and I'd probably wallow in obscurity only to come out and sing every now and then. That's why I don't like interviews. But I've had to learn, I've had to learn because it was part of the job."

"Oh, I thought it was because if you didn't you fell into long convoluted sentences requiring several dictionaries and a thesaurus to completely comprehend and apply to the subject matter at hand."

He could make his nose wrinkle when he grinned! "You noticed that, did you?" he asked, slightly embarrassed.

"Well, it was kind of hard not to. I had to keep you focused somehow."

"I admit I have been called verbose, and worse, before. Let's just not go there. But it's all part of that one-on-one thing. I just don't do well in personal conversations."

"So how come you didn't have a problem with our interview, Colton?"

He thought about it for a moment. "I don't know, I really don't know. Maybe the accident...I mean, it was like we knew each other already. It was more like chatting with a friend."

"Like it was meant to happen? That we would meet before and get to know each other?"

"Meant to happen? I don't know. What I do know is that I can talk to you like a good friend."

"Why thank you."

"I mean it Reanne. I would like to count you as a friend. When you're a public figure it's sometimes hard to separate all those fans from your true friends. But I think we have the start of a wonderful friendship here."

Reanne focused on the street ahead of them and let the wind mess up her hair again. Friendship. She decidedly didn't want to go there. Not after that kiss they had just shared. How could he do that and then go on talking about friendship? Why did he want to confuse her like that? Perhaps he was sorry to have kissed her, maybe he wanted to forget he'd done it. Well if he could ignore it, so could she. She looked at him out of the corner of her eye so he wouldn't catch her staring. It was obvious why women fell for him so easily. He had that devastating combination of talent, good looks and incredible charm. It was foolish, she told herself, to believe that she would ever have a chance for anything else but friendship with him.

"Do you like Italian food?" he suddenly asked.

"Pardon me?"

"Italian food, do you like it? You see there's this little hole in the wall Italian restaurant a little ways down the road here. I tend to go there when I want to be alone. The food is great, there are hardly ever any reporters...I mean, if you'd like some dinner."

Reanne forced a smile and nodded. Better to enjoy whatever he was ready to offer at this point. If it was friendship, then so be it. All of a sudden she felt that even just friendship with Cole would be better than nothing at all. Cole was her first link to the music business again. And even if she never did get to perform again, as long as she managed to stay close to him, maybe she could live a little of the stage magic through him. If she stayed close to Cole she would never have to try and expose herself to a public again. *Wimp,* a little voice inside her scolded, but that little voice had been around for a long time and she had learned to ignore it. So she was a wimp, so what?

"Lead on," she said to Colton, pointing her index finger straight ahead, whatever lay that way, they would figure it out.

Chapter Six

"Reanne? Hello Reanne. Are you going to join the meeting mentally as well as physically?"

Reanne started at the motion of somebody's hand waving in front of her face. "What?" she snapped out of her reverie and stared directly at Jack, who at this point had both eyebrows raised to where they disappeared under his hairline. He hadn't been happy with her all morning and her distracted attitude wasn't helping things. Well, let him be mad, she couldn't help that. After last night her mind was on anything but the morning show. Last night...

"What's the matter with you?" Jack's voice intruded into her thoughts again. "Hot date last night? I'd be willing to bet you missed the entire last fifteen minutes of the meeting, we'll have to do it all over again. Would you just concentrate before you miss the rest."

"No, no, of course I haven't missed anything, what makes you think that?"

"Well, for one thing your eyes were glazed over and you look like you're barely awake. You're a thousand miles from nowhere to paraphrase a famous song and you haven't made one contribution. Reanne, this is not the behaviour I expect..."

"Let it be Jack," said Sasha. "You haven't said anything worth repeating in the last fifteen minutes anyway." Reanne shot her a thankful look. Sasha had been there for her first interview, she was Rod's executive secretaries and one of the few friends Reanne had made on the staff of KSOM.

"Well, you get her up to snuff, I'm getting more coffee," grumbled Jack as he left the room in search of more fuel.

"Thanks for saving my butt," Reanne said after he closed the door behind him. "To tell you the truth, I really am not quite with it today. What was he going on about?"

"Don't let him get to you, he's having a bad day today. Every now and then he takes pleasure chewing out everybody. Now about that date you don't want anyone knowing about…"

"What date?"

Sasha began counting off on her fingers.

"First you left the building rather suddenly yesterday, which isn't like you at all, second you didn't come back after lunch, I heard you call in for messages, third you weren't home all night, as I was calling you at least—oh three or four times, and fourth…"

"There's a fourth?"

"Fourth, you have this look on your face that can only mean you met someone really special and you're trying to decide if he's the one."

"Oh, all right, I was out with someone, ok."

"So? Details, details!"

"Nothing special, really. Nothing to talk about anyway. Sasha, if it was anything I'd tell you," Or not, she thought. Imagine telling her best friend she had been out with Colton Wright, everyone's dream date. Not only would it be all over the station on the inside of five minutes, but the next time she left the building somebody would probably follow her, never mind private phone calls. No, at least until she figured Colton out she didn't want to tell anyone, as much as she might want to. "Now can we get on with the meeting…please?"

Last night with Cole intruded on her thoughts again, though. They had indeed gone to the Italian restaurant, which was as good and as private as promised. Neither of them had wanted to go home, so after dinner they had gone to a little out of the way club to dance.

Somewhere along the way Colton had ditched the hat and transformed himself into the ordinary guy he wanted to be so badly. No one recognized them and they had had fun all night meeting peoples' sideways glances, trying to figure out if they were a famous couple or what? Still no one had approached them and they had gone on dancing until the early morning hours. Dancing and talking about everything and anything.

They found they liked a lot of the same things, dogs, Thai food and nature, and disliked the same things, phony people, spinach and clowns. They had laughed about the last one forever, and then danced some more. In the end Reanne forgot all about being out with a celebrity and let loose, having a good time with a friend. She had shared things with him she had never told anyone before. The fact that he had told her very little about himself didn't feel too important right now.

Reanne had barely got two hours worth of sleep before having to report for the Morning Show. She had dragged herself through her broadcast by the skin of her teeth, flying on the emotional high from last night but the planning session had got the better of her.

Jack was right, she had missed most of what he had said in the last fifteen minutes. "Can you just get me up to date so I can get this meeting over with and out of here, Sasha", she said, pressing the heels of her hands into her eyes. The intercom quietly piped in the current KSOM program, and Reanne caught herself listening to a particular song. Cole and she had danced to that song last night. He'd held her in his arms, slowly dancing her across the floor, close enough that she could smell the spicy scent of his cologne and feel the play of his muscles through his shirt. Oh, the feeling of being swept away in his powerful arms, of dancing with the best dancer, the best looking guy in the whole club. Oh yes she had enjoyed the envious glances of the other women and just for one night she could say *hands off, this one's mine.*

"Reanne!" Sasha was looking at her, bemused. "Man oh man, you've got it bad girl, just look at that silly grin, that is just too much girlfriend. And you're still not paying any attention whatsoever."

Reanne felt herself flush crimson. "Is it that obvious?"

"Let me put it this way, I am insanely jealous. So either you tell me all about it right now, or we're going to have to postpone this session until tomorrow, because I won't get any decent work out of you today. But I still want to know who the mystery man is. "

"Oh, Sash, I'm sorry."

She was tempted for a moment, if only to share the unbearable joy in her heart, but no. There was really no way she could tell anyone, not even Sasha, about Colton Wright, not until she was really sure about him. Or about herself and how she felt about him for that matter. For starters she was totally swept away by a flood of conflicting feelings, joy, happiness, doubt, fear. The list was endless and changed from moment to moment. Mostly, everything just felt unreal right now. Things like this simply didn't happen. Not to girls like herself. Sure she bought a ticket in the power ball lottery some times, but she never really expected the big win. Things like that didn't happen, did they? Average girls from Atlanta didn't get to date country music's biggest star, did they? There were actresses and models and other singers who got to be the lucky ones. A one in a million chance that she might be the winner, or that he might be...

No, until she had all of this sorted out, until her thoughts stopped racing and chasing their own tails in her mind like a litter of unruly puppies, she couldn't really tell anyone about last night. And how did he feel today? Would he carry one like he never met her, would he phone her? Would he want to see her again? But oh, how nice it would be now to have someone to gossip with, share all the juicy details of a wonderful first date with. All morning thoughts of Cole had intruded into her mind, and now...

"Well, Jack, I think she's got it bad, you won't get a decent hour of work out of her today, that's for sure," Sasha said, and Reanne looked up and only now realized that Jack had returned with three large mugs of coffee. He was grinning from ear to ear, his earlier annoyance having been forgotten. He seemed more amused than anything and Sasha, well all Sasha wanted was details. She had a huge list of single male friends and she had tried for the longest time to fix Reanne up with one of those really nice guys. Usually there was a good reason why there were still available...

"So what's wrong with him?" Sasha asked "What is it you're not telling us? He's not married is he? I told you to stay away from the married ones. Is he ugly? Crude? Hunchbacked?"

"None of the above Sasha. I'm just not sure.

"Ladies!" Jack came to her rescue. "Not in mixed company please! We have a show to do tomorrow, we have tons of this Colton Wright merchandise to give away, so can we get back to the planning session at hand, before y'all embarrass me to death."

"Yes, let's." Reanne took a deep drink of her coffee and forced her mind away from last night and back to the present. She picked up a handful of Colton Wright key chains and his smile looked up at her, giving her heart a happy little tug—Cole...

Just then the phone on her desk rang. Reanne picked it up quickly, glad for the interruption.

"There's a gentleman on line one for you, Reanne," the receptionist said to Reanne's horror. Everyone would recognize Colton Wright's voice on the phone. The gossip would be all over the building in ten minutes flat!

"I'll take it here," she said, trying to sound as nonchalant as possible, as there was really no way to slip out of the room.

"Reanne Parker here."

"Good afternoon, I'm calling from Mr. Wright's office. Mr. Wright is on the line for you, would you like to hold?"

"Yes, certainly."

She just barely kept herself from shouting *of course, of course, hurry up,* that would have been gauche. At least no one would have recognized his voice. He came on the line quickly.

"Hi, how are you doing? Is this a bad time?"

"Define bad."

"Are you still awake and alive? I forgot all about your having to start your morning show that early. You couldn't have got more than one or two hours of sleep."

"Two to be exact, but I'm hanging in."

"Oh poor you. Well, judging by your answers you're surrounded by people so I'll make this short. Are you free this afternoon?"

"Sure, what's up?" In vain she tried to deny the huge leap her heart took at the fact that he had called, at hearing his voice, and the fact that he wanted to see her again. Perhaps she had won this particular lottery after all. She was more than a few hours of a good time to him.

"I've got the outlines for the video shoot here, I thought you might want to see them."

"Oh."

"Oh? Well that doesn't sound too excited. As I said if you're too busy over at the station I can…"

"Oh no, don't you dare, that's not it…"

That's not it. I just thought you wanted to see me perhaps, not just hand me contracts and plans…that's all. I was hoping you would feel the same way, that you had thought about me all morning too. And you would feel… My heart got a little ahead of itself is all. They were all the things she wouldn't, couldn't say out loud.

"No, I mean I just was distracted for a second there, what did you have in mind?" *Anything to see you again!*

"That little café around the corner, four o clock this afternoon?"

"You got it, see you then."

Carefully she replaced the receiver and looked up, staring straight into Jack and Sasha's faces. There was curiosity and intense attention there

"Ok you guys! I can just see what you are thinking, so I'll tell you! There are some papers I have to look at and I'll be doing it this afternoon, that's all! Nothing else, got that!" she spoke more harshly than she had intended. "Does that satisfy everyone's curiosity about my life? Anything else you want to know?" she finally added, a little embarrassed.

"Sorry, Reanne," Sasha said. "We didn't mean to pry. I'm sure you'll tell us when you're good and ready."

"No, I should be sorry, for blowing up at you guys. I'm tired, I didn't get much sleep last night. You're concerned for me and I overreacted."

Jack started to say something but a pointed look from Sasha held him back. It took only another half hour of concentrated work to get them through the rest of their program sessions, and he left immediately afterwards, mumbling something about women and how one never knew where one stood.

"So," Sasha said when they were finally alone, and walking down the hall to the lunchroom for a final cup of coffee. "You want to tell me what's going on?"

"Not really, though it's nothing sinister."

"I can see something is bothering you. Something is on your mind that has you off kilter."

"Sasha, I think it's just a case of me not reading signals right, or getting the wrong signals, or sending them—aaaargh, I don't know, I'll figure it out…eventually."

"Maybe. Sometimes you can't see the forest for the trees. Kid, you know I'm always here if you want to talk."

"Thank you, Sash, I mean it. One day I may take you up on that, but now if you'll excuse me, I have to be somewhere."

"Reanne?"

"Mmm?"

"Be careful, before you get into something heart over heels that you can't get out of."

"I'm not…I'll be careful. Thanks though. See you later."

Colton carefully replaced the receiver and spun his hat in one hand, before putting it back on his head. "Well, I'm off," he said, rising.

"Where to?" Ken asked. "Or, should I ask with whom?"

"There's nowhere I need to be this afternoon. Production on the album is in full swing, I have no interviews that I know of. I think I can afford to goof off a little, spend some time fooling around with some new songs."

"Colton," Ken carefully lay down the pen he was holding and moved it around his desk a little, searching for words. "You made your point quite clearly the other day— no more arranged dates for the sake of your publicity image. I agreed to that, so tell me, what are you up to now?"

"What are you talking about?"

"I mean the little girl from the radio station, Reanne Parker. That was her I got on the phone for you. And if I'm not mistaken, you just set up a date with her."

"There were papers…"

"Papers that are completely irrelevant. Don't get me wrong, I'm not butting into your personal life, I'm not trying to tell you who you should be dating, but as your manager, and friend, I should know what's going on. And I should find out before I read it in the gossip rags. Even if you're not taking it seriously, there is still your image to consider. You're not as free in your personal relationships as you used to be, you know."

"Ken, you're taking this whole thing wrong. I'm not dating Reanne."

""Well it sure looks like it to me, Cole."

"Okay, so she has a story that intrigues me. Did you know she used to be a singer? First time on stage she froze, couldn't get out a single word. She's never gone back again, though her voice is quite good. I'd like to help her get her back on her feet. That's the ten second version, but essentially that's it. That's all there is to it."

"So she's a cause to you, nothing more?"

"A cause, yes, but she's also becoming a good friend. You know I have precious few of those still around."

"And how does the young lady feel about all this, Colton. Is she aware of your feelings? I don't want to read some lurid article somewhere—'Colton Wright used and abandoned me'."

Colton laughed. "Ken, you're overreacting, she'd never do anything like that. Don't worry about it so much. We're just having some fun, that's all. As for getting serious with anyone…don't even think about it. It's not going to happen. You were there for me after…when Amber…well you know what it was like, and you should know it's not going to happen again."

Ken nodded slowly, "I hope you know what you're doing Colton."

"You worry too much Ken, maybe that's why you make such a good manager. I'll see you later, phone me if something comes up, ok."

With that he was out the door. Ken still sat at his desk toying with the gold pen in his hand. It was engraved '100,000 Albums – CW.' Colton had given it to him when his first album went gold. They had been together from the very beginning, almost from day one and he loved that boy like nobody else did or ever was likely to. Although Colton hated it when Ken referred to him as a boy. "I'm only 10 years younger than you are, you know," he would say, but there was still a boyish, mischievous quality about him that kept him from completely growing up. Perhaps that was the source of the energy, the creativity that allowed Colton to withdraw and exist in other worlds, different spaces from the rest of us. But that was also the reason Ken felt a little overprotective of him.

He would tell Ken not to worry and, like a good manager, Ken always did, but right now he worried seriously. There had been something in Colton's voice and demeanor that hadn't been there for a long, long time. There had been a bounce and vivaciousness there that he had seen only once in Colton's life and it had hit Ken like a ton of bricks when he recalled the last time he had seen Colton act like this.

It had been ten years ago, at the Blue Oyster Café, when he had met Ambhara von Granville. That disaster would not be allowed to repeat itself he vowed. He needed to act now, even if Cole didn't think it was necessary.

"She's just a cause, is she Cole," he mumbled flipping through his Rolodex. Then he dialed a number.

"It's me," he said after the person on the other end answered. "I need you to find out all you can about someone. Her name is Reanne Parker..."

Chapter Seven

The door had just closed behind Reanne when the phone rang again. "Sasha here, can I help you?"

"It's Jack, Reanne leave already?"

"Yeah, you just missed her, you want me to try and catch her."

"No it's just as well, I want to talk to you."

"Go on."

"Did Reanne seem odd to you today?"

"Distracted, sure, but odd? In what way, odd?"

"I don't know, I've never seen her act like this. I feel responsible for her in a way. For all her bluster, Reanne has a certain naiveté to her. I'm just worried that she's got herself into something that's way over her head."

Sasha toyed with the phone cord and looked at a KSOM advertising poster across from the desk. It showed a number of country music celebrities, amongst them Colton Wright, playing around the huge call letters for the station. Something about the Colton Wright image bothered her, but she couldn't quite put her finger on what it was.

"Jack, I talked to her earlier, but I couldn't get anything more out of her either. She says she's okay, nothing to worry about. She's old enough to know what she's doing, I'll keep an eye on her though, if you want me to," as if she could actually leave it alone! Sasha was just as curious as Jack to know what had caused the change in 'their' Reanne.

"I'd appreciate it, Sasha."

At Merielle's, meanwhile, Reanne sat toying with a cardboard coaster and her cup of coffee. Her heart was beating double time in anticipation of seeing Colton again but at the same time she was confused. Did he truly want to see her again or was it just business? Did he want to spend time with her or was he just passing time with a little distraction? And should she ask him directly about it? The only women he had been seen with over the years were drop dead gorgeous actresses, models and other personalities who were at least equally famous. The question begged itself, what did he want with her and did she even have a chance with him? If not, then what the heck did he want with her? And regardless of the answer to that, wouldn't it be worth it to just play his game for a little while. Round and round her thoughts went, circling the same questions like a pack of wolves around a fire, never really getting to the heart of the matter.

That thought about playing his game was mostly empty bravado, in her heart of hearts she knew she wouldn't be capable of doing that. Perhaps it just took a much colder person. As for the woman beside Cole in her imagination? No matter how hard she tried, all she could picture there was a blonde beauty who could attend all the galas and award shows with him and always know exactly what to say, someone who would always wear the latest designer fashion and would be respected by absolutely everyone, including the gossip rags. Now that was about as far away from Reanne Parker as one could get and still be on the same planet!

A hand fell on her shoulder. "Did you wait long?"

She looked up from the hand that was burning a brand into her shoulder to the handsome face above hers. His face had a dark shadow of beard that meant he would have to shave again in the late afternoon if he was to perform tonight. Today he was a study in black. Painted on, knee blown, black jeans, crisp, black shirt and black boots.

He carried a motorcycle jacket casually over his shoulder by one finger and topped the whole look off with a silly little black ball cap that bore a feed store logo. He could have been standing in a cigarette ad or a poster shot for motor cycles and it would have been a perfect fit. Everything about him said that he wasn't taking himself too seriously today, he was out to play and, still, something about him kept the outlaw biker look from being trashy and made it work somehow.

"Hi!" she said, trying to work her tongue around her suddenly dry mouth. "Where'd you park the Harley, out back?"

"Yup, right with the other hogs," he laughed, turning a chair around and straddling it. "What do you think, I was hoping I was beyond recognition today."

"I thought you were just dropping off a contract."

"That and a few other things—oh all right it was a ruse to get you out of that office of yours."

"All right, what do you have up your sleeve Colton Wright?"

"Sssshhh." He put his finger on his lips. "It's Cole, I'm incognito, remember."

He looked so cute sitting there it made her heart ache, he was the guy you dreamed about at five in the morning when you couldn't sleep. At the same time the word incognito set little alarm bells ringing all over her head. Perhaps the reason he didn't want to be seen was Reanne herself. He didn't want so much not to be seen, as not to be seen with her.

"Are you out playing hooky again?" she asked, putting a false note of cheer into her voice.

"Guilty as charged," his right hand went over his heart. "Also, I have a surprise for you."

"A surprise? I like the sound of that."

"Then, my lady," he stood and bowed from the waist. "As they say in the movies, let's blow this joint."

"But you just got here."

"Come on, no dawdling."

He tossed a bill onto the table and held out her jacket.

"Off we go."

"Slave driver," Reanne muttered, but obeyed. There he went again, she thought, ushering her out of a public place as fast as possible. The only places they had been together were either incredibly private or incredibly crowded, like last night's dance club. And yet there he stood, with that engaging smile and those impossibly blue eyes, and she knew that there was no way she could tell him no. Just being with him would be enough, no matter where.

Out in the back parking lot he opened the passenger door of the Cadillac for her, then literally threw himself into the driver seat. He drove off smiling, excited yet utterly mysterious about their destination.

Once again Reanne let herself admire the car. "This is such a beauty," letting her fingers explore the fine details on the curved dashboard and the old radio.

"Yeah, ever since I was about ten years old I've wanted one of these, and when my first album went platinum, I made it a reality. Ken, my manager, he thought I was absolutely nuts to put that much money into a mere vehicle. 'It's a car' he would say, 'it's just a car,' but it wasn't you know. To me it was like another dream come true, like my own proof that I had arrived. I'd get stared at and I'd pretend they were staring because they recognized me."

"Not anymore?"

"Naw, nowadays they stare at the long white limos. They figure country stars don't drive themselves— they have people for that, don't you know?

"Well I could drive for a little while if you want to get the hang of the having people thing."

"Nice try Red, but it's not going to work. Then I'd have to tell you where we're going."

"Red? RED? Isn't that a bit of a predictable nickname?"

"You don't like it? I had a dog named Red once when I was about …oh…"

"Oh, a dog, that's just wonderful, thanks!"

"Relax, I'm just kidding you, anyway, we're almost there."

Reanne looked around to find out where exactly 'there' was. All the talk about the car and her new nickname had distracted her from paying attention to where they were going. They were in a remote area of Nashville, a collection of mostly old warehouses and industrial buildings. One day, someone would buy up the whole quarter, renovate and turn them into 'loft apartments' and make a killing of it. But for now the whole area had an ambience of charming dilapidation about it. What exactly did Colton Wright want with her in an area like this? A momentary sliver of alarm passed through her, but one look at Colton's amused smile drove it away. He wasn't that kind of guy…couldn't be.

"Cole, where are you leading me?" she asked.

"Astray. Are you worried yet, or have you decided I'm not an axe murderer after all?"

Damn, how do you always manage to read my thoughts? Never mind, I think I would follow you anywhere, any time, no questions asked. Why is this happening to me right now, and why with you?

Out loud she said "I haven't decided yet, but I would like to know where we are anyway."

"Well, we're here."

He stopped the car in front of a one story non-descript industrial building that sat squarely in the middle of a fairly large lot. The lot was paved carefully all the way around but there were no parking spots marked off or signage of any kind. And Reanne couldn't make out a front door anywhere, just a large overhead garage door.

Colton reached into the glove compartment and fished out what looked like a little remote control. He pressed the button and, slowly, ever so slowly, the garage door rolled up. The area behind it was in complete darkness, and it was into this darkness that Colton pulled the Cadillac.

Reanne turned around, but Colton had already pressed the button again, and the garage door rolled back down and the daylight outside turned into a small bar of light that got smaller and smaller, finally disappearing.

She was still feeling nervous when Colton pressed another button and strong overhead lights flickered to life. They were in what was essentially a garage, though the usual assortment of tools and gardening paraphernalia was absent. On the opposite wall was a set of wooden stairs leading up to a solid, gray aluminum door.

"You did scare me there for just one second," Reanne admitted. "What is this place? It looks spooky somehow—secretive."

"Sorry, I just couldn't resist the theatrical entrance. Normally I turn the lights on before I pull in and close the door behind me. Come on, I'll show you what's behind door number one. You'll get a kick out of it."

Like an excited little boy he was out of the car and bounding up the stairs, putting the key into the lock and waiting for her impatiently. All that was missing was him imploring, 'come on, come on, hurry up.' Reanne chuckled and took her time unbuckling her seat belt, arranging her purse, then slowly getting out of the car.

"Come on, what are you waiting for?"

"You, to get annoyed."

He raised an eyebrow and started tapping one booted foot.

"I guess revenge is sweet, but you must admit I had you there for a second."

"One second, one only, mind!"

She came up the stairs and caught her heel in the top riser; she pitched forward and would have fallen if he hadn't caught her.

"Steady there, these wooden stairs can be a mite rickety."

One of his hands had her by the arm and the other was supporting her in the back. Reanne's mouth went drier than a desert. His hands burned a fiery brand through the fabric of her clothes and right through to her soul. His mere touch rendered her all but helpless to him. She straightened slowly, eyes firmly locked on his.

"Are you ok," he asked.

Reanne mumbled, "Yeah sure, just shook up." She turned away, straightening her clothes quickly, keeping her face averted, lest he see the furious blush on her face and, from the very sight, read her thoughts…again. She'd be mortified if he knew how she was starting to think and feel about him. Surely he would feel she was betraying their friendship. If she just had some idea how he felt about her…

She looked up and ran her fingers over a small brass plaque by the door. "ALWYS U Entertainment," she read out loud. "*Always You*, that was your first big single, wasn't it?"

"Good memory…welcome to my sanctuary." He opened the door all the way with a grand flourish and led her inside.

They were standing in a small foyer, and the first thing Reanne noticed was a small fountain splashing merrily right beside the entrance. All around she saw lots of greenery and small groupings of comfortable couches and chairs. One wall held a bookcase crammed with books, magazines, a small stereo and dozens and dozens of CD's in merry disarray. There was even a new flat screen TV's on the wall, a fridge, and what looked to be a well stocked wet bar. The whole room had the ambience of someone's living room or perhaps the den for a group of party-hearty single guys. When she stepped further in she saw several different guitars resting on a couch and on stands beside it and a large pad of sheet music scrawled with hand written notes. As if the musicians had just up and gone for a break.

"Who lives here," she asked, for certainly this was no ordinary office or industrial building. She looked up at him and saw something like embarrassment in his eyes, despite all his earlier excitement at showing it to her. Somehow this place held something special to him and by sharing it with her he was sharing a piece of himself, this much she realized. He looked around with an obvious love in his eyes. Everything he touched was with a special look of appreciation and she felt almost silly for envying everything he touched.

He spread his arms wide. "Welcome to sanctuary. This is where I write songs, practice scores, unwind, and prepare for a show—anything really. Anytime I get bummed out or angry or upset, this is where you'll find me."

"Don't you have a home?"

He smiled indulgently, like one would at a child who does not understand. "Yes, but it's a place to live. This…this is all about music. Anything that has to do with my music—that's what happens here. Here, let me show you the rest."

He crossed the room to the far side and opened one of the doors leading out of the room. Stepping beyond he hit another light switch and it immediately became obvious where they were. The room was full from top to bottom, wall to wall with electronic equipment. One wall was entirely made out of soundproof glass, and behind it was a console that looked like the cockpit of a 747.

"A recording studio," Reanne breathed, completely in awe. "This is unbelievable, look at all this equipment." Her hands flew expertly over the console. "This is state of the art, is this all yours? I thought you recorded at SoundMaster studios? How much…?"

"Sssssh! Too many questions!" He laughed with the pride of a father. "Yes it's mine, but I don't record my albums here. This is strictly my personal space. I write my songs, I record some demos and, sometimes, the band and I fool around with different arrangements. Having this gives me the freedom to experiment with a song, without necessarily having to reveal the end product to anyone, or the different stages of a project for that matter. I can work by and for myself here, I can…create! Nothing leaves this studio unless I deem it absolutely perfect. And if it's not," he shrugged, "the tape goes into the recycling bin and no one is the wiser."

"They said you were a perfectionist," she quietly stepped up to the glass wall, peering into the second part of the studio, the performing area. A powerful microphone stood right in the center and various instruments had been shoved into a corner to get them out of the way. She spotted a keyboard, a huge set of drums, different types of guitars, a fiddle, an accordion, even a saxophone.

"Do you play all these instruments?"

"Only on the synthesizer" he laughed. "These real instruments are mostly for the rare times that I invite the band here to work on some arrangements with me. Although the odd time I have studied a single passage for a particular song on most of them."

"Unbelievable," Reanne said, twirling around like Alice in Wonderland "Even at the station we don't have all this electronic equipment, do you realize what we could do with all this?"

She turned in a slow circle and found herself face to face with Colton again. He was smiling and he obviously enjoyed her appreciation of his sanctuary with a certain pride. His eyes were on her as she surveyed his domain and suddenly Reanne found it hard to breathe. He was too close, too intense, and they were completely alone in this building in a remote area of Nashville. He drew a forefinger down her cheek and rested it under her chin, his eyes never leaving hers.

"Few people have ever seen this place," he said softly. Reanne stood rooted to the floor, a trail of fire burning on her face where his finger had made its mark.

"And now that I have, will you have to kill me," Reanne croaked, futilely trying to stop the crackling energy that was passing in the small space between their bodies. He didn't answer, just raised one eyebrow in careful assessment.

"So what are we doing here?" Reanne tried again but still her voice was not her own, couldn't be for surely she was feeling too much all at once to even speak.

"Did I not tell you," he murmured quietly, not backing up even a single step. "We're going to re invent you."

Suddenly he pulled her into his arms and held her tight. Her face rested against his shoulder, the crisp fabric of his shirt caressing her cheek and the spicy scent of exotic cologne tickling her nose. His hand forked though the length of her hair and nothing mattered anymore, nothing at all.

Just as suddenly he drew away from her again. Reanne, almost dazed, swayed for a moment and stumbled to find her footing again.

"What are you doing?" she asked.

"I told you, we're going to re invent you. Today, you will sing again!" There was a certain pride in his voice.

"Cole, I…"

"You'll start in here, sing just for me."

"Cole, I…"

"Then, maybe we'll do a duet, we'll get the band here if you feel up to it, we'll let you do some backup and then…"

"Cole, please!"

"Then before you know it we'll have you singing in front of an audience again."

"Colton David Wright, will you listen to me!"

"What?"

"Whatever gave you the idea that was what I wanted?"

He looked at her as if she had walked up to him and tweaked his nose. The thought of a talented singer not performing—it just didn't seem to have entered his head.

"I had just made peace with the thought that I would never perform in front of an audience again—ever and the hurt was finally starting to fade more and more every time I thought of it. It was starting to be a fond memory, like at least I had tried, even if I hadn't succeeded, you know. And there you waltz in like a great big grizzly bear and tear down everything I've built up, digging up all the old hurts again. I wish, I just wish you had told me what you were doing."

Colton had been accused of rushing in without thinking before. It was an old impulsiveness that he was struggling to contain. In his music it served him well, he was known to fly with an idea when it occurred to him, it made his live performances extraordinary. The musicians in his band knew to respond to the slightest of cues from him and, since he had surrounded himself with the best, they worked together like a well-oiled piece of machinery. In his personal life, however, it didn't always go quite as smoothly. He sometimes hit a wall when he picked up an idea and ran with it. Even Ken had to sometimes remind him to stop and consider the full consequences before he acted. Of late that particular trait had been euphemistically termed 'creative genius' by one of the trade publication and his stardom forgave many little sins that a lesser man would have had to pay for. Rarely, though, someone like Reanne confronted him head on. Oddly, the opposition only set him more firmly than ever on his original goal. Where there was an idea there was usually a way and he was here to find it.

"You have an amazing voice Reanne. Not only would it be a waste, it would be a terrible shame not to use it."

"Lots of beautiful voices never get heard Cole, except in the shower I don't see anything so terrible about that. Audiences are your life, I can see that, there's something you get from them and that they get from you. You're one the best performers I've ever seen, live or otherwise. Can't you understand that it's not the same for me? The spotlight is not a place I'm comfortable in, matter of fact I'm terrified of it. I don't know if I could learn but, to tell you the truth, at this point in my life, I don't think I want to try."

Colton traced the spaces between the dials on the console with one finger. Fascinated, Reanne followed the progress of the long elegant finger with the blunt cut nail and remembered the magic it could work on the strings of a guitar…or drawing a line down her cheek. Finally he looked up at a spot somewhere behind her.

"I never thought of it that way," he said thoughtfully, "I automatically I assumed that you…"

"That I would want to perform the same way you do. I'm sorry."

"Don't be," he said. "It was me who rushed in where I had no business being. I seem to do that a lot around you."

Glad for the lightening mood she elbowed him in the side gently. "Well at least you're getting good at it then."

"Hey!" he elbowed back, a little more insistent.

"Just kidding, Cole, just kidding." She laughed, glad that the tense moment had dissipated. "While we're here anyway, why don't you show me your sanctuary? I'd pay money to get my hands on a bundle of electronics like this."

"You've pretty much seen all of it. Most of my songs start out here, cobbled together from bits and pieces of ideas I've scribbled down on countless pieces of paper everywhere. The band comes here sometimes to rehearse with me, otherwise it's really just my own little toy."

"Pretty neat toy, if you ask me." She looked around again, this time noting and appreciating all the state of the art technology that had found its way into this room. At the same time she was struck with a certain sense of loneliness. Here was a man who by any measure could have just about anything that money could buy. Yet his sanctuary was a lonely studio on the outskirts of town, filled with every electronic recording gadget he could others, they sang the last verse, hand in hand, face to face, heart to heart. All too soon the final chords of the song faded out and the red light above the window went out.

'Recording complete' the little screen read. The passion of the song still hung in the air all around them. Reanne took off her headphones and turned to leave the studio. What she felt inside her at that moment was so intense she had to get into the outer office. Too intense, far too intense. She had hardly reached the far door when the sounds of a piano and slack key guitars echoed back at her from all sides. Colton had rewound the tape with his little remote control and cued up their recording. She stopped cold in their tracks as she heard their voices fill the room. The addition of a second voice brought an emotion and an essence to the song that had been missing before. Their voices wound around each other, toying and teasing, playfully touching, separating for a moment only to come back together in a wondrous dance. Unable to tear herself away she let the full impact of the song sweep her along. She could feel Colton rather than see him, stepping up behind her. He stood too close, far too close, she could feel his breath tickle her ear and his arms wound around her.

"That was magnificent," he said close to her ear, "We were magnificent."

"Cole, what's happening?" she whispered as he turned her to face him. His blue eyes had gone dark and there was desire etched in every line of his face.

"This," he said simply, "Just this."

He started to kiss her again, gently nipping at her lower lip letting his tongue find hers and finish the dance, the never ending age old dance that their voices had begun. Again and again he slanted his lips over hers, blocking out every sensation save the one he was creating. She heard a little whimper when he finally let go of her. Was that really her own voice on that great sound stage? But he left her no time to think as he swept her up into his powerful arms and carried her into the front and set her down on the couch she had first seen when they walked in, He traced a line from tracks. Colton had spared no expense in his private sanctuary.

Ever so gently, Colton fit the headset onto Reanne, effectively shutting out the world. From now on only each other's voices and the instrumental track existed. He punched some buttons on a tiny little remote in the palm of his hand and indicated the microphone with the other.

There it was; the piano intro, guitars, her cue.

"When I look into your eyes
I see my private paradise,
When I take you by the hand
You take me to another land,
Your magic makes my world go round,
You are my paradise found.

Our hearts live in a place
That knows no time and space,
And though on earth the day is rough
Being with you is enough,
Your magic makes my world go round
You are my paradise found."

Reanne got caught up in the song, the picture that unfolded in her mind of the couple that had created their own paradise no matter what life threw at them. At the end of the day they walked hand in hand off into the sunset. She looked up into Colton's eyes and knew that at this moment they truly were creating a world of their own. Every word he sang to her, gave to her, she gave back in kind.

"Let the world do as it likes,
We are in our own paradise."

On the studio console columns of green lights flickered, reaching for the line of red above them. But in the studio itself only Colton and Reanne existed. He reached for her hand and, with their eyes locked on each for Reanne, from never wanting to sing another note again, she had gone to singing for Cole in the car and now in his private recording studio in a matter of days. So much for best intentions. She watched him from under lowered lashes while he led her through a few trial runs of the song. His very intensity about his music, the emotion, and the passion he brought to it made it easy to see why he had reached such stardom. Every note and every phrase of his song meant something to him and he didn't just sing the song, he expressed it, acted it out and told the tale with his entire being. In the end you felt like you had been right there in the story from the very beginning.

Every time she would get hung up on a particular spot in the song he would bring out the old, battered Gibson guitar that was his obvious favorite and show her over and over how it was supposed to sound, completely absorbed in the music. Music, Reanne began to realize, music is how he communicates. Words are essentially meaningless to him, unless they're strung together into a song. It's only in his music that you see the real Colton Wright. That's his world. But what does that mean for the duet he wanted her to sing?

"Ready?" he finally asked.

She nodded. "Ready as I'll ever be I guess. Do you think I've got the gist of the piece?"

"We'll soon see."

He led her into the soundproof room on the other side of the two-way glass. If the electronics out there were the beating heart of this studio, this room was certainly its soul. The angled walls and floors were solid concrete, and there were blocks of different heights and sizes mounted on the ceiling, all to allow for better disbursement of the sound. In the center of the room Colton had set up two high-powered microphones on identical stands beside each other. The capsule shaped microphones with their circular nylon mesh to filter out hard t's or p's were some of the best money could buy. As were the huge headsets that would provide them with the instrumental and background possibly cram into it, everything except a friendly face or voice to say hello and good-bye. She was about to ask him about it, when yet another idea hit him. She could almost follow it cross his mind and light up his eyes.

"I have an idea."

"Not another one, couldn't you just send it home?"

"Just for fun, Reanne, just for fun let's you and I do a tape of *Paradise* together. No strings, just so I can see what it sounds like as a duet."

"Colton."

"No strings attached, scout's honor."

"I don't know, I really don't think we should…"

"The lyrics are right here," he started digging in stack of pages covered in that odd jumble of letters and numbers that served as a sort of musical shorthand among Nashville songwriters. It freed up writers to put the rough outline of a song on paper regardless of their ability to write music. At the same time it freed up the session players who did the final recording to improvise and imprint their own personal style onto a piece.

"I've taped the background instruments," he said. "I've wanted to experiment with another voice on this for a long time. So come on, say you'll give it a shot—if I promise you no one will ever hear it?"

"Colton Wright, how do you always manage to get your own way?"

"Don't know, just lucky I guess."

"All right, but only…"

"Great, come with me."

He had done it again, somehow there was no way for her to deny this man anything, and from popular press there were a lot of folks in the same boat. Colton, so the press went, had a way of getting an idea into his head and simply running with it, pulling everyone in his wake along with him, like a great powerful tidal wave. His enthusiasm, his very belief in the ideas he was selling you made it hard for anyone not to want to be part of one of them. So it went her ear to the base of her throat, and followed the hot fiery trail with a trail of little kisses, nipping and teasing until he reached the top button of the simple shirt she wore. His eyes were on hers, searching, silently asking permission as he opened it, and every one beyond that. Her own eyes, her own hands gave that permission and asked the same of him, as around her the entire world disappeared. Her hands fisted in his long blond curls as her back arched to get closer, ever closer to him.

The loss was almost overwhelming when he left her to kick off his boots and jeans, then he was back, his hands and eyes roaming over her naked body.

"You are so beautiful," he murmured, his fingers drawing a little curved line underneath each breast, kissing and teasing their sensitive tips until the sensation became unbearable. Still he tormented her, letting his hands and lips explore her body like a blind person. The world turned into a giant orchestra for Reanne, every note reaching for a huge crescendo. "Cole," she cried out, when he finally found that center of her that ached for him so sweetly und unbearably.

"Don't worry, love, I've got you, just let yourself go," he said softly, and then he was inside her with one long smooth stroke. Reanne cried out, wanting him so much she thought she could not bear it. Her body answered his silent call and together they found their own pace of giving and taking, faster and faster. The drums were beating a rhythm in their heads until they found that final note together, a chord of perfect harmony and everything ceased to exist for them.

She was still locked into his arms when she recovered her senses enough to move. Colton's head lay on her shoulder, his golden hair slicked to his forehead with dampness. Gently he blew at a strand, making it flutter up and tickle her eye. Giggling, she reached up, brushing it out of his face and tracing the line of his jaw and mouth. He captured her finger with his lips gently nibbling at it.

"Cole," she said, enjoying the sound of his name on his lips. "You're wonderful."

I think I'm falling in love with you, don't ever let me go, she thought, not daring to say it out loud. She couldn't—she couldn't possibly fall in love with this man, this star, who had no use for someone like her. Someone as absolutely ordinary as he was spectacular. Cole and she were yin and yang, black and white, two ends of a straight line, never destined to meet. Then why did he make her feel things she hadn't ever felt before, why did he pull her close one moment and seem so distant the next, what was his game and would she ever understand him. She turned her head so he wouldn't see the love in her eyes but he used his thumb to smooth the lines on her forehead.

"Now what's going on in that busy little brain of yours?" he asked softly.

She smiled, not knowing how to answer and he kissed her nose carefully. "Don't analyze it to death Red. Let's just have some fun, some good times together, hmmm?"

Fun, good times, no strings. Each phrase was like a little stab into Reanne's heart. He obviously wasn't feeling the things she was.

"Sure," she said with a little defiant head toss. "Laissez les bon temps roullaux."

"Oh my, my lady speaks French."

"Just that."

"Well what more do you need to have a…"

His focus was captured by a monitor across the room, where a little red light blinked on and off urgently.

"Damn," he swore softly, "I forgot that was on."

Chapter Eight

Reanne raised her head and watched Colton cross the room, toward the monitor with the rapidly flashing red light.

"That's on?" she asked. "Please, Cole, tell me that's not a security camera!"

"No, it's a phone! It doesn't ring in here in case I'm recording something."

She pulled on her shirt and watched him gather his scattered clothing on the way to the monitor phone. He pressed a button and Ken's voice came over the loud speaker, "Colton, I've been looking for you everywhere! I hope you get one of my messages. Don't forget your date tonight with Ashley Bowden, for the Recording Industry Reception and Awards. We'll be expecting you at the office at seven. I'll send a car for you. Call me to confirm. Later!"

The remaining messages were inconsequential. Most everyone knew he wouldn't answer the phone in his studio. Colton fiddled with the keyboard and monitor and muttered something unintelligible.

Another one of those parties, they were starting to get on his nerves. Indeed he had forgotten the Awards dinner. Another interminable row of speeches to sit through, eat some rubber chicken and listen to the insipid prattle of his escort, Ashley Bowden. If he remembered correctly he had met her before at one of these functions. She had made a distinct non-impression on him. All he remembered of her was that she was an up and coming fashion model.

Apparently she had decided getting her picture taken and being linked with him romantically for a while would boost her career enough to make it worth her while. Presumably it would also enhance his lady killer image. "This could be the last time," he hummed while searching for Ken's cell phone number. Funny that for years he had enjoyed, even reveled in these types of galas. Now they had become such a chore. For the past few months now, he had been feeling that the business side of country music was becoming far removed from the reasons he had gotten into it in the first place—for the music. He didn't have any allusions about being a great businessman, that's why he had joined up with Ken, that's why all the smart singers found themselves good business managers, but even the marketing and selling of his own celebrity required a lot of his time and dedication lately. Time he would rather spend holed up in his studio writing, only to emerge for the spotlight of live performances.

"Well, I guess one more won't kill me, will it, and, after that…"

After that we'll think about cutting back on the publicity for a while he meant to say, but he realized that he was talking to an empty room.

"Rea? Reanne."

He peeked around the corner into the studio and then had the presence of mind to finish getting dressed, before he went looking for her.

Now where could she have gone? Probably went looking for a washroom while I was listening to my messages, he thought, forking his fingers through his hair.

"Reanne," he knocked on the door to the washroom. "You in there?"

"I'll be right out."

Did she sound odd? Choking? No, probably just the acoustics. "Might as well deal with Ken first," he mumbled and sat down at the desk with his back to the washroom door. Dialing the number he doodled around on a pad in front of him and never noticed the door behind him opening just a crack—his conversation with Ken had another listener.

"Ken? It's me, Cole. Sorry, I had the phone off. I was working on...something. I kind of did forget the Awards tonight—so I'm escorting another beautiful blonde, am I?...Yes, yes, I understand, it's been arranged for a long time, I won't argue...this time.

Can you send the car to the apartment, maybe 6:30, I'll pick up Ms Bowden on the way to the Awards. Anything I should know?—Ok, I'll see you tomorrow in the office then."

With a flourish he finished the little doodle of a guitar on his pad and turned around.

"Reanne?" he called out.

She opened the door fully and stepped into the office. "Right here, I was just fixing myself up."

"Not that you needed it, but I appreciate the effort." He tried to pull her close to sit on his lap but she evaded his arms and picked her purse up off the ground, rummaging for a hairbrush.

"So you've got a big date tonight?" she asked as nonchalantly as she could. *Some big official function that will end up in the papers and you'll have someone else on your arm,* she thought, watching him out of the corner of her eye for a reaction.

He shrugged as if he didn't care. "Another Awards ceremony. I'm not even sure what it is or who's getting an award. Anyway I don't think it's all that exciting—what's wrong?"

"Nothing is wrong, why do you ask."

He sat in his director's chair with his arms spread wide, but Reanne continued to ignore him in favor of folding her jacket into exact quarters.

"You're acting rather strange."

"Strange? I wouldn't say so. Of course if you expected me to fall to my knees and say oh thank you, thank you, thank you great and mighty *Mr. Right*, well then of course it could be considered strange. But don't hold your breath for that."

It took an effort to keep her voice steady but she would eat nails before she let him see how hurt she was. The fact that he could sleep with her one moment and then, a minute later, pick up the phone and confirm a date with another woman—well, it cut like a knife. The little voice in the back of her head that had been taunting her all along was by now screaming at her. *You're not at all what he's looking for? He'll bring you here to his little hideaway, but he won't take you out in public.* The taunting voice rang so loud that for a moment she was afraid Colton could hear it too. For years that voice had told her she wasn't good enough for this and for that and for just as long she had tried to ignore it. It was the voice of her mother and her father, all the relatives back in Atlanta, 'you can do better Reanne, I know it.'

Coming to Nashville on her own was supposed to have erased all that, let her start over. Her experience with the stage had been bad enough and now, just when she had started to recover, someone like Colton Wright had to come along and tear all her defenses down again. Someone who had probably never doubted his own abilities for a single moment. Well she wasn't going to give him the satisfaction of seeing her hurt, of seeing her doubt herself. Let him wonder for a change if something was wrong, if he was losing his touch.

"Reanne?" he touched her arm ever so lightly. That little touch burned her like a liquid fire all the way down to her toes. Every inch of her skin remembered the loving touch of his hands. How easy it would be to ignore the voice in her head and to seek the comfort of his arms.

"Are you just about ready?" she forced herself to ask in a voice that dripped ice. "Would you mind dropping me back at the station again? I still have work to do for tomorrow's show."

His hand withdrew instantly and a flash of pain crossed his face, so briefly she couldn't be sure if it had even been there or if it was just wishful thinking on her part. He would get over it, no doubt. Guys like him didn't get rejected.

He reached into his pocket, pulled out the car keys and tossed them into the air, catching them with the other hand.

"Fine, let's go."

He turned on his heels and headed for the front door. It obviously bothered him that she wouldn't talk to him even though he could sense something was wrong and, despite everything, she felt badly about treating him this way. She could have told him, could have explained...but no, he was the one with the explaining to do!

They settled into the car in silence and barely said a word on the way back. Colton tried once more to break the ice asking Reanne what was bothering her.

"Did you feel I was pressuring you? Did you think...?"

"Colton will you stop it already. Nothing is bothering me. We had an afternoon of fun, that's all. It's time to go back to work. I have a show tomorrow, you have a...an event to attend tonight. What exactly is it you don't understand?"

By then his face had become an unreadable mask. He stopped in front of KSOM and reached over to kiss her cheek, but Reanne twisted away and opened her door.

"It was a delightful afternoon," she said with a false note of cheer. "Perhaps we can do it again some time."

"I'll call you," he said quietly as she turned to leave.

"I have a lot of shows in the next few days and that on location broadcast to prepare for—we'll see."

The car door slammed and she was gone. She didn't turn around to watch the car leave, she didn't stand on the steps and wave, she simply stormed through the glass doors with the KSOM logo, very quickly flashing her employee badge at the guard.

She took the stairs two at a time and headed into the nearest empty broadcast studio where she fell into the chair and rested her head on her forearms. Finally alone she allowed the tears to come in dark heavy sobs that came from deep inside her and went on and on forever. Her tears carried all the pain and hurt with them that had been inside her for years, a thousand times of trying to be the perfect one, the good one, until finally she thought she didn't have a single tear left. She crossed the room to the window and looked out at the evening descending on the city of Nashville. Everywhere people were getting ready for an evening out—a big date perhaps. And inside an empty studio at KSOM Reanne Parker cried again and again—for a lost heart that had fallen in love, reached for a star and found that nothing on this earth could ever lift it high enough to reach that star.

Colton rounded the curves in the underground garage with squealing tires. He carelessly put the caddy into its accustomed spot and banged the doors shut. With the elevator taking its sweet time reaching him he repeatedly stabbed the button with his forefinger, muttering something indiscernible but distinctly vile. All the way through the seemingly interminable ride up he drummed his fingers against the shiny brass rail and frowned at his own reflection in the polished mirror.

The security system asked him for the pass code for access to the penthouse level and he had to try three times before he got it right. Anger had him behaving badly today, he realized. Anger at himself for getting carried away with Reanne, anger at Reanne for reacting the way she did and anger at Ken for setting him up on another date. Maybe he should throw in anger at Amber too, he thought, just for screwing up his love life forever.

He must be doing something wrong, seeing how Reanne had changed from one second to the next. When he finally did reach the penthouse he gave the door another slam and threw his jacket and hat on the couch, making a satisfying mess. The cleaners must have been here, he noted. For a change everything was in its place, neat and clean. A distinct counterpoint to everything else today.

He poured himself a drink and wandered out on the balcony terrace. From here, on the twenty fifth floor, Nashville looked tiny and unimportant.

"A fine mess you made again Wright," he said to his reflection in the window. A fine mess indeed. He should have never let himself get carried away with Reanne the way he had. But with the intensity generated by their duet and the emotion Reanne had poured into it—his head hadn't been exactly the one leading the way.

"It's your music, you get carried away in your music and you don't care about anything or anyone. The only number one in your life is always going to be music. Everything else stands in line behind that."

Another woman had said those words to him a long time ago, in another lifetime. And another memory forced itself into his mind; of the only woman who had taken second place to nothing, not even his music. But Ambhara was gone from his life. She had gone forever and taken everything inside him that was kind and gentle, everything that was able to love another human being.

And so, music had filled the void and become the passion in his life. Reanne had picked up that passion in his song and had reflected it back at him perfectly. "I shouldn't have led her on," he continued to the silent reflection.

Silently he toasted Nashville's skyline with his glass. *Now if Reanne is any indication at all we may have another platinum single on our hands.* Perhaps he would sound out some female colleagues and give it another try as a duet. The irony of that, of course, would be lost to his fans. That he should be able to write the most beautiful and successful love songs—songs that would be played at weddings and proms everywhere, songs that would be requested on the radio and live, to turn a ladies head and heart. Songs that a Nashville reviewer had once called the second most passionate thing he knew. Oh yes, the man in the reflection could write those songs—and put his heart and soul into singing them. But that is where his heart would stay, Amber had seen to that.

Funny thing, in all those years, through song after song, every time he had stopped and listened for his heart—he had found nothing. Nothing at all that would move him to love again. He lived through his music and through his fans, letting them supply the passion that was missing from his life.

That arrangement had worked quite well until Reanne had shown up with her innocent enthusiasm. She had an openness and basic honesty that he had searched for in the celebrities of Nashville without success. He had let those qualities temporarily carry him away.

He finally turned away from the view and strolled through the apartment to his cavernous dressing room, turning on lights and the stereo as he went. His thoughts were still with Reanne, who intrigued him to no end. Where he used music to bring passion to his life she had used her own passion and brought it to his song, to his music and created an unbelievable energy. Truly amazing—now if he could only figure out why she had reacted like he had slapped her in the face after his phone call.

His mind replayed every moment of that afternoon as he went through the motions of selecting a fitting Colton Wright outfit for the evening. Super tight, black leather pants with huge metal studs along the side seams, a soft, white shirt, a western style jacket. Add a western string tie, his cowboy boots and a Stetson hat—more or less battered, depending on the occasion—and the legend was ready.

Finally he turned to leave his dressing room and stubbed his toe on the slightly open door. He was still cursing, hopping on one foot, when a flash of insight reminded him of another door, opened just a crack. The door at the studio! Reanne must have opened the washroom door at the studio just a crack and heard him arranging a date with another woman. Or at least that's what she would have thought she had heard. He slapped his forehead. No wonder she had reacted like that. He was lucky he hadn't got his face slapped.

"Colton, you are an idiot!" he told himself. "If stupid was dirt, you'd own half of Texas, that's for sure!"

Reanne's behavior became absurdly clear and Colton felt suddenly guilty at the thought of how hurt and used she must be feeling, He of all people certainly knew that feeling and the sheer cruelty of being rejected.

He was halfway to the phone to give her a call when the doorman called and announced the arrival of his car. He hesitated for a moment, his hand poised over the telephone, but there would be nothing he could achieve in the few minutes before he had to leave. He would call later he thought, when they could talk a little longer. Perhaps he and Reanne could have a good laugh at some of tonight's celebrities together. Yes, that would be more like it. He would call her and explain the situation to her, perhaps even bitch about his ruined evening. They would both get a good laugh out of it.

Chapter Nine

"And tonight's recipient of the distinguished musician of the year award—Mr. Colton Wright." Cole rose from his seat waving to the cameras and the crowds and went to accept the award.

Quite a surprise, he thought. He had known that he was to be a presenter tonight, but no one had bothered to tell him he was also to receive an award himself. Oh well, another piece of crystal to weigh down his growing display at the CW Management offices. *Whoever heard of a distinguished musician award?*

He spread his arms in a helpless gesture, as if to tell the spectators—*I can't help it, you just keep giving these things to me*—fixed that famous enigmatic smile on his face and strolled to the stage.

The crowd stood as one, cheering and whistling, and he played to them, tipping his hat, and putting a bit of a macho swagger into his walk. This was Colton in his famous celebrity persona. To the left and right of the narrow aisle, hands reached out to touch him and he acknowledged them with a smoldering look from below his hat brim. Dozens of hands held something out to be autographed as he made his way slowly but surely to the front of the hall.

Finally, having reached the stage, he swung up on it rather than use the stairs and, to the thunderous applause from the guests, took off his Stetson and let it sail into the crowd. He couldn't see the lucky lady who caught it, but her delighted squeal rang through the auditorium. He bowed again, waved and delighted in the cheers and applause that brought him. Tonight he reveled in their accolades.

On the stage the spotlights brightened, and there stood Reanne…dressed in a long, silver lamé dress, tiny jewels in her hair sparkling in the reflected lights. She looked like a column of sparkling diamond dust. She smiled radiantly and her eyes shone with a special light just for him, as she held out the award to him, a crystal guitar with golden strings.

So much glitter, so much sparkle, he ought to be blinded. But his eyes saw only Reanne, her bright red lips smiling, competing with the red of her hair, every trace of anger gone.

"Congratulations Mr. Wright," she said as she presented the award to him.

He took it from her hands and raised it high over his head, and then amid the wild cheers from the crowd bent to kiss her. Her hair smelled like a fresh summer meadow and her lips were soft and inviting. All around them the cheering and applause rose to a thundering crescendo as he set the award down and drew her closer into his arms. He gently coaxed her lips apart and nipped them playfully, drawing her as close as he could to his length and deepening the kiss passionately. She made a tiny little sound in the back of her throat, returning his passion with equal desire, until somewhere some joker started banging his glass with a spoon. They all wanted to see them together, they all wanted to see a true fairy tale kiss.

Colton released Reanne and turned to face the crowd, but sometime during their kiss the entire hall had emptied, silent except for the insistent ringing that went on and on. With the spotlights blinding them in the middle of the stage, Reanne covered her face with her hands and seemed to be crying…still Colton could not find the source of the ringing.

Colton opened his eyes suddenly and faced the ceiling of his bedroom. On his nightstand the telephone went on stubbornly blaring. He picked it up, still chasing wisps of his odd dream.

"—lo?"

"And a top of the morning to you too, Cole."

"Ken you bastard, what time is it, you sound disgustingly awake. Lemme go back to sleep."

"It's past noon Cole, if you were still sleeping you deserved waking up."

Colton muttered an obscenity and stretched under the covers. The blinds let in tiny slivers of bright sunlight that glinted off the crystal chandelier, reminding him eerily of Reanne and the award in his dream.

"How did last night go?" Ken asked and Colton grunted an abject response.

"Boring, but ok, I suppose the guests enjoyed themselves. I handed over the award, gave my speech, pressed the requisite hands. It was all right as these things go."

"And your date?"

"Ah, Miss Bowen. She was so worried about wrinkling her dress, or herself ,she wouldn't even dance. As for conversation—I think she left her brain home by mistake."

"Cole, you're not being nice."

"Believe me Ken, believe me, I am being nice."

"Well, some of the gossip rags got some nice pics of the two of you, chalk it up to publicity."

"That type of publicity I don't need. That was the last time, all right?"

"I know, I know, the new image. We'll talk about that when you get to the office, spin it into the right direction. Are you coming in today?"

"I might and, if I do, I think I'll have a story of my own for you."

"Yeah? What kind of story and do I really want to hear it?"

"You'll find out later, Ken you'll just have to wait."

"I see", Ken said guardedly. "Anyway, that radio station contest is progressing as planned. The winners have been confirmed, the reservations for the hotel have been made, the video shoot has been arranged—all you have to do is look over everything and sign the stuff."

"Right."

"You still sound like you're half asleep Colton, get your ass out of bed and into gear, I'll see you later."

Colton replaced the receiver carefully, stretched again and folded his hands behind his head. Idly he imagined what Ken would say when he heard the story of the duet he had done of *Paradise* with Reanne—and that weird dream. Never mind Ken, first thing he would have to do was square things with Reanne herself. It was after noon, so the morning show should be over by now and Reanne and Jack off the air. Too bad, he had been half planning to phone into the show under a disguised voice and request a song for her. Would she have recognized him?

Now at this point she was probably still at the station, didn't they plan the next days show in advance? He reached for the phone, but slowly withdrew his hand. Phoning KSOM looking for Reanne was probably not a good idea. For one thing what kind of message would he leave, for another the gossip would spread like wildfire if Colton Wright phoned and asked for her personally? He had developed a thick hide against the gossip mills, but how she would react to it was anyone's guess. Private number? Darn, he had forgotten to ask her. Damn, he would have to get a hold of her somehow. Perhaps he could ask one of his people at CW Management to track her down.

Satisfied that he at least had a plan he finished the business of completely waking up, getting out of bed, dressed and ready for the day.

Several messages awaited him already, but he chose to ignore them while he phoned the deli downstairs and had some coffee and pastries delivered. Then he assigned one of the young men at the management office to the task of finding Reanne. A mountain of paperwork had been delivered in the over night mailbag and he sat down to it unwillingly. That even an international recording star still couldn't get away from paperwork seemed like one of the world's great injustices to him.

Mentally he prepared himself and took a deep breath when the phone rang. Here goes...

"Hello there," he said as pleasantly as he could, expecting Reanne on the other end of the line.

"I'm sorry Cole, its Mike from the office, but the lady in question would not take the call."

"She what?"

"She refused to take the call, sorry."

"Well what the he... What did she say?"

"I don't think I would want to repeat that."

"Well try again."

"Rightoh."

All right, maybe this was going to be a mite more difficult that he had imagined, she could be just a touch madder than he had first thought, heavens it was just a little mix-up!

As an afterthought, he phoned up Nashville's best florist and ordered an outlandish bouquet at an outlandish price and had it delivered to her. The card he had them sign 'From your duet partner—who has a lot of explaining to do.' Maybe that would work.

Within the hour, Mike had tried 8 times to get Reanne on the phone and been turned down just as often, each time a little more forceful than the one before. The last time, he admitted, he had learned a few words even he hadn't heard before. The flower store phoned back because the delivery had been refused, wondering what they should do with the flowers, and Colton was pacing his study, cursing quietly.

"All right Reanne," he mumbled, "so you're angrier than thought. I was being insensitive, but at least let me explain!"

He should be getting some work done, pacing his study was not accomplishing anything. He sat at the grand piano and began some ham fisted two fingered tinkering.

He had no illusions where his piano playing was concerned, his playing sucked, but he found that it did help him concentrate. None of his work was getting done, he had several live appearances to arrange and get ready for and Reanne was acting just simply foolishly. Well, he thought, who needed her anyway, there were dozens ready to take her place. His thoughts, however, had a different opinion and kept returning to Reanne. No matter what he did, in a matter of moments he was thinking of her again. Finally he muttered a minor curse, it was obvious that, for the remainder of the day at least, he wouldn't be able to get the woman off his mind.

He left the shambles of his office for the cleaners, grabbing the keys for the Cadillac off the board by the door.

"So, you want to tell me what this is all about?" Jack asked, putting down some notes he had been working on and looking across the desk he was sharing with Reanne.

"What what is about?" she asked, knowing full well.

"The phone calls, the flowers you returned, your general distracted, scattered mood, the funk you're currently in."

"Nothing, Jack", she said, looking straight at him. "At least not any more, so I'd appreciate if you would simply not mention it. The situation has resolved itself."

"Yowza! I heard from Rod you tried to get out of the on location in Hawaii. Pardon my butting in, but I don't think that is very smart. Does this have anything to do with…"

"I just didn't feel like it Jack, there's stuff going on that I…"

"Don't kid a kidder Reanne. That is probably the most unprofessional thing I have ever heard you say. This assignment is going to be a major career boost for you and I'm not going to let Colton Wright screw this up for you."

"What? How did you…who told you"?

"Get real, no one had to tell me. I could see that for some reason you and he took an instant dislike to each other and you've been off your game ever since. Now, as a professional, I expect you to stand back and work with people even if you don't like them. I'm not mentoring you for you to throw it all away, is that clear? Anyway, the guy did one show here, we're spending a week in Hawaii, it's not like you have to be attached at the hip or anything."

Reanne's heart beat a mile a minute. For a moment she had honestly thought Jack had caught on to her real feelings about Colton. Joined at the hip, now there was a joke! Right now she wouldn't be attached to Mr. Jerk Wright with shackles! Not that it mattered—it was over, but it would be just as well to keep it buried and written off under embarrassing experiences.

"Jack, Rod turned me down anyway. So, yeah, I'm going to be there. No matter what, I'm doing that show. And I'm going to make it the best damn show we've done yet. So please don't worry, none of your tutoring is going to go to waste."

Thoughtfully Jack rubbed his chin for a moment. "That wasn't the only thing I was worried about. I didn't know what was going on with you and Wright, just that you seemed to hate each other's guts, and I also don't know what's going on in your life right now—it might be better that way—but if it brings out that fighting spirit in you I'm all for it, so keep it up and pretty soon you're going to sit in this chair." He pointed to the old and battered swivel chair he occupied.

"Thanks Jack but I think I had better get my own."

At the end of the day, when Reanne finally let herself put away the last file, the last notepad and the last tape for tomorrow's show, she could barely contain a yawn. If she was really honest about it, in the dark corners of her mind where no one was looking, she had worked like a mule all day to avoid having time to think about Colton, having time to think at all. She had already made up every vile name for him that she could think about, and was finding out that perhaps now was not the right time to work at a country radio station. Every song seemed designed to make her cry today, *What do you Know About Love, For my Broken Heart, Sad Side of Town* and on and on it went.

On the other hand she had come up with a few true heartfelt commentaries and in a weird and twisted way the whole thing had given her a new ease on air today. Well, maybe that wasn't such a bad thing either. For a moment she was tempted to volunteer for the late show and put a few more hours of work in, but she would be absolutely no good tomorrow and eventually there did come a time when she had to go home.

She packed her purse, looked around the office one more time and turned out the light. Time to go face her empty apartment. At least he had stopped phoning, that was a good thing. He had finally got the message—now if she could just get it through to her heart too.

And still…for a day she had let herself dream. Dream of being with Cole, of falling in love with him and he in love with her. In her dream she was sitting in the audience while he played live. Thousands of women screamed at the man who would go home with her. During his songs he would give her little signs from the stage, a wink here, a wave there, a subtly altered word in the lyrics—all just for her. And then, just before the end, he would introduce her to everyone in the audience as his girl, he would ask her to come up on stage with him, would give her this incredible kiss that branded her his, right there in front of the clapping audience. The flashbulbs would pop and the headlines would scream, "Small town girl woos big time country star!"

That was the Cole of her dream, unfortunately today he had turned out to be just a jerk who used his stardom to surround himself with beautiful women like fashion accessories. And just as easily changed. Yep, just another jerk with a hat and a guitar she reminded herself all the while scolding herself that she should have known better. She should have known that her reach was exceeding her grasp, as they said. A guy like him probably pointed into the audience during a concert and his goons would go out and bring those women to the dressing room after the show. It happened. No one really talked about it, but it happened. Why should Colton Wright be any different? Because he seemed like a nice guy? Fat chance!

So, a lesson had been taught and learned today and, once again, it was time for Reanne Parker to put aside her dreams of stardom and to concentrate on life—that thing that happened while you were busy making plans.

When she arrived home the first thing that greeted her was the "Elevator out of Service" sign. "Not again." Sighing, she began to climb the stairs to her fifth floor apartment. This was the third time this month. She was sure looking forward to the time that KSOM would give her a raise and she could leave this dump and find a better place.

When she finally put the keys into the lock and opened the front door she noticed immediately that something was out of place. There was a fine floral scent hanging in the air, and she had the distinct feeling someone was in the apartment. Warily, she reached around the corner and flipped the light switch without stepping further into the room. What she saw almost took her breath away. Every available surface was covered in flowers of every kind. There were roses, lilies, carnations, mums, and orchids—on the table, the dresser, in shelves on ledges, even on the floor. Every available inch of flat space in her apartment covered in flowers. There were even some succulent cacti perching on the windowsill.

Reanne, awestruck, put her hand to her mouth when the kitchen door opened and a certain cowboy stepped into the room, careful not to crush any flowers under his size ten boots. His expression hovered somewhere between contrition and pride over what he had done. He reminded Reanne of a big clumsy puppy who has chewed up your best dress shoes. He knows he shouldn't have, but he's too proud of his achievement and he just had to show you. And, of course, you always forgave the puppy.

Colton? For a moment she was tempted to forgive and throw herself into his arms but the memory of yesterday quashed the impulse quickly.

"How did you get in here and what do you want?" she asked and flung her purse aside, deliberately not caring where it landed. It fell onto her couch, knocking over a particularly lush bouquet of yellow roses in the process. Colton followed their progress to the floor with a pained expression.

"Your land lady is a great Colton Wright fan," he said. "Now if you just let me explain…"

"I really don't want to hear another tale of how you used your stardom to get what you want. Get out of my place and take your…your botanical garden with you," she sneered. "I have no use for either."

"Reanne, what you heard was…"

"A misunderstanding?"

"Well, yes, but…"

"Not what it sounded like?"

"Not at all, you see…"

"I see that I've heard it all before. Now please get out."

"Will you just listen for a moment? It wasn't real!"

"Which one Cole? Sleeping with me or making a date with someone else, immediately after?"

She started pulling handfuls of flowers out of their vases and throwing then at him and he had to raise his arms to deflect the floral artillery.

"Or maybe, Cole, maybe you don't know any more, would you like some time to think about it?"

Finally he crossed the room and grabbed her firmly. His powerful hands imprisoned her wrists by her sides and even though she tried to fight him off, delightful little shivers ran up her arms from where he touched her, straight to her heart. Once again her traitorous body was disobeying her.

"There was no date for crying out loud," Colton hissed, staring straight into her eyes.

"Oh yeah, I sure heard you make one," she said, fighting against his grip and her feelings. "And no matter what you thought it was, I would still like you to leave and leave me alone—forever—you got that? I'm not into these kinds of games."

"They are games all right, Reanne. They set these things up between my management company and my publicist. I have nothing to do with it whatsoever. I simply take the bimbo of the month out, get a few pictures taken and that's it. It's been done for my so called image for a long time."

"That's disgusting."

"I agree, that's why I stopped it, image or not. I'm just sorry it's taken me so long to realize that. The awards date had been set up a long time ago, or so I had been told. It would have caused more trouble to try and get out of it than not. This was the last time, I swear."

Reanne sat down heavily on her couch, belatedly remembering the poor roses and pulling a bedraggled bouquet out from under her.

"Look, you've got to believe me Reanne, none of this means anything."

She looked up and realized that he was kneeling beside the sofa—in amidst a sea of rapidly wilting carnations. In his blue eyes she saw genuine regret, and, again, she had to squelch the impulse to just fall into his arms and let bygones be bygones.

"I can't play these games," she said, "I can't wonder every time something like this happens and worry what's going on, sorting out what's real and what's not."

"No more games, I promise."

"No more games? Cole everything is a game to you, a show you're putting on. Is there a real you in there somewhere? One moment you're hot then you're cold. One moment you sing with me, then you sleep with me. Then you go out in public with someone else. What is it you want? Do you even know?"

There was a long silence as Colton plucked apart one of the roses, petal from petal, leaf from leaf.

"Maybe not," he said finally. "Believe it or not I'm kind of new at this too. All I know is that we've got something here. A good something, a great something maybe. I might not know where it's heading, but I'm willing to follow for a while and find out, are you? I don't want to kick myself in a few years for passing something up that could have been wonderful."

"Colton," she shook her head. "Colton, right now I don't even know what to do or what to think. When I thought you were making that date I was incredibly hurt and angry. Now I know that you didn't but I can't just stop and let everything be all right. "

She looked up and saw a little of the hurt reflected in his eyes too. "So I'm a wimp, I don't do well with— uncomfortable feelings, with rejection, I never have. I need time to sort this whole thing out in my own mind. Will you at least let me have that?"

"Just as long as you're not saying no to me right off the top, of course," he said, trying to hide his disappointment. "But I need you to know that…"

"That the date wasn't real, yes Cole, I know that, but I still need time to set this right in my head and to find out what I'm feeling myself, okay?"

"Okay." He pulled her close and rested his chin on her head. For one moment, for one insane moment she thought he was going to tell her he loved her, just so she could look at him and say *me too, my love, me too*, in this breathy, seductive voice—and then he would kiss her and they would…*Never mind!*

"I'm not going to push you. Really I'm not. Take all the time you need. Are you going to be all right by yourself?" He looked around sheepishly, "I did end up making a mess in here didn't I?"

"No, it's ok, just leave, just leave for now, please."

"All right. I will…reluctantly." He stood up, found his hat and jacket somewhere in that botanical mess he had left and went to the door.

"I'll phone you tomorrow," he said tenderly, "see how you're doing" He laid two fingers to his lips and then he was gone.

Reanne waited until the door clicked into its lock behind him and then broke down on her couch, beating the pillow beneath her with both fists in a mixture of anger and frustration. All through the day anger had sustained her and she had not let herself cry. She would not let herself cry and she had been proud of it! Then in the space of moments Cole had moved in and turned everything upside down. As little as a week ago she had known where she was headed and what she was feeling. Now? Almost hourly her emotions changed from denying she ever felt anything for Cole to being deeply in love with him. One moment she wanted to slap him, send him back to under whatever slimy rock he had crawled out of, the next he was her white knight, come to carry her away on his white horse.

One voice told her he had at least come to her and apologized, explained, filled her place with roses and given her the time she had asked for, shown how he felt. Another voice asked whether she was out of her mind, envisioning any kind of future with him. His words were still hanging in the air, "just follow this thing and see where it leads."

Reanne got up from the sofa, straightened her clothing and started organizing all the flowers in the room. Even storing their vases and various containers after the flowers were gone would eventually require an extra cupboard. Such a sweet, impulsively irresponsible, typically Cole thing to do. Sometimes he reminded her of a headstrong impulsive boy who refused to grow up—and the question still remained, did she allow herself to fall in love with him—did she even have a choice?

If she gave her heart away, would she get his in return, or would he eventually figure on finding someone more suited to his celebrity persona? Reanne stopped in her flower arranging efforts when the full truth of that thought hit her. Reanne Parker and Cole might be a wonderful match but Colton *Mr. Right* Wright showed up wherever he went with someone glamorous enough to match his own fame.

And deep inside Colton was his music, he lived for his performances, he had probably never even thought about separating one from the other. His very celebrity allowed him to do what he did. She wondered if Cole even realized these two distinct sides of his own personality. And of the two sides, which would eventually make the decision?

Standing there she pictured him in her mind and smiled. I can only hope that it's you who calls the shots Cole, she thought, and a fifty-fifty chance is worth the gamble. Whether she liked it or not, that was the very moment she fell in love with Cole, aka Colton Wright, heart and soul, no way back and she would do anything she could to live up to his ideal.

The Cadillac's headlights cut a bright swath through the night, illuminating a small part of the lonely road ahead of him while leaving the rest in darkness. Just as part of his mind concentrated on driving while the other mulled over the mystery that was Reanne. In his entire life he couldn't remember apologizing to anyone else as much as he had to her in the last few days. It brought to mind an article that Zeta Daly from *Country Insight* had written about him a while ago, "We forgive him a lot because he is *the* Colton Wright. He demands and gets an indulgence of his whims and we go along with it because we know that once we sit in the audience at his concerts he will give back to us a thousand fold."

She had made him sound headstrong and spoiled, not exactly a flattering assessment. At the time Zeta Daly had referred to a minor incident over album cover shots with his label that had resulted in a month long delay of a new album release. Yes the album had been worth it a thousand times over and yes he had used the extra time to put that special oomph into his live show, but there was a nagging voice reminding him that he had been accused before of insisting on his own way, and of using his celebrity status to get it.

Not until Reanne, however, had it become this noticeable to him. A long time ago, when he had sworn off love and marriage for good, a lot of close relationships had gone by the wayside as well. Perhaps his stubborn streak had already been getting in the way back then. Perhaps around the time when he started to referring to himself in the third person—*'we are working on a song right now'*— he had stopped feeling personally responsible for everything he did while being in celebrity mode.

Just like this business with the set up dates. Reanne was right, it was disgusting, and no one but a celebrity would get away with it. It had kept him from getting too close to anyone, protecting him from emotional closeness at the same time. His life and work style catered to his basically solitary nature and, for the longest time, the only person he had to worry about was himself. Stars seemed to be expected to worry about no one but themselves. He spent a great deal of his day in his own head, creating. Until the stage lights came on and he let loose and let the wild ride start.

Then *Mr. Right* emerged on that stage, a maniac, throwing his hat, the odd set of drum sticks and, sometimes, himself into the crowd and reveling in their adoration from the opening note until the last fading sound of their cheers. Over the years it had been a luxury to indulge both sides of himself at will, being able to choose when and where.

Lately, though, something seemed to be missing. An emptiness where he didn't know a need had been. An inner longing for something he had yet to define.

Perhaps putting a stop to his so called dates had been a first step. A first step to what? The idea that he might be opening himself up to a real relationship scared the living daylights out of him. He depressed the accelerator quickly, trying to outrun that particular thought.

Fun, that was the best answer to such dark musings. Fun, unbridled, uncensored fun. That's what he had told Reanne, that's what he should really stick to instead of trying to read a dark and heavy meaning into everything that happened.

And where did he usually find this brand of fun? Bingo! A quick check in the back of the car revealed that his trusty Gibson acoustic guitar was with him—not that he actually ever went anywhere without it—and he turned the caddy around smoothly, heading for the Barn Door, a country music bar. A dive really, on the outskirts of town. He knew the owners and he knew they would welcome an impromptu live act on a night like this. Marc Bannon, that old, grizzly bartender-turned-club owner, would be thrilled to have him. Some of his very first live gigs had been played there, Marc having a nose like no one else for new acts, and he indulged in revisiting his old stomping grounds every now and then.

The crowd at the Barn Door that night was your typical weeknight crowd, regulars, a few working men having a drink after the end of their shift, some couples on a shy first date and a few characters he wouldn't have cared to have an argument with. This was the type of Honky Tonk where he had gotten his start, singing for a few dollars at night, and getting fired frequently because he insisted on playing his own stuff instead of the standby favorites the bar owners wanted to hear. Not that the crowd ever seemed to mind, but the owners had their opinions. Opinions, which by now, had been thoroughly revised.

The Barn Door even featured the requisite hand painted wooden sign "Live Country Music—Every Nite". Young hopefuls played their hearts out in places like this night after night, in Nashville and beyond. Often they played for little more than the hope that one day the right record producer would be sitting in the audience, and their big break was just three minutes away. Outfits like this had honed Colton's talent with a crowd to the sharp blade he now wielded with impudence.

Here he had discovered his need for an audience, for that special give and take between audience and performer that, in rare cases, can create pure magic. Colton Wright possessed such magic. The houselights dimmed for a moment and a lone spotlight wandered onto the half moon wooden stage. The band playing there tonight, *Not Quite Dwight,* a Dwight Yoakam cover-act waited with anticipation—in high spirits over a chance to play with the famous Colton Wright. Marc Bannon, now a good friend of Colton's stepped into the spot light and hushed the crowd with one hand. "Ladies and Gentlemen, for your listening pleasure tonight I am most proud to present a special guest. He's a great singer, a great songwriter and a very special friend of mine. Lets all give a hand to the one, the only, the incomparable Colton Wright!"

There was a moment of silence as if the bar patrons couldn't believe what Marc had just said, then the whole room erupted in pandemonium. They were screaming, whistling and banging on tables with everything they could get a hold of. In the back of the bar a chorus started that quickly passed on to the front, multiplied and became a deafening roar:

"Col—ton, Col—ton, Col—ton!"

The house lights dimmed again and when they came back up, there stood Colton in the middle of the stage.

"Helloooooo everybody!" he screamed, swung his guitar in front of him and launched into one of his favorite drinking and party time songs *Honky Tonk Hardware*.

As the tempo picked up, so did Colton, running over the stage, dancing, kicking his feet—he physically covered the tiny stage from one end to the other as if it were a ten thousand seat arena, all the while playing the guitar. It was hard to tell who was having more fun, the performer or the audience. He created that special rapport with everyone in the crowd that made them feel he was playing for only them.

Immediately he segued into a medley from his first album and then some old classic country and rock and roll favorites. He was getting into the act by now. It didn't matter what he was thinking or feeling, what was going on his life. As always, the music itself took over and used him as a conduit.

Everything that was Colton Wright condensed and concentrated into his music. By the time he launched into a smoky voiced version of Aerosmith's *Don't Want to Miss a Thing* every man and woman in that bar was either squeezed in a tight circle around the stage or standing on tables, chairs and barstools, anything to get closer to the singer. Their screams in his ears were deafening, their voices calling his name, their hands reaching for him and clutching at him. And all of it charged him with an energy that made him want to go on forever, as if he could do anything, climb any mountain, conquer any obstacle.

Hundreds of hands held out something, anything for him to autograph, a few flashbulbs were popping, momentarily blinding him, a young girl who happened to have brought a Polaroid camera made a fortune selling his picture, but Colton didn't mind, he put down his guitar and stepped forward into the throng to receive their adoration, their love. He was at home here, in the middle of a crowd, being the performer, the man on stage. He didn't have to worry about relationships or hurt feelings or rejection here, all he had to do was show them a great time, that's what he was born to do.

Across town, in his elegant penthouse condominium, the telephone rang...once, twice, three times without an answer. Finally the answering machine kicked in and an unfamiliar, automated male voice answered, asking the caller to "please leave your message after the tone." It was an impersonal message, giving no clue as to the owner, but it didn't really matter, only fifteen or twenty people knew that particular phone number. They usually didn't bother leaving a message.

"Hi Cole...I'm sorry I missed you. It's me— Reanne. I don't know when you'll get this message, but I want you to know..."

There was a long pause.

"I'm sorry about freaking out on you Cole, I guess I have this thing about rejection, about being good enough, you know," she laughed nervously. "Anyway, I want you to know that...well, you're right, we'll never find out what is between us unless we follow it and find out. So I hope you'll phone me, and we'll go...and we'll go find out. Good night Cole...Call me."

And I love you, my God I love you. Why now...why you? Will you ever find out how much?

Chapter Ten

"That was a good show Reanne, I'm glad you got whatever it was out of your system and you're the girl we all know and love again."

"Oh? Is that so I can pick up the slack you're leaving, Jack?"

"Watch it missy."

"Jack, if you ever make it out of bed and to the studio on time I will eat this microphone!"

"Tomorrow, bring the pepper!" Jack grinned and slapped her back, laughing. He preferred treating Reanne as one of the guys, instead of worrying about hurt feelings and other problems. "Honestly, I'm glad you're yourself again. Whatever was going on, I trust that it worked itself out?"

"You worry too much," Reanne evaded. "Right now I'm just kind of psyched about that Hawaii trip. Can you imagine—our morning show in Honolulu?"

"Well actually our morning show will turn into our afternoon show once we get there. Since they're six hours behind us, we'll be the morning show on WJKT, Honolulu and the afternoon show on KSOM."

"What about the web cameras, the web site deal?"

"As far as I know, there'll be a couple of cameras around the KSOM/WJKT transmission booth and a couple around the stage by the beach where they're filming the video. As far as I understand there'll be a continuous feed from those cameras to both Colton Wright's and our KSOM websites. Basically our listeners and his fans can tune in twenty-four hours a day to find out what we and our winning listeners are up to."

"OK, but there's not going to be action there twenty-four hours a day."

"We thought about that, we'll have a camera crew with a few portable cameras. When there's no action either at the booth or the stage we'll have some events: a barbeque, beach volleyball game and such. That should keep it interesting."

"And there'll be live chats from time to time?"

"Yeah, at odd intervals one of us or Colton will do an impromptu fifteen minute chat. Nobody knows when or who it's going to be. The idea is to keep the listeners tuning into the web site to find out."

"Well, we're certainly going high tech aren't we? I can't tell you how excited I am about this Jack. This is going to be incredible."

"I'm glad, because that Rea, is the future. The future in radio and perhaps in general. You're going to see this type of thing more and more. Now I'm an old fashioned DJ—set in my ways, late most mornings. But you, you can go places in this business."

"Thanks Jack, only because I learned from the best, you know that."

"Well it's another week, and then we are off."

"Are we all—staying at the same place?" Reanne asked carefully, trying to find out whether she would have any chance at all to be together with Cole, without being surrounded by cameras—web or otherwise.

"Well, we and our ten winners will be staying at the Kahala Mandarin—nice hotel, by the way, beautiful grounds. That's where we'll shoot the video, poolside and by the beach. As for Colton Wright and his crew, who knows? Probably somewhere secluded I imagine. Wouldn't do to mingle too closely with the common folk. Why do you ask?"

"No particular reason, just nosy."

Exceptionally nosy she thought, as she lovingly brought a picture of Cole to mind. After her message on his answering machine they had had a few dates, talked on the phone, nothing heavy, nothing difficult. Both of them moving carefully around each other, as if on eggshells. No one wanted to rock the boat, and both were wondering where they were headed. On the surface they had a good time together, listening to music, checking his newest compositions and demo tapes at the studio, going out for dinner. Still she couldn't help being bothered that they always went to places that would be quiet and out of the way. He made sure to dress down in one way or another, always being careful not to be recognized. They'd get the odd sidelong glance, someone wondering who the good looking guy reminded them of, but Colton never encouraged any of it.

When they were alone the lively, carefree and mischievous Cole came to the surface. The Cole who could laugh and joke and say what was on his mind without worrying what the press and, by extension, his fans would think. And she loved that side of him. Yet there was always a guarded layer over top when they were out in public, as if one eye was always looking over his shoulder—who is seeing us, who is watching? Or perhaps I'm just paranoid, she thought, perhaps I'm just upset because he doesn't call *People Magazine* to announce we're a couple. Is that really what I want? And, as always, after her thoughts had chased each other in a circle, around and around, they came to rest at the same spot. What she wanted was to be with Colton, plain and simple, and it didn't matter how.

"So that's where that expression came from—Nosy Parker"?

"What?" Reanne pulled herself back to reality. Jack was asking her something. "Oh, my question about the living arrangements, ha ha Jack, like I haven't heard that one before. No really, I'm looking forward to this, it's going to be fun."

"That it will be kiddo, that it will be."

"Now, here's your itinerary and your ticket," he handed her a package out of his briefcase. "I'm taking a few days off so I'll see you at the airport."

"More holidays, huh? Well you enjoy, and be sure not to miss the plane, ok?"

After Jack left she leafed through the tourist brochures of Hawaii and the Kahala Mandarin for a while. It all looked exciting, alluring and fascinating from a dark broadcasting studio in Nashville, but to be that close to Colton every single day, from morning to night, and not let on to anyone how she felt, it would be difficult at best. But, perhaps Cole had changed his mind in the meantime about letting others in on their secret. They had fun together, more than anything they enjoyed each others company, no matter what they were doing. Reanne rested her head in her hand and let her thoughts wander to all the things they had done together.

Just yesterday, Cole had driven her a few miles outside Nashville to the Bar M. The Bar M was a ranch owned by one of his friend who had invited them to spend the day. He didn't ask any questions and Cole didn't offer any explanations, but he had looked Reanne up and down very carefully while Cole selected two horses for them.

Reanne's skills on horseback were rusty at best—sorely lacking was probably a better term—she hadn't been on one in ages. Despite her protests though, Colton had a beautiful, gentle mare saddled and ready for her in moments.

He took her around the corral a few times, to make sure she wouldn't fall off before the morning was over and then they were off along the trail. It was like they were alone on this world and in this beautiful valley. Their path wound through the pastures and into a little forest following a babbling creek. They let the horses have their head and moved at a comfortable tempo. The path was wide enough so they could ride abreast and talk if they wanted to, but for long stretches they simply enjoyed the ride and nature and the companionable silence of two who don't necessarily have to speak to understand each other. Reanne wished the ride could go on forever.

It was just after noon when they reached a little sun dappled forest clearing. Colton stopped the dark stallion he had selected for himself, a horse that matched him in temperament as well as good looks, and Reanne's mare pulled up beside him. All around them was nothing but green forest in the warm glow of the early afternoon sun, the sounds of a few birds and small animals in the brush and the soft jingle of their horses' bridles.

Colton slipped off his horse and easily grasped Reanne around the waist and lifted her down. For a moment she stood completely still, her head leaning into his shoulder, inhaling the spicy fragrance of his cologne. Could there be a moment as perfect as this? The only living things in their world were themselves and their horses, with the clearing forming a magical circle around them, impenetrable to all, save themselves.

"I could stay here forever," she said, and Colton touched his nose to hers.

"But then you would miss the picnic."

"Picnic? What picnic?"

"Come and see." He tied the horses properly to a tree with a long rope so they could crop the fresh young grass under the trees and removed his saddlebags.

"Over here, have a look," he beckoned.

"This is like Christmas."

"You just wait and see. Item number one, a red checked tablecloth." He handed it to her, snatching it away as she reached for it. "Come to think of it, I think each of these items is going to cost you a kiss, so let's have it."

Laughing, she paid him his tribute and took the tablecloth from him.

"You are incorrigible."

"You bet, I think I see a good flat spot over there."

Cole had packed for an army and expected, and received, the appropriate payment for each item he removed from the never ending saddlebags—champagne, grapes, cheese, crackers, and paté. There was an endless array of delicacies. At one point he frowned at a quart of strawberries with intense concentration.

"Now, do you think that's one bowl of strawberries or about forty berries?"

"Oh, definitely by the berry, Cole, definitely."

"Really?"

"Really."

"All right," he sighed, "if you insist, over here then."

They acted like little children, kissing and laughing and, for all the world, they could have been alone on the planet.

"Is there no end to your magic saddle bags?"

"No ma'am." He laughed and finally turned it upside down and shook it, looking inside again.

"Too bad, I think that's it. Well, maybe just one more kiss, just for thinking about it. He caught her about the waist and slanted his lips over hers, drawing her into a kiss that made her lose all sense of time and space.

He stretched out his full length on the blanket, lying on his side his head cradled in her lap, nibbling strawberries. Her fingers played with his long golden hair, winding curls around her fingers while he told her about the new album, the song he had started writing today, the time he had spent with the band, rehearsing with them, and the tour he was preparing. When he talked about his music his eyes lit up and his voice became soft and gentle. Reanne listened with one ear, simply enjoying the feel of his head on her lap, the look of his long graceful body sprawled out beside her and his fingers pulling out blades of grass and splitting them, and the soft feel of his hair she was winding around her forefinger.

"Ouch, that hurt, what are you trying to do, scalp me?"

"Sorry!"

"Don't be." He pushed the rest of the picnic out of the way and patted the ground beside him. "Lie here, there are better things you can do with those talented fingers."

"Oh yeah?"

"Oh definitely yeah!"

He pulled her down beside him and kissed her again and again, silently guiding her hands down the buttons of his own shirt and Levis' while he pulled the end of her sweater out of her waistband and over her shoulders. Her hands found his manhood hard and ready and she stroked and gentled him, innocent of the power she held over him. He groaned impatiently and his lips barely left hers long enough for her sweater to clear her head and he tossed it somewhere behind them. His own clothes followed and soon enough they lay side by side, running their eyes and hands over each other's bodies. He bent his head to her breasts and teased their nipples into tight little buds with his expert tongue. His fingers found her already hot and ready for him and he rubbed and teased her mercilessly drowning her little cries with his kisses. She arched her back, the need to have him inside her so great she thought she would die of it and still he showed her no mercy bringing her to the brink over and over and pulling her back again.

Just when she thought she couldn't handle any more, he grabbed hold of her sides and rolled them both over, impaling her on his length. Reanne's eyes flew open as she took her fill of him. His hands were on her breasts and their eyes were locked on each other as she rode him on and on in the brilliant sunshine. She took him inside her as deep as she could again and again, until the valley, the forest, the horses, everything faded and there was only the sensation of themselves as one. They created one body and one soul in a place that needed neither time nor space, with one final thrust he took them both over the edge and they truly joined together as their cries echoed through the silent forest, proclaiming their union to one and all.

The memory of their beautiful magic raised goosebumps on her flesh—they were incredible together, as long as they were alone. Their time together held a special place in her memory, a once in a lifetime moment. No matter what happened, their hearts always seemed to find a common ground a place away from time and reality but, ultimately, the time came to return to earth and, when they turned around and faced their respective realities, inevitably the awkwardness returned.

She had observed the tenderness his face had held on the way home, and how he had chewed for a long time on something he needed to say.

"I don't want to you to read anything into this, please don't be upset," he said softly, "but I'm not quite ready to go public with our relationship. The press would be all over us like ants at a picnic and I don't want to do that to either you or me. Give us both a little more time, time for it to be just like today, just us."

He wasn't too specific about what it was he didn't want the press doing to them, and why he didn't want their names linked for the foreseeable future. He simply asked her specifically to not reveal their relationship while they were in Hawaii, but why? That was the central question her mind had been turning this way and that, ever since. What could he possibly have to be afraid of? And perhaps afraid was not really the right word, perhaps he simply didn't want to ruin his chances at someone better suited to him.

"Ah Reanne, don't go neurotic on me and ruin everything, not again," she muttered to herself.

"Sometimes that's good advice," someone said behind her and Reanne turned to see Sasha standing there.

"Trouble, Reanne?"

"Not trouble specifically—it's really kind of complicated."

"I'm good at complicated. Want to tell me about it?"

"Sasha, I don't know. Ok, what exactly does a guy mean when he's dating you for a while and everything is fine, except he doesn't want anyone to know about it?"

"Geez, Rea, you don't ask the easy ones, do you? I can see what you mean by complicated. Ok, what does it mean—depends on the guy. If he's married or gay he's covering his butt, if you are, he's covering yours. Any other case—I'd say…he might be out playing the field keeping his options open, he might be commitment–shy, he might have an entire harem of ladies—am I close with any of these?"

"Oh thanks Sasha, that's just what I wanted to hear?"

Sasha put an arm around her shoulder. "You know, that sounds like an awful mess you've got yourself into, Reanne, is there anything I can do for you?"

"Thanks Sasha," Reanne rubbed her eyes with the balls of her hands, trying to get rid of the constant fatigue in her head. "That's kind of you, but I don't think there's anything anyone can do right now. It's something I have to figure out for myself, I guess."

"Reanne, are you sure about this guy? Whoever he is, he's got you jumping through hoops, I mean it sounds a bit odd to me, and he is definitely not treating you the way he should. I want to tell you that. If it's meant to be, it's going to happen, but I don't know…"

"He's ok Sasha, he's not into anything weird or anything, he's just got this thing about no one knowing."

"Well, that's wrong. He should be proud of being with you, he should want to show you off. Don't bury yourself in this, Reanne. Take a step back and take a look at what it is the two of you have. Then if you decide it's good enough to fight for, that's what you're going to do and, if you don't think you can live with that…well I guess you know what to do.

"Thanks, I think."

"I mean it, if you ever need anything, even some advice you don't want to hear…"

"I'll remember."

She gathered her belongings and rose from her chair.

"I guess it's time to go home now and get ready for Hawaii."

"Oh, I envy you Reanne. And you'll see, a few days away from it all will do you a world of good. And who knows, by the time you get back mystery man may be ready for some serious commitment. Absence making the heart grow fonder and all that. Maybe your little vacation is going to fix everything just right."

Reanne smiled and left the office with a little wave. Good advice, except instead of getting away from each other, she and Cole would be together every hour of the day. Either they would both become very good actors or some gossip rags would have a very juicy story pretty soon. And why not, there were worse stories the papers could write about her than going with Cole. Oh sure, they might dig up her past attempts at a singing career, but so what. And suddenly she realized that when she thought about Cole, her past failure on the stage didn't sting quite so much.

Chapter Eleven

"Ladies and gentlemen, we have arrived at Honolulu International Airport. Please remain in your seats with your seatbelts fastened and your tray tables in the upright position until the aircraft has come to a complete stop in front of the terminal building."

Reanne couldn't help grabbing Jack's hand. "We're here, we're here!" she said excitedly.

"Yes, we're here," he grumbled. "Just about time too, I don't think I'll ever walk upright again."

He kept grumbling all the way through the unloading of their carry on luggage and filing out of the Airbus.

The first thing that struck Reanne as they deplaned was the light breeze and the fragrance of plumeria. After the humid heat of Nashville that could hang over the city like an inverted water glass, Hawaii's gentle breeze made a welcome change. Their arrival had been coordinated by the marketing company that was sponsoring their trip and they were checked through and ready with their luggage half an hour later.

Jack had apparently recovered. Reanne found him chatting animatedly with some of their guests, keeping one eye out for a likely pub or other watering hole. Reanne took the time to look around the terminal building. Absolutely every space that didn't serve some utilitarian purpose was covered in greenery. Palm trees, ferns, orchids and lovely white plumeria flowers grew in abundance everywhere and their subtle scents hung in the air. Everyone seemed to be wearing a version of the standard Hawaiian dress, colorful shirts or dresses with flowers on everything. And smiles, all the Hawaiians were wearing huge smiles on their faces. How could anyone help but be in a good mood with all this beauty and all this happiness around? While she was looking about, a young Hawaiian with a big, white-toothed smile came over to her and stuck a plumeria blossom behind her ear.

"Why, thank you," she stammered, blushing furiously, but the young man was already gone. A honking horn brought her attention back to the front of the terminal building. The bus for their transfer to the Kahala Mandarin Hotel had arrived, and out jumped a group of girls in brightly colored dresses welcoming them, smiling and giggling. They placed a flowered lei around everyone's neck and kissed their cheek. "Aloha, welcome to Hawai'i."

Aloha! Reanne raised the lei to her nose and inhaled its rich fragrance. It reminded her of the flowers Colton had filled her room with and instantly she smiled. In a few short hours she would see him again.

"Oh, my gosh, oh my gosh, this is so exciting," the lady beside her said. "Hi, I'm Emily, I listen to your show all the time. It is such an honor to finally meet you. Do you think we'll see Colton Wright soon? I think this is so exciting. Oh my gosh, I don't think I can stand it."

"Well, thank you," Reanne laughed, touched by the woman's excitement. "Thank you, I think Cole…Mr. Wright will join us for dinner.

"Aw, you know him, what's he like, you must tell me everything about him, I am such a fan, such a fan, do you think he'll let us take our picture with him?"

Most of the guests were couples staying two to a room, but both Reanne and Jack had a room to themselves. After the cramped atmosphere of the plane, her room was a soothing refuge. It looked like a study in soft pastel, with whitewashed wicker furniture. Pearly pink, light blues and creams dominated the cushions and bedspread and, of course, there was a profusion of flowers everywhere.

Reanne left her luggage where the bellboy had set it down, rushed to the balcony and threw the slatted wood doors open. The sun was getting ready to sink into the ocean just beyond the horizon and there were quite a few couples out strolling the beach. Her balcony had a magnificent view of the gardens and a beautiful stretch of white sand beach. The salt tang of the air filled her nostrils and the steady rush of the tide provided a constant background sound. Oh, I'll be sleeping like a baby with all that in the background, she thought, that is if there is much sleep with Cole around. Right away her naughty thoughts made her smile and wonder where he was at that moment.

She went back into her room and decided to turn the air conditioner off for good and leave the door and windows open instead. Maybe she and Cole would be able to sneak away from their group once in a while and go for one of those beach walks themselves. The gardens had plenty of little paths meandering through the greenery with a little river that wound through the grounds, emptying into small ponds with fish, turtles and penguins. In the middle was a large lagoon with dolphins. Everything just looked exactly like paradise. No wonder Cole had chosen it for the *Paradise* video.

She was sitting in one of the wicker chairs on the balcony when she heard the phone ring in the room. Who knew where she was? Jack maybe.

"Hello?"

"Aloha. What were you doing, sitting on top of the phone?"

"Cole, that was fast. No I was admiring the scenery, it's just so beautiful I don't think I've seen anything more gorgeous before, where are you?"

"Next door, Kahala apartments, I'm renting a condo. Hawaii is beautiful isn't it?"

"Just breathtaking."

"Well it's one of my favorite places in this world, I wish I could show it to you, just you and me…maybe next time. Now how is my best girl? Did you have a good flight?"

"Not bad as flights go, I'm just a little tired…not too tired to you see you though, when are you coming here?"

"Well, I don't want to just stroll into the hotel like that, I'm sure all your guests are on the lookout for me, but I'll see you at the welcome dinner tonight."

"Oh."

"Don't sound so disappointed, we'll manage to get away by ourselves a few times, I promise."

"The wages of dating a star I guess. I can't wait to see you…at dinner then?"

"You bet, I'll see you later."

"Bye Cole." *I love you Cole.* Of course she only said the first part, but between the flowers, the sunset, the breeze and the ocean, falling in love was the natural thing to do. She stepped back out onto the balcony, holding a picture of Colton in her heart. Out in the gardens, she heard the faint strains of a group of slack key guitar players, including Keola Beamer, who had set up on the patio in honor of Colton Wright.

He had used them on his newest single because he loved the harmonies they produced by literally loosening the strings on their guitars. He was fascinated by the legends that slack key was drawn from the heart and soul out through the fingers of each player, and Keola was one of the masters. As she stood on her balcony listening to the sweet and soulful melodies she had never felt more content and at peace than she did now, and she had never felt closer to Cole before, as if in showing her a piece of the Hawaii he loved, he showed her a part of himself.

She let the wind and the setting sun caress her and allowed herself to daydream of the times that were still to come for them, all the firsts they would have as a couple, starting with their first solitary beach-walk in Hawaii.

A good half hour later Jack knocked on Reanne's door.

"Ready?" he asked "Let's go down to the reception and dinner, and shake some hands." Reanne nodded, nervous all of a sudden. She didn't know how she would react seeing Cole with all those people in what he called his full *Mr. Right* persona. He laughed at it when they were talking about it, but Reanne couldn't ignore the fact that *Mr. Right* and his attitudes sometimes scared her a little. He was just too much the star, had too big an ego when he was in that mode.

Jack and Reanne rode the elevator down to the lobby and, again, Reanne admired the rich dark woods and polished brass that spoke of a quiet elegance.

Down in the lobby their twenty guests had already met and were chatting away amicably. Everyone was excited about being in Hawaii and had nothing but wonderful things to say about the hotel and the grounds. Excitement was also building up. They were about to meet Colton Wright any moment. Jack started handing out diamond shaped badges on a white silk cord that read 'Paradise Found Video' on them. They also bore the CW logo in a hologram and everyone's name and position. The back carried a magnetic strip that could be read by their security scanners and would set off an alarm if someone wandered into an unauthorized area. A little over the top, Reanne thought, but then again, a lot of what *Mr. Right* did was over the top.

"Now," Jack explained, "you will have to wear these around your neck at all times during the video shoot, as certain areas of the beach and the gardens are off limits to the general public while we're filming. These will grant you access to pretty much all areas, except Colton Wright's private trailer of course."

A few of the women were giggling at that idea, and, even as they spoke, a bus pulled up under the hotel's

Porte Cochere and disgorged a never-ending stream of people, all wearing identical ID badges, the only difference being in the color of the stripe around the edge and the cord they were carried on.

"Who on earth are all those folks?" Reanne asked Jack quietly.

"Wright's people."

"His people?"

"Well yes, his management team and their assistants, his publicist, wardrobe person, hair stylist and all their assistants. His photographer, videographer and who knows who all they brought. All the choreographers and the Blonde Strangers band members and their families, not to forget the record label representative and all of his assistants. There's a probably a few journalists and photographers for *Country Music Magazine* and *CMT*, and I believe the folks with the gold badges are his private guests."

"Good God Jack, there's a whole town here!"

"Did you think it was just going to be us?"

"Well," Reanne felt foolish for her naiveté. "I never thought much about it, and never in my wildest dreams would I thought there were so many people involved in a single video production."

"That's just the beginning Reanne, all the technical people are already down by the beach setting up the stage, and the broadcast booth and the computers for the live web chats. Oh, look, over there are the reps from WJKT, let's go say hello."

The hotel's lobby and patio began filling up with more and more people. Reanne realized that she, Jack and their guests were just a tiny cog in this huge machine that was Colton's video shoot. Jack, she noticed, was visibly wilting in the heat, repeatedly wiping his balding head with a handkerchief and still there was no sign of Cole.

Finally, after the cocktails had been consumed, introductions been made, and a pro forma pecking order established, they were all invited to the patio buffet to find their tables. The patio was covered with a wooden roof in case of rain but three sides were open to the gardens, the beach and the ocean beyond.

Today the white covered tables spilled out onto the lawn beyond, and each table had a carefully designed seating order and placement. No doubt designed by Colton Wright's social director and his assistants, Reanne thought wryly. Jack, Reanne and their guest found themselves at a table with the reps from WJKT near the entrance.

Just as everyone had taken their seats the doors opened, admitting Colton. He was dressed completely in white, from the lace up ropers to the dimpled crown of his Stetson and he wore a fragrant lei of white plumeria around his neck. All in all he looked more like the wealthy, no good son of a plantation owner than a country singer.

He strolled into the room purposefully and everyone rose and began applauding. He raised one arm accepting their homage for a moment as his due and then picked up the microphone an assistant handed him.

"Welcome, welcome one and all to this video shoot for *Paradise Found,* We certainly seem to have arrived in paradise so I won't make a long speech at all."

"Except," he laughed, "Except to thank y'all for coming out and to wish us all good luck or knock on wood or whatever it is you do at home for luck. Let's make this the best damn video we've ever shot. Thanks everyone!"

He sat at his own table briefly to have a bite to eat then quickly proceeded to make the rounds. Reanne watched him, fascinated. He called almost everyone by name without visibly reading their ID tags, he had a personal word for everyone and knew who had just got married, had a baby or a sick relative. He made everyone feel special, as if they were one of his closest friends and Reanne realized she was watching part of the famous Colton Wright magic in action.

"He's coming here." The woman beside Reanne whispered excitedly and elbowed Reanne in the side. "Oh my gosh, I think I'm going to faint, isn't he gorgeous? Oh, I'm gonna faint."

But of course she didn't. Cole came round to their table, blue eyes sparkling with energy and drive. When Jack made the introductions Colton repeated everyone's name, kissed the women on the cheek and made a point of chatting with everybody, Patiently he signed everything they stuck out to him, all the while chatting away as if they were at a neighborhood barbeque. He hugged the woman sitting next to Reanne, thanking her personally for coming down to be in his video. Now she really did look like she was going to faint…and said so. Colton merely laughed, whispered something in her ear that made her blush furiously and kissed her on the cheek again.

Reanne was again impressed. She had heard of this special way he had of interacting with his fans but she had never seen him in action. These people would walk away feeling they had made a new friend in addition to meeting a multi-million selling recording artist.

"Miss Parker, nice to meet you again." he said. But when they shook hands he gave hers a little extra squeeze and winked almost unnoticeably. His way of telling her, 'hi there, I'll talk to you later'! Reanne watched him go from table to table until he had greeted the last person and then disappeared behind the greenery.

A few minutes later he stepped out again, this time carrying a white guitar. It all looked so natural it was hard to believe it had all been set up in advance. The host was entertaining his guests.

"I heard a little dinner music improves the digestion," he said and flashed that famous rogue smile. From somewhere an attendant brought a microphone again. "So I just thought, seeing as there are so many fans out here tonight, I'd sing a few songs." He grinned again, "If you don't mind that is."

Laughter and polite applause. He looked over the crowd and zeroed in on Emily the woman beside Reanne. "Emily," he said, "Why don't you go first, seeing how everyone is so shy tonight, so please, tell me your favorite song. Emily blushed furiously and said "Mah favorite song, gosh I like em all, but my favorite is *Always you.*"

"Well you have excellent taste Emily, that happens to me one of my all time favorites too. All right folks, here it is, just for Emily from Nashville, *Always You.*"

Accompanying himself on the guitar he ran through a few request and some old favorites. His own favorites, other artists' songs, everything and anything someone called out to him. If he could play it he would sing. He mesmerized the crowd; many of whom had been with his organization for a long time and surely had seen him perform before. It didn't matter, every time you saw Colton Wright live it was like the very first time.

As dinner finished, a circle of chairs formed around with Colton in the middle. Someone stuck a few torches into the ground and someone called out, "Thank God the Tiki Bar is open."

Reanne watched Colton from the shadows of a potted palm tree. The torchlight played on his face, lighting up his handsome features and putting a glow into his eyes. The shadows played in the angles and planes of his face and body, reflecting off his year round tan making him look like a sun god tonight.

He sang, chatted and laughed with his guests and seemed totally comfortable in the huge circle of people, at times using his guitar almost like an extension of himself, pointing its end, twirling it, hiding bashfully behind it, winking around the corner—he was definitely right in his element.

Even after he finally begged off singing—to save his voice for the next day and the video shoot—he was still surrounded by people. Reanne retreated further into the shadows. It didn't look like she would ever get a chance to see Colton alone tonight. She moved off a little and began to chat with some of the people KSOM had brought to Honolulu. Emily was near tears from the excitement.

"He's just so wonderful," she gushed "I cannot believe how nice and how amazing he is. I'm going to remember this forever!"

The others pretty much echoed her sentiments, ranging from gorgeous to delicious to absolutely, unbelievably great. And while a part of Reanne swelled with pride, the other grew more and more disheartened at the idea of measuring up to such an idol. Finally, when Jack suggested they retire for the evening, she gladly agreed, casting one glance back at Colton. He was still surrounded by admirers, presently telling a story of the time he had met the president of the United States, the president for crying out loud, Reanne had yet to meet the president of the network.

But tonight was not a night for worrying. Tonight was for enjoying Hawaii, for reveling in the breeze and the smells and sounds of the ocean. Tonight was simply for enjoying and for knowing she was in love, in love with Cole.

The next morning the steady rush of the tide and the time difference woke Reanne early. She stretched under her blanket, savoring the warm fragrant breeze and the cries of the seabirds that came through the open windows. Some folks closed up their rooms and shut out nature keeping the air conditioning on, but Reanne didn't want to miss a moment of this. Not one smell or sound or feeling would be sacrificed.

Her thoughts turned to last night and Colton's impromptu concert. Now that had been a true Colton Wright moment, the ruler paying homage to his admirers. Thinking of Cole made her heart sing and she couldn't wipe the smile off her face.

Almost immediately the telephone by her bedside rang as if summoned by her thoughts. "Hello?"

"Hi sweetheart, what happened to you last night, all of a sudden you were gone and I missed you."

His voice sounded mellow, warm and relaxed, just like Hawaii itself. Not a trace of the stress and tension he carried in Nashville survived.

"Hi Cole, you were pretty busy from where I was sitting and it was getting late."

"I'm sorry sweetheart, everybody wanted me last night, there was no getting away from it, but I'll steal away tonight, I promise."

"Yes?"

"After the video shoot, we'll take a car to a little out of the way spot I know, away from all the hustle and bustle down here."

"Sounds good, I'll be looking forward to that. I really really missed you. Hawaii puts me into a certain kind of mood—very romantic."

"Me too, Reanne, and if you keep talking like that I'll be at your hotel in about ten seconds and we'll both be late this morning. Go do your broadcast, I'll see you at the video shoot."

"I'll be thinking of you all day."

"I think you had better!"

The WJKT/KSOM broadcast booth was a relatively simple affair. In essence they had a ten by ten foot booth with a backdrop that was half Honolulu, half Nashville. Superimposed over all of it was the unmistakable silhouette of Colton Wright.

The electronic setup was pretty straightforward. From the transmission booth the signal was being picked up by WJKT in Honolulu, which in turn provided a satellite feed for KSOM in Nashville. Thus their listeners could pick up their morning show live from Honolulu. The prospect of a simultaneous show was incredibly exciting to

Reanne. The time difference gave everyone a little bit of a headache, and a certain amount of foul ups were most certainly going to be a part of this show. But then again, even that kept their listeners tuning in.

There was no sign of Jack yet, so Reanne checked herself out on the electronics. She gave a thumbs up to the other DJ's in the booth with her and, as the guest, took the honor of opening their first joint broadcast.

"Good morning Honolulu, good afternoon Nashville. I'm Reanne Parker whishing you a good day, wherever you are listening to us. We're here in beautiful Hawaii at the Kahala Mandarin Hotel and let me tell you what a wonderful time we are having. Right now it's eighty five degrees and breezy. You know, after the heat of Nashville this steady ocean breeze is really fantastic…and, best of all Colton Wright is here with us…how exciting can it get?"

Out of the corner of her eye she saw Jack amble up to the broadcast booth and she winked at him. "We're here on our first day of the *Paradise* video shoot. Jack have you been down to the beach yet?"

"You bet, Reanne, there are just wall to wall people down there. Keoki and Maria from WJKT were gracious enough to show me around and I am just stunned. You wouldn't believe how many people there are involved in a video like that."

"Well I just bet you liked two beautiful Hawaiian girls showing you around the beach, Jack. Did you actually see anything? What's new at the video stage?"

"They're setting up for some of the early dance scenes right now, so why don't we put on a Colton Wright song and then we'll have us a little chat with some of our winners from Nashville who will be in those dance scenes."

"Well Jack I'm sure they'll be just exhausted from all the choreography practice they've had to endure. I've got *Paradise* right on deck for you, so go ahead, sing along—and just remember, if you want a live look at what's going on here at the Kahala Mandarin, log on to

KSOM.COM or MRRIGHT.COM for a view from our twenty four hour video cameras. I'll see you there!"

Reanne tried to keep an eye on their music selection, provided by an engineer at the WJKT building, and at the same time be on the lookout for Colton. She hadn't seen him all morning, but of course he was staying at the condominium complex next door and he must be wiped after last night's performance.

Down by the beach they had set up a gigantic stage. She could just barely see a little of it from where she was standing. Lighting and sound technicians worked on it from all angles, crouching under the stage, and hanging suspended from giant steel girders which held a number of lights and cameras. In essence the video would feature Colton and his band, the Blonde Strangers, performing *Paradise* live, while a group of performers, including the folks from Nashville, danced on stage. Interspersed they would show clips of Colton and a girl walking through Honolulu or along the beach. Most of these clips had been shot previously and were ready to be spliced into the video and, truly, Reanne was quite happy she didn't have to watch them shoot those segments.

When choreography finally let their exhausted guests go for a break, Reanne signaled Jack and the WJKT crew, excused herself for a moment and headed for the hotel lobby. Jack would take care of the interviews while she grabbed a quick coffee and a moment of rest.

She brushed her hair off her forehead, exhausted. The simultaneous show required split second timing and she always had to be on her toes checking the monitor in front of her to see which songs were coming up, if WJKT was receiving a clear continuous feed, and a myriad other details. The tiny screen in front of her had her squinting most of the time, and her eyes were quite simply dog tired. The outdoor acoustics and the wireless microphone she wore made it necessary to speak clearly and enunciate more carefully than normal. In short, on location broadcasting was a lot more demanding than studio broadcasting.

Reanne had barely stepped into the hotel lobby when the doorman approached her with a portable phone. "Miss Parker?"

"Yes?"

"Phone call for you, it's urgent."

Now what? Did they already need her at the broadcast booth again?

"Thank you…This is Reanne."

"Good morning my darling."

His voice felt like the warm and soft, a reprise after the stressful morning.

"Hi Cole. How did you catch me so quickly? I just stepped out for a break."

"The web camera Reanne. I had the computer locked on our own website this morning, just to see what it looked like. I've been watching your broadcast on my monitor all morning while I was having breakfast. One feed is fixed on our video location the other on your broadcast booth."

"Wow, I haven't looked at it yet, does it look good?"

"Fantastic. It is so cool. I actually saw you walk out of the frame, I guessed you were going for a break, you look awfully tired."

"Oh thanks I guess. I can't believe this stuff they are doing with electronics these days.

"Never mind electronics, how did you like the party last night?"

"We had fun, really. Except, you were surrounded by people Cole, I didn't think I could get you to myself for even a second."

"That's life with a singer, darling, but I did miss you. I looked around and all of a sudden you were gone."

Reanne looked around for a moment to make sure no one was listening in, but the hotel lobby was busy with dozens of people all following their own business.

"I missed you too Cole, incredibly, but I was afraid that I would give myself away." She paused for a moment, "and you didn't want that to happen, right?"

There was a momentary pause on the other side. "I just don't think right now is the time to tell the press we're dating Reanne. They'd have a feeding frenzy. When we get back to Nashville I'll have Ken draft a statement, ok?"

Well, dating was ok, drafting a statement was ok. It might have been nicer, Reanne thought, if it wasn't your manager who told the press, it would be better if his statement said we were in love, not we were just dating, but I guess for now…

"Reanne?"

"I'm still here."

"Are you sure you're ok? You sound a little down."

"Just tired, Cole. Do you think I can see you today? Alone I mean. Are they going to let you out for a little while?"

Colton laughed. "I'll figure something out. After all, I am the boss around here. Don't worry It'll all work out."

It'll all work out, Reanne thought after she hung up. The question was, did they both have the same definition for *it*?

Chapter Twelve

Reanne was already needed badly again when she returned to the broadcast booth. Between finishing the show, interviewing some of their guests and some of the folks working on the video and coordinating the next day's show, it was early afternoon before she had a chance at a few more free minutes. Taking advantage of these, she decided to stroll down to the beach where they were shooting the video.

The whole area bustled with excitement the way only a live show can. The stage had been set up as a giant beach bar with plenty of bamboo, straw, silk flowers and drinks with little plastic umbrellas. Set designers were swarming all around trying to make sure everything looked authentic—only a producer could decide that a genuine Hawaiian beach was not authentic enough.

Still, there was an aura of enjoyment surrounding everything. Everyone was dressed in sarongs or bright shirts sporting at least one lei around their neck or in their hair.

"All right!" the choreographer called. "We're going to take one more run through from the start up to the first chorus. Everyone remember their steps, let go, have fun…you're on vacation, try to look like it."

Nods all around. Everyone, of course, was nervous and they had been working all morning on getting the stiffness out of their actions. Fortunately Colton's choreography group was patient and friendly with the newcomers and, after only a few hours, there were already giggles all around.

"Somebody get Colton, I want him to do this one with us."

A visible sigh went through the ladies' side. They had been waiting for him all morning. The young dancer who had been acting as a stand in for Colton jumped off the stage and dashed to the edge of the property where they had set up a small trailer. It served as a conference room, lunchroom, film storage and a retreat for Colton. As much as he wanted to get closer to his fans, he tended to hide when he wasn't working, to avoid getting mobbed.

The dancer knocked on the trailer door. "They want you for the final run through."

Reanne couldn't hear the answer but moments later the door opened and Cole strolled out and toward the stage with that confident swagger he had. He wore white jeans and a retro Hawaiian print aloha shirt. His white Stetson sported a lei instead of a hatband and he completed the look when he picked up a lime green fender stratocaster with a white faceplate, checked the amp and let loose with a few notes.

"Final check!" the producer called, giving Colton a dirty look for distracting everyone. Especially the women, they were shuffling and giggling, trying to keep their eyes on Colton.

"Action!"

The band started the famous piano intro. Reanne could have sung along, she remembered it so well—the song and the afternoon that had followed it. The white grand piano in the middle of the stage slowly swung away on a moveable piece of stage as Colton stepped forward easing into the piano solo with his guitar, then taking over, lovingly caressing the guitar, the strings. Reanne shivered, despite the heat, at the memory of those fingers on her skin.

Then he lifted his head just far enough that his blue eyes were barely visible under the wide hat brim. He looked directly into the camera and began, "You take me away to paradise." Reanne found herself mouthing the words as he sang, flooded with the memory of that song as a duet. Colton was completely wrapped up in the moment—the beach, the visitors, the cameras, they all faded away, such was his concentration on the music.

Reanne hardly heard the producer call out to the cameramen, cueing close-ups. All around her the activity of the shoot ebbed and flowed like the great ocean beyond, but she only had eyes for Cole. He had disappeared into his song while he acted out and expressed every note and phrase. Time and space condensed down to a point and expanded again, filling her world with one song. Humming and vibrating with it until the producer called a stop. Then the magic vanished like Cinderella's carriage. They were just over dressed actors on a makeshift stage at the beach.

"Beautiful, people that was just beautiful," the producer called. "Let's call it and keep that take. Colton you were absolutely hot in that scene. We'll take the next one by the beach…let's move before we lose the light people. Dancers, I won't need you again until tomorrow morning, get off my set. Stagehands! Move! Light is wasting—I want that beach scene in now. Makeup!"

Like a well-oiled machine a dozen or so technicians ran to dismantle part of the set and prepare the next shot right on the beach. Power cables rolled like huge black snakes across the pathways, pieces of equipment and stage sets were being rolled, carried and dragged. If they were lucky they would get the shot done before the sun set. Time was of the essence.

Reanne felt herself being jostled from all sides and stepped out of the way only to realize that put her right in someone else's way.

Move, move, move. Everyone had a specific task and the feeling of being out of place began to bother her again. When she looked for Cole she found him surrounded by assistants. The hairdresser was giving his hair more bounce and shine, the makeup lady took the shine off his face, and the wardrobe consultant held up three identical shirts in case he sweated through the one he was wearing—she was in the middle of a general pandemonium that centered around Colton, but he was taking it all in stride, he seemed to be the only one who was cool and collected. He was the star here, so sure of himself and his place in this huge circus.

After a few futile attempts at getting close to him, she had wandered back to the broadcast booth where Jack and two of their Nashville guests were working on a live chat. They sat in a circle around a computer set up in the shade of a huge banyan tree and Reanne sidled up behind Jack to look over his shoulder.

They were all hooting with laughter.

"Okay, Okay," Jack said and continued to read off the screen. "This guy wants to know if the dancing in the video is really difficult."

"Yeah, definitely," everyone chorused, "But it's fun," one of the women said.

'You bet it's hard, everybody screwed up at least a hundred times today,' Lily, the girl at the keyboard typed, 'But it's also a blast, nobody gets mad at you and we're having like a great party every day.'

"All right, next one is a lady, she wants to know how close all of you have gotten to *Mr. Right*?"

Giggles and laughter ensued, a few hushed comments.

'Well if you ask me, not nearly close enough.' Lily typed amidst the laughter.

"Is he as gorgeous in person?"

"Oh, even better, definitely." The girls laughed while a few of the men started to boo.

'He is absolutely dreamy,' Lily typed 'and you wouldn't believe how nice he is in person.' After a moment's pause she added, 'Makes me glad I'm still single.' Which made the girls erupt in even more laughter.

"Ladies, ladies, now let's try and keep our G-rating, no description of body parts, please." Jack said, eliciting more giggles.

Reanne felt a tiny stab of jealousy. Forever after she would have to put up with the fact that Cole was an idol for thousands of women. The most beautiful women tried to get close to him. Not an easy thing to compete with, even if one wasn't already a bit shaky in the self-confidence department.

She wandered away and sat down beside the dolphin pond. Throughout the day the dolphins and their trainer performed for the hotel guests, but while the CW Video team had taken over the hotel the show was probably suspended. Right now all she could see were a few lazy turtles sunning on a hot rock. The scene had a sense of peace and tranquility to it, embodying Hawaii and the spirit of Aloha.

Behind her, the video shoot was going on, the Nashville group was having a great time with the web chat, while the web cameras captured all this fun and transmitted it to the websites. Everything just made one giant statement: 'We are having a lot of fun!' So why did she feel so out of place right now? Having to share Colton with a dozen or so members of his staff and all those adoring fans was proving to be a bit more difficult than she had imagined.

The serene, light sunshine falling on the dolphin pond, and the lazy quiet movements of the turtles finally conspired to soothe her spirits. Getting up, she dusted herself off and walked back to the hotel. In a week or so this would all be over and then she could have him all to herself again—in the moments he had to spare for her.

Thousands of miles away, in a small apartment in Hollywood, a beautifully manicured hand tapped out the address for Colton Wright's website. It was an older computer so the pictures took forever to load. The monitor was also in bad shape and kept flickering on and off. Once or twice she thought she was going to lose the feed completely, but finally the woman was looking at live pictures of Colton practicing for the video.

"Well, what do you know?" the woman said quietly, addressing the screen. "He's having a ball in Hawaii while I sit here in this dump twiddling my thumbs."

"Are you still obsessed with that guy?" the half naked man on her sofa bed asked and took a swig from a beer bottle. "You ask me, I think he looks like a wimp— just look at the long hair."

"Shut your mouth," the woman said sharply, brushing her own long blonde hair out of her face. "I'm figuring out a way to get us some money here."

"Why don't you go marry the guy," the man laughed.

"Ya know," the woman twirled a length of hair around her finger "that is not a bad idea. Not a bad idea at all."

Chapter Thirteen

Colton silently thanked his own genius for filming this video with a group of fans. Their enthusiasm and simple joy brought an energy to it that he wouldn't have found using professionals. He had an inkling this video might get nominated in the best video category at the next CMA. He could almost treat the whole shoot as one huge live show, drawing on his rapport with an audience—his audience—to bring the song to life. For once, making a video wasn't tedious and exhausting, he was getting a kick out of it.

He saw Reanne out of the corner of his eye and sent a loving thought in her direction. Failing any kind of private moment with her, that would have to do for now. The memory of their lovemaking stirred something powerful in him and made his performance all the more passionate. How could that woman, in such a short time, stir feelings in him that had been dormant for so long?

When they went on break he asked someone for a cell phone and disappeared into the trailer.

The phone in Reanne's room rang once, twice. She didn't really feel like talking to anyone.

"Hello?"

There was a moment of silence. "Hi!' I've been looking everywhere for you. How come you're in your room? I was just going to leave a message for you."

"Oh, I was just…resting, the sun got to me," she fibbed, not wanting Colton to know how out of place she had felt earlier. How she had thought that everyone had a place and a job to do except herself. Colton Wright was used to being the center of attention, he could not possibly know what it felt like to feel redundant, unnecessary in that huge machinery that surrounded him.

"What's up?"

"How about sneaking away for the evening? I have a little outing planned for us. Are you up for a little excitement?"

"Oh? What did you have in mind?"

"I hired a car for us, and I'll take you to my favorite spot. Something you've never seen before, be ready at eight. "

"I will," she said, and just like that, all was right with the world again. While Jack and the Nashville group made plans to see one of the hula shows in town, Reanne begged off to stay in her room. She had the hardest time convincing everyone to go without her, that she would be fine, but finally they all set off, leaving her alone.

Eight o'clock came and went with no sign of Cole. Knowing that the video shoot might have gone into overtime, she settled in and waited, watching CNN on her TV, checking the clock every five minutes. Oh yes, she understood Colton was the star here, but there was that nagging little voice again, telling her that she was playing second fiddle to fame, fortune and stardom. And a very poor second fiddle at that.

It was almost nine o clock and she had long since tired of CNN, when the doorman buzzed with the news there was a car waiting for her downstairs. In her excitement she raced for the elevator, forgot her purse and had to go back to get it.

She headed at a dead run though the lobby, colliding with some annoyed tourists in the process of checking in, and out to the waiting car, which turned out not to be the expected limousine but a non descript white, little rental car.

Confused, she let the doorman help her in then buckled her seat belt. The driver wore one of those chauffeur caps pulled low over his face with dark aviator glasses, despite the lateness of the night. Probably trying to look cool she scoffed.

"'Allo, miss," he said with a heavy accent.

"So, where are you taking me?" she asked, as the driver started laughing and took off his glasses and cap. Pale curls tumbled about his head.

"Colton!" she squealed." She was so happy to see him it took her a minute to remember she was angry with him for being late.

"Where have you been? I thought you'd stood me up."

He shrugged apologetically. "The video shoot ran over and we had to do the beach scene five times. Kenny nearly had a fit and he had everyone jumping through hoops. Same old, same old. Where were you all afternoon? Not in your room while you're in paradise I hope."

"Well it sure didn't look like you were lacking for company."

He chuckled. "You're not jealous, are you? I work with these people every day. You know you're the one I want to be with."

"Humph." She looked out the window at the passing scenery. "So, you never answered my question. Where are you taking me?"

"Wait and see," he grinned mischievously.

Wait and see, wait and see! Well she had been waiting all day, miserable, and here he was charged and full of energy after spending the day being adored from all sides, and that just wasn't fair.

She stayed silent as he pulled the car onto a small winding road that slowly grew steeper and narrower as they climbed one of the many volcanic mountains around Honolulu.

'Tantalus Peak' she read on an old wooden sign. Colton sped the car up and took the hairpin turns at a heart-stopping angle.

"Careful, my God, you're scaring me, what are you doing?" she cried out.

"Life's not for being careful darling," he said, speeding up even more, and sneaking his right hand onto her knee.

"Cole, for God's sake be careful, and use both hands."

"Sorry honey, I've got to keep one on the wheel."

They entered a stretch of road where the foliage grew so dense and dark they might as well have been in the jungle.

"Aiee!" Cole called, and took another turn so tight she swore two of the wheels left the ground.

"Stop this car right now, Colton or drive like a normal person. I mean it. What has gotten into you?"

"In a minute, girl, in a minute."

They emerged from the foliage onto a small parking lot. Ahead the ground dropped away suddenly, protected by the flimsiest of wooden barriers. They were high above the city and beyond the fencing was the most breathtaking of sceneries. Honolulu lay like a jewel in all its glittering beauty with the dark ocean in the background, and Diamond Head just to the left. The towering hotels and condos looked like toys and all the people with their problems and worries had dropped away. Reanne felt as if a mere slight of hand could change the world up here.

"Tantalus Peak," Cole said quietly.

"It's magnificent. How did you ever find this?"

"It's sort of a secret place. Even the natives don't like to talk about it—afraid the tourists will ruin it. I believe it used to be a gathering place of the ancient kings. I got lost one day and ended up here."

He stood so close behind her she could feel the space between them crackle with energy. His hand came around and caught her about the waist.

"It's easy to see why the kings would gather here. It feels like you could command the world from up here," Reanne said, turning around to look into his eyes. "One word and everything would be yours. Thank you, thank you for showing this to me."

She put her arms around his neck and buried her face in his shoulder. "I'm sorry if I've been out of sorts all evening, I haven't exactly had the greatest day today."

"It's ok." He put his finger under her chin and lifted her face to kiss her. "This ought to make it better…and this…and this."

He conquered her mouth relentlessly, leaving her breathless and incapable of speech. Meanwhile his hands freed her flimsy shirt from the waistband of her skirt and found their way up to her breasts, teasing the sensitive tips into tight little buds.

"Cole," she finally managed to protest, breathing heavily, "someone might come by."

"Nobody ever comes here. Tonight this spot belongs to just you and me." He kissed her again, this time tracing a line with his tongue from her chin to the sensitive spot just below her throat. He drew a few lazy circles there and she completely surrendered herself to his arms. She heard herself moan deep in her throat and his raw little chuckle.

"That's it honey, just let yourself go. Turn around."

Willingly she obeyed, her hands gripping the railing in front of her as the cold night air touched her skin. His hands caressed the length of her legs and slid her panties down. Blindly she stepped out of them and leaned back into his embrace. He brushed the hair off her neck and kissed her. "My girl," he whispered into her ear and gripped her shoulders. His lips were nuzzling her ear as he molded her to his length, running his hands down her body again and again. "Cole," she whimpered, "now, I can't wait."

She heard his low throaty chuckle as he entered her with one smooth stroke. Her hands gripped the railing so hard her knuckles turned white and she threw back her head as he picked up the pace with a ferocious passion. It was a coupling of pure need and desire. Their bodies craved a desperate release and raced toward a final peak. Their moans filled the night air faster and harder until they finally crested the wave together and cried out in unison.

They collapsed in each other's arms, holding on to the flimsy wood in front of them, feeling the universe stood still for them and the stars in the heavens stopped for one perfect moment in time, while before them, beyond the cliffs of Tantalus, life went on without notice.

I love you her heart beat a rhythm, *I love you, I love you so much.*

"My girl," Colton whispered in her ear when they had recovered enough to speak. "My best girl, you are wonderful."

"Cole," she chided, "someone could have come."

He chuckled. "Someone did, I believe."

"Be serious." She tried to rearrange her clothing in the dark. "You always do this to me."

"Do what to you, make you feel good?"

"When we're alone you make love to me and everything is great, but when there are other people around…"

"Yes?"

"It's like I don't exist when there are others around. I was so mad at you tonight, I was sure I wouldn't let you do this again."

"You didn't want me to"?

"That's not the point."

"Then what is?"

"The point is that you're only mine when we're alone. You belong to everyone else all day long."

"That's the life of an entertainer honey, I don't even belong to myself in those times, you know that. That's the way my life works. I guess that's why so many entertainers are single—or divorced—I'm sorry, but that's who I am."

"I know that." She kicked little pebbles with the toe of her sandal and watched them skitter down the cliff. "I know that, but it would be easier if…if I could stand there beside you. If I could be…with you, if I didn't feel that you're trying to hide us."

There was a long pause. Colton turned away from her and looked out over the glittering band that was Honolulu. The night wind ruffled his long hair and Reanne had to keep her hands at her side to keep them from running through it.

"I'm not trying to hide you," he finally said, "I'm trying to protect you, because I know what this business can do, especially to someone who is…sensitive. I didn't realize you would take it this way. You know, when I told you that I wasn't ready to go public with the fact that we were…dating, I was really thinking of you."

"How do you figure that?"

"I wanted to spare you the ferocity of the press until we were…well, maybe more secure with each other. Believe me, once they know we are dating, you won't be able to go to the grocery store without some press goons being there. They'll keep phoning the radio station when you're on air, they'll be at your house trying to get a quote. You might lose your job. I know, I've been there. The public loves a Cinderella story."

"I'll handle it."

"Are you so sure? It took me years to be able to handle it. And still, to this day, I'd just as soon be by myself instead of braving the press. They've helped me get where I am today, true, but at the same time they've made it very hard for me to be…myself, to even know who that is."

"Cole, listen to me," she gripped his hand and forced him to turn to face her fully. "I don't know what it's going to be like, but as long as you're there with me, I'll handle it, I'll deal with it. You once told me that you didn't know what we had or where it was leading, but you were willing to follow it all the way to find out. Well here I am, and I am willing. Colton, I don't want to hide any more, please."

There was another long silence, while he caressed her cheek with one gentle hand. "Okay," he finally said, "Ken should still be up when we get back."

"What are you telling me?"

"I'm telling you, that once we get back, we'll tell Ken the truth, I think he suspects anyway. Then I think you should stay with me at the Condo tonight."

"Yes Cole."

"By the time we get down to breakfast tomorrow morning, all of Honolulu should be buzzing with the news."

She hugged him to her tightly.

"You know what?"

"What's that honey?"

"You're making me the happiest woman on earth tonight, I love you Colton David Wright."

There, it was out before she had a chance to think about it. She had finally told him. At the same time her heart felt like it was falling off this peak. What if he didn't answer her, or what if he answered, but it wasn't what she wanted to hear? For a long moment none of them said anything.

"I still can't believe it—you're going to tell everyone," she finally said to cover the awkward silence; perhaps they could both pretend she hadn't said anything.

"Is that not what you wanted, for everyone to know about us?"

"Yes. But Cole, I want you to want that too. I want you to be proud of me standing beside you, not to have to hide me away in some corner or…" she indicated the dark parking lot with a nod of her head "or in the dark night somewhere. All of this is going to change your image quite a bit," she laughed nervously. "I never thought I was asking you to give up anything, but I guess there it is."

Colton leaned with his hands against the railing, looking at nothing at all. How could he possibly explain to her that after years of being locked away behind a solid wall his heart was slow to emerge from its self imposed exile? 'I love you' she had said just a moment ago and his first impulse had been to tell her *I love you too, with all my heart,* but almost automatically he had bitten his tongue before he could answer her aloud. Years of not allowing himself to feel anything for anyone had created an automatic response. Now, as he looked at her in the soft moonlight, standing there, her red hair tousled by the night wind and their love making, her eyes at the same time loving and fearful, something squeezed his heart powerfully.

For the last few weeks he had felt drawn to her, her freshness, her honesty, her openness. Nashville and its business of music had failed to make her jaded and hard, despite the disappointments she had had to endure. Every time he looked at her his heart did a little jump and he felt drawn to her with an energy that he had felt only one other place in his life, when he was on stage.

Now as he brushed her hair and held her small face in his hands he saw the love and the question in her eyes. He wanted to tell her he loved her so badly he could almost taste it. If this is what love feels like, he thought, then I do love you, Reanne Parker. He almost started to tell her,

"Honey, I…"

"Yes?"

He shook his head, when the words wouldn't come, words that would roll off his tongue in a song almost every day.

"Be patient with me, will you?" he finally asked, relieved at not having given himself away and still feeling like a coward. He put his arm around her shoulder and pressed a tender kiss in her hair.

"Let's go home, shall we," he said quietly.

He put his arm around her shoulder and led her back to the parked car.

"This is it, things are never going to be the same once we hit town, are you sure you're ready for all this?" he asked.

"Ready for what? For being with you?"

He laughed dryly. "Hardly. I mean ready for the reporters asking you what color underwear I prefer."

"And I gather you would not care for me to answer that question."

"That would not be my first choice, no."

Colton opened the doors and helped Reanne into the car. "Don't take this the wrong way," he said, "but I think Ken and my publicist Reece are going to give you a few lessons in talking to reporters."

"Do you really think it's going to be that bad?"

"Reanne, once we hit Nashville, with the publicity for the new album about to start, the tour beginning—oh yes, there are going to be quite a few nosy questions."

"Cole," she squeezed his hand for reassurance, "as long as you're with me, I'll handle it, ok. I'll do whatever is necessary."

That feeling of cowardice continued to nag at Colton. There was Reanne sitting in the car beside him, looking so innocent and trusting. She thought he was going to be her hero, standing beside her through everything, but he didn't even have the guts to return a simple 'I love you'.

Reanne played with the radio until she found WJKT and they spent the rest of the drive just listening, pointing out the scenery to each other—hanging on to their own thoughts. Anything to avoid talking about how they felt.

Finally, after they had left the Waikiki strip behind them and were following the curve of the beach, the hotel complex came in to sight.

"Ready?" Colton asked again. "There's still time to back out of everything and return to the peaceful quiet of your own room."

"Not a chance, I'm ready for anything," Reanne said placing a quick kiss into the palm of his hand and folding his fingers over it. "Ready for anything with you Colton David Wright."

There was no room under the canopy and the entrance and walkways were crowded with people. The hotel grounds seemed abuzz while, here and there, flashbulbs were popping.

"I wonder who's here," Colton muttered. "At least our entrance should go unnoticed."

"What? Are you jealous of someone stealing the spotlight?"

"No, but a good chunk of the rooms here are reserved for our people working the video shoot. Call me pessimistic, but this much attention not centered on you and me can only mean trouble."

He looked truly concerned, and a slow feeling of dread began to settle in Reanne as she watched him craning his neck to see through the throng of people. His hands gripped the wheel with steely determination. Mentally she tried to count through the people at the hotel. Who was here warranting this much attention? Certainly no one associated with the CW group. It had to have something to do with Colton. She couldn't fight the feeling that something truly awful was about to happen. Cole beside her was fidgeting nervously, trying to catch the attention of one of the valet parking attendants.

Finally he managed to leave the car and they threaded their way back to the hotel entrance. Someone called out to Colton from the crowd but he was headed straight for the entrance. It was all Reanne could do to hang on to his arm and follow him as fast as her high heels would carry her. People were pressing in on them from all sides. This was not the way it was supposed to happen, this was not the way they were supposed to come home.

"Cole, wait." She called out but he didn't hear, he was headed straight for the lobby his arm as tight as a bowstring while she stumbled behind him, trying to keep up.

She wasn't looking ahead and almost ran into him as he suddenly stopped. If it hadn't been for his protective arm steadying her she would have fallen headlong onto the red carpet. As it was, she stopped, looked up and straight into the eyes of one of the most beautiful women she had ever seen, apparently the center of all this attention.

The gorgeous creature smiled angelically at Colton and opened her arms to him. Right about then a reporter stuck a microphone into Colton's face.

"Mr. Wright, did you ever think your wife would come back to you?'

"Why did you keep this marriage from your fans?"

"What's going to happen now?"

The voices rose to a clamor in Reanne's head. The words *your wife* reverberated and echoed until she thought her head would explode. Her eyes couldn't focus and the room seemed to be swimming around her. All the voices came at her through a huge dark tunnel. She looked at Colton, his lips seemed to be moving, forming words but she couldn't hear anything. "Cole!" she heard herself call out his name, then nothing. Nothing but the powerful rush of a huge tidal wave as the floor came closer and closer and she passed out.

She was lying on one of the wicker loungers in an anteroom to the lobby when she woke up again. Jack sat beside her, holding her hand.

"Hey there kiddo. Are you with us again."

"I think so. What—what happened?"

"You passed out, apparently."

Oh God—Cole. They were going to come back together, announce their relationship—the crowded lobby…his wife! It all came rushing back to her in one single jumbled thought.

"Oh God, tell me I was dreaming," she said.

"I don't know what you were dreaming Reanne but you and Colton Wright walked into a hornets nest tonight, together I might add."

"Oh no, it wasn't a dream! Then that angel was really his wife?"

"Ambhara Kensington Wright. Angel is a good name for her, if not an apt description. The lady has been spitting venom all night, ever since she got here. Who knew *Mr. Right* was married, that there was a Mrs. Wright somewhere?"

Reanne rose carefully, holding on to the back of the lounger when she got dizzy.

"Whoa," Jack said, sit back down, you're not going anywhere."

"I need to get back in there, find out what's going on."

"Whatever is going on there, and I have a feeling I don't even know the half of it, you are not going back into the middle of it Reanne."

"Jack…"

"Sit back .down Reanne!"

Reanne pushed Jack away as forcefully as she dared.

"I need to find out what's happening, Jack, all right."

She reentered the lobby, shaken to the core, her nerves so raw she was almost sick to her stomach. Colton was still surrounded by photographers and reporters, the gorgeous blonde was hanging onto his arm with proprietary zeal. Again Reanne was struck by the thought that this must be the most beautiful woman she had ever seen. Tall and slim, as beautifully proportioned as any model, her long blonde hair brushed to perfection shining the spotlight, every strand in place. Reanne was keenly aware of her own disheveled red locks and her wrinkled clothes. The Angel's huge cornflower blue eyes wandered in Reanne's direction, as if she had noticed the scrutiny. Then she detached herself from Colton and approached Reanne.

"Are you feeling better?" she asked, "I was terribly concerned when you fainted." She smiled, oozing concern, but her eyes remained cold as ice and a small shiver ran through Reanne's spine. The beauty stuck a well-manicured hand out.

"Let me introduce myself. I'm Ambhara Kensington Wright, Colton's wife. You're with the radio station from Nashville, aren't you?"

Ambhara—Colton's—wife. The words hit Reanne's brain like hammers on an anvil.

"Reanne Parker," she managed to stammer, sure that she looked like a complete moron beside this exotic bird.

"I see you have met my ex-wife."

Reanne spun around and saw that Colton had joined them.

"Now Cole," Ambhara lightly slapped his arm, as if she was correcting a willful child. "You do know that divorce was never final my dear, don't you?"

"That remains to be seen," he said tightly. His face was an unreadable mask, his usual rich baritone voice a rasp of tightly controlled fury. The reporters closed in on them again, peppering Colton and Ambhara with questions. Reanne felt a hand on her arm and turned to see Jack standing there, concern in his face.

"Come on," he said quietly. "This is a mess that doesn't require our presence."

She could only nod and follow him as if she was on autopilot. At the door to the elevator she glanced back into the lobby one last time just to see Colton looking back at her. He shook his head almost imperceptibly and she desperately wanted to see love in his face, or guilt or sorrow, anything but the cold dead mask that was there. When the elevator doors closed with a quiet ping, Jack's calm vanished and he turned on her.

"Just what was going on out there a minute ago?" he spat.

Reanne leaned against the wall of the elevator sullenly and only shook her head.

"You and Wright were coming back together from God-knows-where. I would like to know what that was all about! And then to run into his wife in front of all these people in the lobby that just puts the crown on everything, doesn't it? What on earth are you up to Reanne?"

"Jack, I had no idea that—never mind! Let's just not talk about it, ok?"

"That's not good enough, Reanne. Tomorrow I want to know exactly what was going on, is that clear? You may be putting everything in jeopardy—this project, your job, the station—my God!"

Reanne glared at him and the numbness inside her suddenly turned into helpless fury. "Exactly what was going on is exactly none of your business Jack, okay?"

"If there's a possibility anything you're doing could impact on the station…"

"This is not going to affect the station in any way. You'll get your broadcast, you'll get your morning show, but that's all, you don't own me and, as far as I'm concerned, it was just coincidence that Mr. Wright and I came back to the hotel at the same time. We met in the lobby as far as anyone else is concerned. So just do your job Jack and leave this alone. Now, I believe this is my floor."

She pushed off the elevator wall and stalked out and down the hall to her room without waiting for a response. None was forthcoming anyway, he had stood in the elevator, staring after her.

She let the door slam behind her with as much force as possible and flung herself onto the bed. For once the tears would not come. *Cole's wife!* Did he say he had divorced her? How could he not know one way or another? There was so much she needed to know, so much she wanted to ask but, for once, Jack was right. The lobby was a madhouse right now and not the place to get the information she needed. She could phone Cole later and simply ask him, but with the scrutiny they were under right now, chances of getting him alone were pretty slim.

What to do? She paced her room, thinking, until she was near exhaustion but, still, the answers refused to come. Finally she fell into her bed, too tired to stay up, too wired to actually go to sleep. She lay there staring at the ceiling until she finally remembered where she had seen Ambhara Kensington before:

Of course, Cassandra Asher, the bad girl heroine on the daytime drama 'Five and Dime Heart'. She had been a cast member for almost ten years, developing her character from a minor extra into one of the pivotal characters of the show. Just recently Cassandra had been shot and spent three weeks dying dramatically on daytime television. For all intents and purposes Ambhara Kensington had lost her job. So now that Reanne had worked out where she came from, the question remained, what was she doing suddenly back in Colton's life? And was she here to stay.

Reanne tossed and turned, contemplating the situation. A beautiful movie star wife was certainly the exact perfect match for *Mr. Right*, the sexy superstar of country music. Wasn't that what she had been worrying about for the last few weeks?

Colton watched Reanne and Jack step into the elevator. With one last look he tried to convey all his feelings to her but he knew he failed miserably. Reanne was as pale as a sheet and there was nothing he could do to come to her aid now. The room around him was still in total chaos. Goal number one would have to be to get rid of all these extra people. He held up his hand to command silence.

"Ladies and Gentlemen," he began without raising his voice A few folks continued to talk but were quickly silenced so everyone could hear.

"Ladies and Gentlemen, thank you for coming out here tonight. As you can see, I'm faced with a rather— complicated situation. I would appreciate it if you let my ex-wife," he shot amber a glare that just dared her to contradict him "… and me sort this out in private. There will be a statement released to the press tomorrow morning. Once again, thank you."

Most of the press lingered, hoping for a juicy tidbit, a statement from anyone at the fringes of this scandal, but Colton took Amber's arm with a steely grip and steered her toward the elevators. He stopped by the concierge desk momentarily to make sure she had checked into a room of her own, then they disappeared from view.

Colton slammed the door behind them and stood, still as a statue, glaring at Ambhara. "How dare you!" he finally spat.

"Hello Colton…glad to see you too."

"Hello? After ten years, 'Glad to see you?' Are you out of your mind?"

"Don't throw a fit Cole. It doesn't become you."

"You!" Colton pointed at her, "You left me! Ten years ago you left our home, our marriage and me. You up and left with the producer of that scummy daytime show because he gave you a role. Talk about the casting couch. Not a word from you since. And now you show up here, out of the blue, as if nothing has happened? Are you out of your mind?"

"Colton, don't be so dramatic, that was always your biggest flaw, perhaps it's you who should be in movies. Now come here."

She embraced him in a cloud of blonde hair and expensive perfume and kissed him. And just like that the years fell away and they were twenty again, on the first day of their marriage. With one single kiss he was back in Nashville, so many years ago.

They had lived in a dreadful dump of a one-room apartment, they had no furniture except for an old sofa bed the previous tenants had left behind. They had no money nothing to call their own, but they had each other. Two kids who were going to hit it big.

Colton remembered waking up with her head on his shoulder, her hair mussed from a night of lovemaking. He had watched her for a long time, while the sun slowly rose, content just to look at her. He just couldn't believe that this beautiful, wonderful creature was truly his. Finally she opened her eyes.

"Good morning Mrs. Wright," he had said, relishing the sound. "I love you."

"I love you too," she murmured and snuggled closer "forever and another day."

But forever and another day proved to be much shorter than they had thought. Colton finally had the coveted recording contract in his pocket, but now the real work started—to make Colton Wright a name everyone in county music would recognize.

Colton put in long hours for very little pay and Amber went on audition after audition as an actress and a model...without a lot of success. Money continued to be tight. At the end of every month they had seemed to have a choice of getting the phone or the electricity cut off, or making the landlady wait—again.

Still they had never thought of giving up. They had each other and they had a dream and that was enough. The nights they spent in each other's arms more than made up for the days they spent battling the world. Ken Taylor had big plans for Colton and he had a way of harnessing the energy and drive of the young singer. He found out early on that Colton was at his best in front of a huge crowd and he worked on getting him as many live appearances as possible. Not a day went by when he wasn't out there somewhere, spreading his name, singing his heart out, signing autographs until his hands hurt. Every record store, every Walmart that put out his new record could count on a live appearance by Colton Wright. No matter how outlandish the requests, or what he had to do to win another customer, another fan, he would do it. It cost him plenty, but he knew that this was what he was made for he loved every minute of it, and often he would come home, bursting with stories 'from the road' impatient to share them with Amber.

He would tell her of everything that happened to him and all the things they would be able to do in the near future, all the things they would be able to afford soon. He had painted a colorful picture of their future, and always they were together in that future. No matter what he did, he did it for both of them. Things were truly happening for Colton Wright since signing Ken Taylor as his agent. If Amber's face hadn't show the enthusiasm he had expected, Cole didn't notice, and although she smiled, the smile never quite reached her eyes.

He had told himself that she was just overwhelmed and he promised her things would get better soon, he would take her along on his ride to the top. For a while she sang backup in his band, but her voice and personality refused to blend into the background. Then Cole got her a job recording generic versions of current hit titles for cheap collections, and for dance clubs. That job she quit after a week. The more Colton's star was rising the more Amber's seemed to be doomed to remain in the shadows. By now Colton was in demand more than ever, for personal appearances and the millions of other things required of a new artist to promote his first album.

He personally visited every radio station in the area, to give interviews and distribute CW merchandise. He arranged visits with all the stores known to sell a lot of county music, he worked like a dog to promote this album. There wasn't a day he wasn't out knocking on doors promoting himself and his music.

If Amber was unhappy, he never noticed it. He never demanded of her that she stand beside him during all the functions he had to attend. Perhaps he was too focused on his career, or perhaps he thought she too would find joy in his rise to the top. Little things started to turn into fights, the fights started to become more frequent and more intense. Amber stopped going to the auditions he arranged for her, causing him no end of embarrassment for arranging them in the first place. Finally she announced she had decided to leave the music business to Colton and to concentrate on acting entirely.

With renewed zeal she threw herself into acting lessons and went on dozens of auditions. Their lives grew apart steadily, but Colton believed in their love. Just as hard as he worked on being a musician, he began to work on being a good husband. He could feel her grow distant to him and he tried to love her all the more to pull her back to him. Yet the higher his star rose the more she resented him for it. One day in late summer they were going to record the final tracks for the next album. The studio had been booked, the session players hired, and Colton was nervous as all get out. The first album had performed adequately, but certainly had broken no records, there was a lot riding on this session. Moreover, this time around Ken had hired the best of the best to produce the album. If it didn't perform, they were tens of thousands of dollars in the hole. That was the day Amber finally threw his success into his face.

"I don't want to be a star's wife, I want to be the star myself," she had screamed at him

Still Colton thought his love strong enough for both of them. He would do anything for her. He never realized how strong her anger and resentment truly were. The hell with the recording session, he told her, the hell with the money, he would stay with her until they had talked out everything, settled this problem once and for all.

They argued for hours, then argued some more. Argued and drank until they had both passed out, exhausted and drunk—causing him to miss that important, very expensive recording session.

It was only a few weeks later that he had come home unexpectedly to pick up some new song lyrics he had left on the dresser by mistake. What he found caused the blood in his veins to freeze and his heart to lock itself behind a wall so high and thick as to be impenetrable. He had opened the door to their bedroom to find Amber in bed with a TV producer. He stood there, watching his world crumble around him, watching her calmly get dressed, watching her walk out of his life.

"You do know that I still love you," he had told her, "even after everything that's happened."

Amber continued packing her things, almost as if she was glad he had caught her. "Have a nice life," were her last words, walking out arm in arm with her new producer.

The last he had heard of her she had changed her name to Ambhara Kensington and made it big in daytime television.

Colton pushed Ambhara away from him, angry with her, but more angry at his body's sudden reaction to her. That reaction hadn't been lost on Ambhara.

"Ah, but you do remember the good times," she purred and ran her hand down his side.

He caught her hand and held it in a vise like grip.

"No more games! For the last time, what do you want?" he growled.

"Why, to be your wife again, of course."

"I divorced you ten years ago, remember? After you walked out on me to sleep your way to the top. You can't just walk in here and pretend nothing has happened. Things don't work that way."

"Colton," she said, and sat on the sofa, stretching her endless legs, "We were so young then. We've both grown up don't you think? As for the divorce—it never happened."

"What are you talking about?"

"I never signed the papers dear Cole. I was betting you would be too busy to check and that you'd be so intent on hiding your ex-wife from everyone, you wouldn't have somebody else do it. God, music was everything to you, of course you wouldn't check on a little thing like a signature. Now, wasn't it smart of me to figure that one day it would come in handy being your wife again?"

"You're lying."

"Suit yourself Colton. Have someone check it out if you want to. For all I care have a whole team of lawyers look into it. I don't care. It's all there in black on white on legal size paper. Meanwhile—where are we going to live, honey?"

She took off her strappy high heels and dangled them from her forefinger. Colton stood as if thunderstruck never taking his eyes off her. After a moment he picked up the phone and dialed Ken's home number. It would be early in the morning in Nashville.

"Ken, I need you in Honolulu. There's a situation here that requires you right now!" he said without preamble.

Amber watched him with a kind of cool detachment. She poured herself a drink from the mini bar and watched Colton pace the room like a caged tiger. She relished his obvious discomfort. She had the upper hand and she intended to play it for all it was worth.

"Just in case you're trying to get rid of me in a hurry," she said casually. "Remember that I still know where some of the bodies are buried Colton. You didn't think I would walk in here without another ace up my sleeve, did you?" she paused dramatically. "Would it surprise you if I told you I know who really sang the lead vocals on that famous *Always You* single. The one you're so proud of, the one that made your career? You didn't think I knew, did you? Well, if you don't want the rest of the world to know, I suggest you don't piss me off darling. That wouldn't be good for your career—not good at all, Colton."

There was a certain sick enjoyment in her eyes as she watched all the color drain from Colton's face—as she watched the phone drop from his hand to the floor.

Chapter Fourteen

A partially closed off area of the cavernous lobby at the Kahala hotel had been set up as a press room for Colton Wright and his entourage. Dozens of gossip journalists were sipping coffee, nibbling on donuts and waiting for the dirty laundry on this story.

Ken Taylor watched Colton step out in front of the waiting mob of reporters. He should have been in there orchestrating the press conference but, as usual, Cole had insisted on and gotten his own way. Deep lines furrowed Ken's face and the shadows under his eyes were big enough to drown in.

He had hired a private jet immediately after their phone call and flown through the night, so he was exhausted. He still couldn't believe the story Colton had told him, it was too bizarre even for Ken, who had seen a lot in this business. Since his arrival he had barely had the time to get up to snuff on everything that had happened here in Hawaii. He hated to be out of the loop and he didn't mind letting everyone know it.

Colton tapped the microphone with one forefinger, testing it. "Ladies and Gentlemen," he began. "Thank you for being here this morning." The cameras ran silently, somewhere the web cameras rolled too, transmitting the whole thing over the websites. The KSOM/WJKT broadcast had been interrupted for this live feed.

"As you have probably heard by now, my wife of ten years, Ambhara Kensington, has come back into my life."

Ken looked at Amber, standing beside him, "Why?" he asked quietly, "You left him ten years ago when his career eclipsed yours, why are you coming back now?"

"I've seen what he's done for the careers of those models and actresses you've made him date Kenny dear, and I want him back."

"As a career booster? You're disgusting! I can't believe he he's going to put up with that."

"Our respective careers have taken us far from each other at times," Colton continued while the reporters scribbled, "but the time has come for both of us to take a serious look at the commitment we made ten years ago—and to work on our marriage."

An audible gasp drew everyone's eyes to Reanne who stood at the edge of the crowd, still pale as a ghost, her hands covering her mouth. Colton's gaze flew to her for a moment and his voice almost broke as he continued.

"Therefore—Therefore we are going to give our life together and our...our." He stopped and closed his eyes for a moment, rubbing the bridge of his nose with a thumb and forefinger. Ken stood ready to interfere, but Colton took a deep breath and went on.

"Our feelings for each other another chance. Ladies and Gentlemen...," he reached out to Amber, "Mrs. Ambhara Kensington-Wright."

Amber stepped up beside him, smiling, laughing, and accepting the public accolades due her. They smiled and nodded, snapping pictures of Ambhara hugging Colton, although Colton stood unmoving, scanning the room for Reanne.

Ken finally raised a hand to stop the reporters from asking any more questions. "That's enough for today. Thank you all for coming out this morning and be sure to partake of our complimentary breakfast in the morning room. Enjoy Hawaii Ladies and Gentlemen, and check out our video production by the beach while you are here."

Then he sidled up behind Colton and Amber. "In the conference room, now," he hissed, even as he dealt smiles and handshakes to the press. They both obeyed, perhaps out of habit or perhaps because one did not argue with Ken Taylor and win very often.

He closed the door, leaving behind them a world of speculation, rumor and innuendo. He whirled around immediately.

"OK", he said, "Why? What I want to know is why?"

"Ken," Colton said exhaustion and defeat in his voice. "She knows."

"She knows, she knows? Knows what Cole, what are we talking about here?"

"She knows," Amber said triumphantly. "She knows that it was Clay Fender who sang lead on that famous single, *Always You*—not him." She paused a moment for effect. "You remember the song don't you Ken, the one that went and debuted at number one in the charts, the one that made Colton's career, and yours by the way. What did *Country Weekly* call it? 'A once in a lifetime gem for the talented singer, the perfect way to showcase this new and refreshing voice of country music.'"

"Oh shit," Ken said. "How Amber—how do you know? You and Cole were both…"

"Wrong, he was passed out drunk when the biggest recording session of his life was going down. I woke up when Clay came to the door to pick up Cole. He'd been waiting and he was worried, the poor idiot. I sent him packing but he decided to stand in for Colton. He had roughly the same build and, with the hat pulled low over his eyes—who would know. He took Colton's clothes and went to the studio. He'd been singing backup, he knew the song, and you…"

"I," Ken said ruefully, "I helped him rig the filters on his microphone so he would sound like Colton with a very slight case of the flu. The technical stuff we could fix in the editing, but the label would have fired us if he hadn't shown up. That was the most important part. God, all these years I thought…"

"You thought only you and Colton and Clay knew."

"Clay never told me he let you in on his plan and when Clay died, when the accident happened…"

"That was no accident, Ken. Clay committed suicide."

"That's a lie!" Colton called out.

"Is it? Is it really Colton? Clay had been on drugs longer than either of you knew. That's what got him out onto a stage in your shadow every night. There's no way he could have accidentally overdosed. Thing was, he knew he could be as good as you, he knew he was as good, but he was stuck in your band—knowing he had made your career—and he would be forever the backup singer being introduced at the end of the concert. That's why he killed himself."

"There is no way you're going to put this on me Amber, you can't prove it wasn't an accident, never mind holding me responsible for it."

"Oh, but I do hold you responsible, and so will the press and your fans and your label. The reporters are going to have a field day I guarantee it. It would only take a little effort on my part to make it look like a murder even. Maybe you were jealous—he sang your song and his version became a hit while you were sleeping off a bender. You messed with his stash, you had someone sell him some bad Coke, God there are so many ways I can fix this story, you can't even imagine. How would the press take that, do you think? I can definitely make this smell at least a little like a murder if I want to, I hold all the cards. All it'll take is for me to plant a few ideas in a few heads."

Colton had jumped to his feet and was about to rip into Amber but Ken stopped him with an upraised hand.

"Never mind," he said. "What is it you want Amber, how much is it going to cost us to get rid of you?"

"I don't need money Ken," she spat. "I have that myself. What I want is what he has given away to all the bimbos who dated him over the years…fame, respectability, a name, and I'll have that as Mrs. Wright, so there is absolutely no way I'll sign the divorce decree now that I didn't sign ten years ago—you get my drift?"

"Shit!"

"You already said that once Ken, and I'll thank you not to do so again in my presence. Now if you will leave my husband and me alone so we can get reacquainted, I would appreciate it."

Ken started to leave and pulled Colton aside.

"When you told me you where still married," he began, out of Ambhara's earshot "I had no idea of the can of worms that stood wide open here. This is an unholy mess, but I'll have it on our lawyers desk in the next ten minutes Cole. I don't care what it costs I'll have them put an army on it, but please do me a favor and try to keep the gory details out of the press. Try to control your temper, I can't tell you how important that is right now."

"Ken, a favor please." Colton said quietly.

"Anything, what do you need?"

"She won't take her eyes off me for one second, she's taking no chances. Try to find Reanne; she must be out of her mind by now. Try to explain this to her, tell her the whole story if you have to, tell her…I didn't mean to…Tell her…" He shook his head, "I don't know—this is not how I wanted everything to turn out."

Ken put his hand on Colton's shoulder. "As fast as I can, I'll have you out of this, I swear."

He left, the conference room door closing behind him with a quiet click, leaving Colton and Amber alone.

Ken looked all over the compound but nobody had seen Reanne. He stood for a moment by the beach, thinking. And having been a victim of many a heartache himself, he started combing the beach bars. Finally he found her in the hotel's dark lobby bar. He picked up her glass and sniffed it.

"Not quite noon yet, but I think I could use one of those myself."

"Go ahead," she said, morosely staring at her drink. Ken signaled the bartender and turned back to Reanne. "I don't know if you recognize me, but…"

"I know who you are, Mr. Taylor," Reanne interrupted, "and if you're here to do his dirty work—don't bother. I have nothing to say to him. His *wife*," there was a whole ocean of bitterness in that word, "his wife said everything that needed to be said."

"I know it looks pretty bad. Even I don't know how he got himself into this mess. What I do know is that he had no idea something like this could happen and he never meant to hurt you. You mean a lot to him. He didn't tell me anything and, with Cole, that usually means he's really into something. He doesn't talk a lot about the things he's really wrapped up in."

"So what we have here," Reanne said, gesturing exaggeratedly, "is another misunderstanding. Another this-isn't-what-it-looks-like thing. Well you know what? What it looks like to me is a lot of pain and heartache. I don't know who told you what I mean to him, but you can go tell him to go and…"

Ken put his hand on her arm.

"He's hurting just as much. Amber destroyed him a long time ago"

"Mr. Taylor, I know you mean well, you're on his side, you should be, but I don't really want to hear it, ok? I've been listening to the reporters all morning, saying how beautiful she is, how the two of them make a perfect couple. Well I'm pretty sick of hearing it. I don't think anyone is ever going to say that about me, so if they make the perfect couple, leave them to it. Now, I have four more broadcasts and a few more on line chats to do, so I suggest you go and tell him…"

"What? Tell him what?"

"Have a nice life," she said quietly and turned back to her glass.

Ken paid for his untouched drink and slid off his barstool.

"Mr. Taylor?"

"Yes?"

"Who told you about Cole and me?" hoping against the odds that it had been Colton himself, that he hadn't kept her a secret from everyone. Ken saw the hope in her eyes and hated to destroy it, but lying would serve no purpose.

"I have my sources," he said carefully. "It's my job to stay informed about what he does."

"Just as I thought, Mr. Taylor, just as I thought. I guess he never did intend to show us off in public."

"That's not at all…"

"You better go now Mr. Taylor, I'm sure you and your spin doctors are going to be working overtime."

Ken searched his mind in vain for something to say, anything to make her feel better. The way she sat on that barstool, all her pain expressed in the rigid set of her shoulders and jaw—but she was right. If he was going to make sure this whole story didn't turn into a disaster he had better go to work, quickly.

An hour later Jack came by the bar to pick up Reanne for the afternoon web chat session.

"I carried most of the morning broadcast for you," he said "I think it's time for you to go back to work."

"I'm not really feeling on top of my game here, in case you hadn't noticed."

Jack shoved her drink away and held his hand out to pull her off the stool."

"I don't know what was going on with the two of you and frankly I don't want to. But if there is anything that I have learned in my life, it's that work is as good a medicine as any. And believe me," he indicated her drink with a shake of his head, "I have looked for answers on the bottom of way too many bottles. That's not where they are. I won't let you go there. Now come on, let's go do some real work."

Reluctantly Reanne followed. She stepped out of the dark cool bar into the brilliant sunshine of Hawaii. People passed by, they were laughing and joking, a gardener clipped the hedges, a bellhop passed them with a message for someone. Would it be good news or would it cause tears? Life went on, crashing against her like the great ocean out there just beyond the hotel grounds. Reanne mentally straightened her shoulders and put her heart and her feelings into a deep and dark place inside herself away from the sunshine and laughter of the world. She took out her compact and fixed her face and slid a large pair of dark sunglasses over her red rimmed eyes.

"Ready," she said quietly and under Jacks concerned eye she took her place at the computer station and logged on.

"First question, what's going on with Colton Wright and his wife? Do you know any more than we heard in the press? Is she really as beautiful as I heard?"

'You know as much as we do,' she typed quickly before the hurt deep inside her heart could act up again, 'I think she left him many years ago and now she's back. And yes, she is absolutely gorgeous.'

"I heard somewhere that she was the only woman he ever loved and that all his songs are dedicated to her."

'I wouldn't know about that, but check out the web page for current shots of the video production and, as always, stay tuned to KSOM/WJKT for today's hottest country including Colton Wright.'

For another hour it went on like that, Reanne and Jack taking turns answering questions and dispensing gossip. When they finally logged off Jack looked at her, eyebrows raised. He rose from his chair and stretched.

"Feel better now?" he asked. Truth be told, he was concerned about having thrown Reanne headfirst into this web chat business. Every question had torn out another piece of her heart, and though she had answered them all quickly, easily and without undue agonizing, every answer seemed to put another brick into that wall she was building around her heart. Right now there was nothing showing of the warm hearted, funny Reanne he had come to know. She looked cold and remote, as never before. She did her job, she functioned, but there was no heart left. Or maybe she was just wishing there were no heart at all, then there wouldn't be any heartache.

"No," she said, "I don't really feel better, but thanks for asking. I think I'll go and lie down for a little while."

"There's a beach volleyball game this afternoon, after they finish filming the video, are you sure you want to be alone?"

"No really, I'm not feeling all that hot. I'll join you tonight for the luau."

Jack watched her walk away and realized what had been missing from his show all morning—the sparkle was gone. The very electricity, the charge that made her such a great radio personality, the thing that made them such a great team, it had disappeared. He recognized the jaded, disillusioned, disappointed attitude as his own.

Down by the beach, on the *Paradise* stage, Colton went over the choreography for the umpteenth time. His mind elsewhere, he had just blown the fifth take on a scene by stepping out in front of another dancer. He swore softly while the hair and makeup people fixed him up again. The producer babbled into his ear but most of it passed Colton right by. His gaze traveled to the stage where Ambhara had managed to insinuate herself into the video and was already in the progress of crowding out the other dancers and calling the shots. Oblivious to the disharmony she was creating, or perhaps simply not caring, she went right on doing what she was doing.

Irritated Colton finally slapped the makeup girl away. "Guitar!" he barked and one of the many faceless gofers brought him his favorite guitar, the vintage Gibson. He carefully took the instrument out of its case; it was so well used the wood of the sounding board had started to wear away just below the strings. He rarely used it in concerts nowadays but, nevertheless, it went everywhere he did.

"I'll be in the trailer for ten," he mumbled to no one in particular and disappeared into the mobile that doubled as command center and storage.

He locked the door and shoved all sorts of video paraphernalia out of the way before settling on a chair. He started hammering away at chords, singing whatever came into his mind at the moment. He considered himself an average guitar player, didn't have the patience to practice endless chord progressions and grips. The guitar was simply there to express the love or anger, the fear or hope he was feeling at the moment. Over the years it had become more of an extension of himself than he dared to admit.

Right now it was receiving all the frustration he poured into it and throwing something out in return.

> "If I could walk away from you,
> I'd take my hat and leave,
> why'd you come in here looking like that,
> hoping for a last reprieve?"

He hit the strings, he caressed them like a gentle lover, he screamed his frustration, he cried his tears. It was all there in the songs, his own and those who had gone before him.

After twenty minutes he emerged from the trailer emotionally spent but in a curious space the music had created. Like nothing could touch him. He waved everyone away and stepped up onto the stage.

"Let's go everyone," he said into the microphone and finished the last scenes of the video in one perfect take.

"Let's wrap it," the producer called, "I'll take care of the rest in editing."

Colton walked away feeling empty inside. The temporary high the music had produced was wearing off and he could see Ambhara headed toward him.

Systematically she was putting her hooks into every area of his life, determined to be Mrs. Wright in every possible way. In every way but one Colton vowed, despite his body's betrayal every time he so much as looked at the beautiful Ambhara.

She had moved herself into his rented condo next to the hotel, stashing her belongings in his bedroom closet and shamelessly sprawled out on his bed last night. For a moment, for just one brief moment, he had been tempted to forget the last ten years and to just pick up where they had left off—in each other's arms, in bed.

His body well remembered the joys they had experienced together but his mind remembered all the pain she had caused him. There was no ignoring the hard lines in her face or the smile that came from her carmine lips only—not from her heart—and it never reached her eyes. He had spent an incredibly uncomfortable night on the couch in the sitting room and was even now trying to secure a second unit in the building. Ambhara would find moving into his life a lot tougher than she thought.

The next important item on his list was to find Reanne and to explain to her what was going on. Her expression at the press conference had broken his heart.

The pain he had experienced ten years ago when Amber left him was reflected in her face. He wanted nothing as much as to go and take her into his arms, to tell her everything was going to be ok. If only he could find a few free minutes between the press and Ambhara watching him, to go and talk to Reanne. He looked for her at the broadcast booth, but today's broadcast was finished. The web chats were over and the equipment was locked up for the day. He stood by the empty booth, letting his hands linger on the KSOM logo for a moment. He could walk into the hotel and go up to her room but that too would cause gossip. Perhaps even more so, now that Amber was back and he had been seen with Reanne the night of Amber's return.

He caught the eye of a few guests on the hotel grounds, and had to give the expected autographs. By now his wanderings were causing attention and Ambhara effortlessly caught up with him.

"If I were you I wouldn't go looking too far for her," she hissed while taking his hand off the KSOM logo on the booth and hooking her arm through his, strolling along, and smiling pleasantly at passersby. Outwardly they made the picture of a perfect couple.

"Why would you care?" he asked.

"Because we are going to be the fairy tale couple again Colton, I can't have you sniffing after that little radio girl."

"You leave her out of this, you hear."

"Ohhh, you've got feelings for her, poor you, and here I thought you were just screwing her. You wouldn't want anything to happen to her now, would you? Well then I doubly recommend you behave, my dear Colton."

Colton tightened his grip on her arm noticeably. "Leave her out of this, you hear me!"

"Certainly, it's all up to you Cole," if she was feeling any pain, she didn't let on. "If you leave her out of this, so will I."

Colton let go of her and stalked away without looking back. Right now, there was no way for him to get to Reanne, he would ask Ken to speak to her and, back in

Nashville, they would work out something. If Ambhara thought she could make him give up Reanne jut like that, she had just made mistake number two.

"Don't forget the Luau tonight, Colton dear, I'm thinking of having us renew our vows," she called after him but Colton set his teeth and kept on walking. No chance and she knew it, she was just trying to drive the point of the knife in a little further.

The Luau that night began with Colton blowing the ceremonial conch shell and making a short speech. He thanked everyone for their participation in a successful video shoot, expressed his hopes that it would become a hit and hoped everyone had enjoyed him or herself. His speech was stiff and devoid of the joi de vivre he had shown just a few days ago, for their opening night party. Had it really been just a couple of days ago? It seemed like an entire lifetime had passed.

"I'd like to turn over the musical part of the evening to the Keanana brothers and their slack key guitars, seeing as how I've been doing an awful lot of singing the last few days." Everyone laughed politely, "After that, we'll have the fire dancers and the lovely ladies from the Honolulu Academy of Dance entertaining us with the hula. Please enjoy your evening." He signaled to the stage where the musicians started playing Honolulu City Lights, and he took his seat at the head table again.

Not a word was said about Ambhara who was clearly miffed about the situation. Just before the musicians could really get into their first number she dashed up to the stage and grabbed the microphone. A hush fell over the room and Colton's gaze was like thunderbolts. Ambhara graced the crowd with her practiced movie star smile. "I couldn't let the evening go by without thanking you all," she gushed. "You've all been so gracious while Colton and I have turned your work and your lives here upside down with our stormy reunion. So thank you all. And in the years to come, both my darling Colton and I will remember this vacation fondly."

"Laying it on a bit thick?" Jack whispered to Reanne, but she didn't answer. She sat at their table like a statue, fixing Colton in her stare. Today he looked like any tourist at the beach, wearing a flowered Hawaiian shirt and white Dockers. Would that he was just a tourist. Reanne had tried to go through the afternoon's activities mechanically, without thinking about Cole. She nodded and smiled at her guests at the table. She said yes and no at the appropriate times but inside she felt as if she was watching herself perform. *Now starring in the role of the radio DJ, Reanne Parker.*

Only this one evening to get through, she told herself, only this one evening. Once she was back in Nashville, she could avoid him and his *darling* wife, avoid thinking or talking about him. She could bury herself in her work and never have Colton Wright or Hawaii cross her mind again. If he just didn't look so handsome sitting there. If the look on his face didn't make her heart turn inside out, if she could just stop thinking he was a victim in this sick game, stop thinking there was a sadness in his eyes— something he was trying to tell her when he caught her eye across the room.

But whenever Reanne looked, his newfound blonde wife made a show of draping part of herself all over Colton, and unmistakably there was something triumphant in her eyes. Reanne had a feeling there was something almost dangerous about the woman. To cross her, to try and take away what she considered hers, including Colton would mean a major battle. And it would be a battle Reanne was convinced she could never win.

On the stage the Hula dancers started to share their elaborate stories woven into a dance. People rose, went to the enormous buffet and came back. Snatches of conversation hit her ears, and Reanne felt again like life was crashing against her in its constant motion. The CW organization had spared no expense with this authentic

Hawaiian Luau. There was the traditional roasted Kalua pig, which had been roasting in a hole atop a pile of hot lava stones by the beach since this morning. There was poi, the traditional taro root mush, Lomi Lomi salmon, vegetables, and an abundance of local fruit. For the less adventurous all the popular delicacies of a standard buffet were provided and, at a thatched bar in one corner, were all the tropical drinks one could wish for.

Their Nashville guests were having a wonderful time, chattering away exitedly, not a word of which Reanne remembered later, but she did act the perfect, gracious hostess. The staff from WJKT provided the background stories and hawaiiana and Jack amused everyone just by being himself. Here and there the website technician with his handheld camera would walk through, peering intently into the top of the camera capturing everything for the website feed.

Somehow there seemed to be a general understanding, as if everyone knew not to touch the subject of Ambhara and Colton in Reanne's presence. Who had told them and how much she didn't know, but she was glad no one mentioned it. Right now she just couldn't handle pretending to be glad they had found each other again. She watched Colton make his rounds again, talking to everyone and he was working his way to their table.

Reanne sat frozen, considering her options. She could sit her and watch him make a fool of himself—in front of everyone or she could get out of here—forever.

She had put down her napkin and was rising from her chair when she felt Jack's hand on her arm. "No," he whispered quietly.

"But he's coming this way."

"Eventually, Reanne, you will have to face him, one way or another."

"Jack, not now!"

But Jack relentlessly pulled her back into her seat from where she helplessly watched Colton Wright come closer and closer. He shook everyone's hand, taking his time to chat with all the guests. Finally he turned and shook her hand. His blue eyes were fastened on hers, his hand held hers just a moment longer than usual. A tiny shiver ran through Reanne again, at the touch of his hand and she remembered the feeling of those hands all over her body, and the gentle touch of his fingers in her hair and face. She remembered the feeling of his lean strong body above her and the long curly hair tickling her bare skin and she ached with the need for him.

I love you, she thought, and even as she dismissed the thought, she could see the same feelings mirrored in his face. Tears stung the back of her eyes.

"Thank you very much," he said quietly "It's a pleasure working with you, as always."

Was it her imagination or did one finger of his dig into the palm of her hand as they shook hands? A silent signal? A moment later it was gone and she might have imagined the whole thing.

"Thank you Mr. Wright, and yes it was an honor working with you."

She used the past tense on purpose and she saw him shake his head just the tiniest fraction.

"I'll make this right," he whispered so quietly even Reanne couldn't be sure he had said it. She was so focused on his face, trying to remember every feature, every line and dimple that she was startled by another hand stuck at her. A beautiful manicured hand bedecked with rings and gems in the colors of the rainbow.

"Let me thank you also," Ambhara, said with cloying sweetness. "You did a wonderful job on the broadcasts."

Reanne shook her hand and smiled thinly. "Thank you."

She couldn't believe it; Ambhara was dressed in bridal white and sparkled with diamonds. Around her neck was a lei of TI leaves, offered by the ancient Hawaiians to the gods of fertility. Ambhara smiled and shook Reanne's hand, but her eyes held a warning.

She knows, Reanne thought, *or at least she suspects.*

Ambhara hooked her arm through Colton's and gently steered him away from the KSOM table, cordially greeting people she knew and those she didn't. The role of Mrs. Colton Wright fit her to a T, and unless Reanne was mistaken, she would not relinquish it without a substantial battle.

I'll make it right. His words rang in her ears. *Oh Cole, I don't think even you can make this right. What have we got ourselves into?* Someone was tugging at her sleeve and she returned to the present, realizing that she still stood where she had been talking to Cole. Jack looked at her concerned. "Are you ok?"

"Just distracted, thank you." She sat down quickly, covering her embarrassment with some mindless chatter. One thing her mind could always be relied upon, to provide some tidbit of gossip or trivia to smooth over a scene. Her eyes though, followed Cole's retreating form

My love, she silently mouthed, *my love.*

She had just turned her attention back to dinner, when Ambhara stepped up to the microphone still holding a reluctant Colton's hand.

"Ladies and Gentlemen," she said, "In honor of Colton and my finding each other, I would like to have a special song performed for us. Would you please welcome Koko Kehalo performing the Hawaiian Wedding Song."

"Oh man," Jack groaned, "now she's going too far!"

But Ambhara relished her role. She took Colton's hand led him out on the dance floor and started to dance.

"This is the moment of sweet Aloha,
I will love you longer than forever"

Her eyes glowed like those of a new bride, or perhaps the cat who had just devoured the canary. Reanne couldn't handle it any more. She got up so fast she had to hold her chair to keep it from falling over.

"Promise me you will leave me never,
Here and now dear,"

"Excuse me for a moment." Reanne said, "I'll be right back."

Jack nodded quietly, at least he understood. He would entertain their guests, make her apologies. Reanne headed up to her room, blinded by tears. The only image in her mind was that of Colton and Ambhara dancing in each other's arms.

She had left so quickly she never saw that Colton only danced with Ambhara for the first half of the song. Then he bowed politely and asked the wife of his record label's representative to dance, thus completely destroying the romantic intimacy of the song. Ambhara was left standing on the dance floor, fuming, until the video producer stepped up and asked her to dance. Other couples joined them on the dance floor and Koko Kehalo performed the song again in the original Hawaiian.

"Way to go Wright." Jack said quietly and raised his glass in a silent salute, "one up for you."

Colton had effectively ruined Ambhara's big moment and he couldn't help to feel a little smug about it, even if Reanne wasn't there to see it.

Reanne had gone up to her room and changed into shorts and running shoes as fast as she could. She headed down to the beach and, trying to ignore all the plans she had made for a romantic beach walk with Cole, she started running. She ran and ran through the damp sand, past volcanic rocks and couples out for a stroll, past private beach houses and estates. Her legs screamed with the exertion of running through the shifting sand and still she went on. The beach curved and became almost impassable with a volcanic rock formation reaching right down to the water. The lights of Waikiki glittered in the distance and still she ran until her legs would no longer carry her. Finally she fell to her knees in the soft beach sand, wiped her eyes and waited for the tears to fall. All the heartbreak and all the hurt she felt inside threatened to engulf her, but she could not cry a single tear. The lights of Waikiki sparkled like diamonds on the water, the surf continued rolling in and out, somewhere a couple laughed...

And life went on.

Chapter Fifteen

Ambhara paced the floor in Colton's beautiful condominium like a caged bear. The walls were closing in on her and boredom made her testy and angry.

"What do you mean he's still in there?" she barked into her tiny, high tech cell phone. One of those little luxuries she could now afford, thanks to Colton's money. "I pay you to keep an eye on him at all times, you hear me, at all times. Are you trying to tell me the man spends hour after hour in that—that music studio?"

She made the last word sound almost like a catching disease. "Don't get cute with me mister. Remember who's paying your outrageous bills. And the next time I talk to you, you had better have a proper report, is that clear?"

She stabbed the end button and resisted the impulse to hurl the phone at something. So far her re-entry into Nashville society was not going as planned. Not as planned at all. For the first few weeks they had been invited to all the hot spots and happening events, wined and dined by everyone who wanted a story or just a quote from the current headliners of society. Ambhara had reigned like a queen and relished every delicious moment of it, even if Colton was surly and short most of the time. Anything he did say came out laced with resentment and irritation. He was careful to never cross the line and annoy her too much, but rumors were already flying that all was not well at the Wright house.

In time, she figured, he would realize that she was holding all the cards. And this, this was most certainly the life she had been born to live, and she didn't intend on giving any part of it up. Colton needed to be kept in line so, just to be sure, she had hired a private detective to keep an eye on him, to make sure he didn't go chasing after that little radio girl, but otherwise everything was just perfect. The little redhead was no match for Ambhara Kensington Wright.

Unfortunately, Colton slept on the couch or in the guest room, if he slept at all. He always seemed to be working. He had gone through great expense and effort remodeling the condo so his studio was as private as possible. In time, Amber thought, in time he would come around. He hadn't been able to resist her the first time around, why should he now.

She had made a few grave errors in those first years. Colton was only supposed to be a leg up on her way to the top. A talented guy who looked great in the pictures. If he was a badass musician that would give the whole thing just a little delicious wickedness. She had never expected him to be better than she was, never supposed to make it to the top as fast as he had. Well, those were the mistakes one made when one was young, especially leaving him—that had been a major misjudgment. She should have seen then what he could do for her, how far she could go by his side, even if she didn't care for his serious, introspective moods. Oh well, she had come back and she would rectify it all now.

Things needed a little more planning. The first strike had gone well but, after only a few weeks here in Nashville, things had begun to change. She wasn't in the headlines anymore. Someone else had been involved in a scandal. Someone else was the news du jour. People began to tire of Ambhara Wright, she wasn't getting invited to parties any more, and all the private little lunches and functions she had been hoping for were still elusive. Society hadn't embraced her as it should have done.

Worse, there hadn't been any offers at acting roles whatsoever; somehow she had hoped she would be a hot property again once she made the gossip columns.

Then there was the fact that Colton led a fairly quiet life. *Quiet?* Boring was more like it. For crying out loud, the man was a superstar, where were the parties, the grand events, and the pomp? Damn, this was not going as planned at all.

Lately he spent most of his days at that awful little sound studio of his and, when he did finally come home, he would read and answer mail for a few hours then fall into bed—alone. Just to be up and out of the house at six am the next morning—like a common working man!

The exception, of course, being when he was giving a concert somewhere, in which case he could be up until the early morning hours surrounded by fans and music business people.

He spent most of his weekends performing, to promote this new album of his and, again, he had shut out Amber. His road manager of all people told her to sit in the audience with everyone else—because she made the crew nervous and it was a security risk for her backstage. *Security risk, nervous,* ha! The few times she had spent backstage they worked around her like a team of ants, ignoring her for all intents and purposes. As for security, there seemed to be just as many weirdoes backstage as there were in the stands. If Colton had put his foot down she would have had a place backstage but, as always, he didn't say a thing.

Anyway, who really wanted to see the show over and over? It was okay—great even to judge by the critiques and the audience responses—but if you've seen one… Now, if Colton had the common decency to ask her up on the stage and introduce her to the audience—like Tim McGraw and Faith Hill perhaps—that would be different. If he asked her to do a duet, let her share some of the spotlights…yes that would be a show worth going to. But to just sit there and watch.! Any show that didn't feature her didn't really register on Ambhara's radar.

There were some interesting rumors going around that a duet of *Paradise Found* existed somewhere. That he had performed it and then locked it away somewhere, never to be played.

"I wonder if that's true, and if so who is singing with him," she mused out loud and resumed pacing the apartment again. It would have to be a female singer. Now Ambhara couldn't really sing worth a lick, but she had other assets to offer and it would have been a nice thing to do to offer the part to her. It would have capped off the story of their reunion beautifully, one of those stories fans told each other with tears in their eyes. But did Colton see the potential? No, of course not. He preferred to act like an oaf.

She would have to take steps to get Colton to act more like a loving husband and less like a martyr. All her seduction efforts had so far been for nought, and Amber was starting to get frustrated. On any given day Colton was polite enough. Inquiring about her day, praising her skills the few times she had actually attempted to prepare a meal, but on the whole he acted like a man with a permanent houseguest. And, he seemed to be working eighteen hours a day. Damn! Ambhara stared at the silhouette of Nashville beyond the balcony.

At least Colton wasn't with that little girl from the radio station, this much she knew. But still, if she had to tell the truth, Amber was bored out of her mind at the moment. On the soap opera she had worked sixteen to eighteen hour days herself, in addition to being one of the reigning queens of society. Here, there seemed to be nothing to fill up her days since Colton had dumped her in this condo.

"Nashville," she grumbled. "Backwater hole in the wall!"

Once, only once she had mentioned moving to LA to Colton and his answer had not given her any hope. "I'm

Colton Wright, I sing county music and I live in Nashville. My business is here and here is where I will stay, you want to be married to me, this is it because there ain't no Colton Wright in LA."

Baloney of course, why shouldn't a star of his size be able to live anywhere he wanted? However this might not be the right time to force the issue with him.

Dang, dang dang, unless country music was your business, Nashville was a bore indeed. Sighing, she picked up the phone and stabbed out the number of her ex-producer and boyfriend. Time to catch up on some good old Hollywood gossip.

Colton, meanwhile, was doing some pacing of his own. Back and forth between the walls of Ken Taylor's office.

"Cole, you're wearing out my rug, will you sit down."

"I'll sit down when we figure out how to get rid of her. I'll get you a new rug if you want one. Now tell me, what can we do that we haven't already tried?"

Cole's face looked gray and drawn, Ken thought. The release of the new album and the accompanying tour had its own set of headaches. Having to deal with the sordid details of his so-called home life had taken more out of Colton than he dared to admit. The dark shadows under his eyes were ever-present, his hair was constantly mussed from running his hands through it, and the fun and sparkle was missing from his eyes. If they'd had to do publicity pictures right now, they would have had to spend hours on him in makeup to get him to look like the *Mr. Right* they all knew and loved.

"Sit!" Ken finally said, pointing to a chair. "Now you know that our lawyers have gone over this thing with a fine tooth comb and the only way to get Amber out of your life is to sue her for divorce."

"At which point she'll release her juicy little gossip tidbits, ruining my career and yours and God knows who else depends on this organization for a living. Do you know what would happen if she started rumors that I had Clay Fender killed? That you were in on it—my God, just by denying it everything could be ruined. "

Ken tapped a folder in front of him. "If she did that, sure, but maybe she won't."

"What are you telling me?"

"I've done some digging into the life she led for the last ten years. All my sources indicate that Amber likes the high life, the jet set, and the parties. She won't find that in Nashville unless you introduce her to it."

"So? She's asked me more than once to move to LA already."

"Which you refused."

"Which I refused, definitely—your point being? I still don't know where this is leading."

"My point being that Amber counts on your name to gain her entry into society. To get her known and loved, maybe even to get her some role offers. So far it hasn't happened that way, because we've buried you in work for a while."

"And thanks to your spreading rumors that keep her pretty much an outsider. Ken, I appreciate what you're doing, but I still don't quite see where this is going."

"I didn't know you were aware of the rumors, I do what I can, thank you. But let me ask you this, why did Amber leave you ten years ago?"

"Why? You know why, my career was taking off hers tanked, what does that have to—oh."

"That's right Cole, we'll just make it happen again. All we have to do is make her want to walk. Show her that there is absolutely nothing here for her. Sooner or later she'll get fed up with sitting in your condo all day, doing nothing."

"Ken, that's a great idea, but, aah, it's a long shot. I mean, it could take years for her to decide she's had it, pack up and leave. That woman is the most mercenary creature I have ever met."

"Well, Cole buddy, you're the one who married her—don't say it—*she wasn't like that then.* I'll buy that, but she is now so, unless you're ready to throw everything away and make widgets for a living I suggest you wait her out."

"Widgets, Ken, widgets?"

"Figure of speech. Meanwhile," Ken tapped a few buttons on his computer where the most recent soundscan figures were updated continually. "Look at this, so far the whole affair has certainly helped record sales. The new album is flying off the shelves, we're headed for a solid platinum, and airplay is most satisfying. The album is steady at number three, the *Paradise* single is number one, and the video—the video is just racing for the top. They call it the hottest thing you've ever done. That at least should make you happy."

"Sort of."

"It's the music Cole, that's what's important, how often have you told me that's why you and I are in this racket?"

Colton pulled a face and started pacing again. This time Ken didn't bother stopping him. "It's hard to think about all that when my life is such a mess Ken. About the only time I leave it behind is when I step on that stage at night. Then it's just me and the music and the crowds. I can't let her take that away from me."

Ken walked around his desk and put his hand on Colton's shoulder. "She won't. We're all doing everything in our power to make sure she won't. Trust me."

Colton didn't answer. He stood by the window looking down at the busy street. The heart of music row. This was where country music happened. For a moment again, he felt connected.

Ken watched him and hesitated. He meant to talk to Colton about the recent batch of songs he had written. One more depressing than the next. Something had to be done, and quickly, or they would play Colton Wright at funerals instead of weddings. He whose trademark had always been upbeat Honky Tonk Party songs and breathtaking love songs. There had been a desperate sadness in his music lately and Ken was afraid to wait for it to pass naturally—it might not. But how could he tell his friend? *Stop being upset and write some happy songs?* Not likely.

"Have you tried talking to Reanne?" he asked instead, remembering the spark Reanne had struck in Colton in the short time they were together. She had brought out a joy in him that was visible in every inch of the *Paradise* video.

Colton shook his head. "No, she won't take my phone calls—can't say I blame her either. I tried to see her but Amber's people are on me like fleas on a dog. Lord knows what kind of sleazy surveillance my money is paying for."

"Well maybe we can do something about that."

"How?"

Ken shrugged. "You don't want to know. Just stand by for the next little while, I've got my own supply of sleazy characters, and for Gods sake hang in there Cole, we'll figure this out somehow, buddy."

"Yeah, and we just hope that it's not too late."

He left the CW Management offices on music row and headed for the studio, knowing that somewhere in the city a phone would ring and someone would report his every move to Amber. She made no secret of the fact that she had him shadowed at all hours of the day. "Just to keep you in line". More than ever he needed the sanctuary of the studio. The cool quiet rooms that were for him alone, where his music was the most important thing and the only constant in his life.

He aimed the old pickup truck west. The caddy had been parked at the studio since before he went to

Hawaii. Somehow he couldn't bear the thought of Amber getting her hands on it. How many more years of this? He found himself longing for a concert, a live appearance, anything he could lose himself in, a performance that would give everything to the crowd and in turn wipe out all the memories and feelings and the pain until only the one bright point of the spotlight remained within him. And from that point he would grow, expand, and become *Mr. Right* to everyone in the audience, and he could sing and dance and give joy to his listeners for a few hours in exchange for being allowed to lose himself in his music for them.

For a moment he thought of trying to call Reanne again, but there was most likely not much point. *She's refused to take any of your calls since we got back from Hawaii, and you can't really blame her. In her eyes you committed the ultimate betrayal— jerked her around for weeks. No, there's no point. You can't offer her anything except more heartbreak and, of all people, you know what that's like.*

Chapter Sixteen

Reanne was sitting at her desk, lost in thought, when she heard someone knocking at her door. Probably another well-meaning soul trying to cheer her up.

"Reanne, are you going to join us for lunch?"

"No, thanks, I need to finish this paperwork first, but thanks for asking." She looked up and saw Sasha framed in the half open office door. "I'll be fine, I brought my lunch, I just really have a lot of work to do Sash."

Instead of leaving, Sasha came into the office and closed the door behind her. "Are you ever going to come out from under that mountain of paperwork there, Reanne?"

"It…really needs to be done Sasha, and you know that as well as I do—some of it's yours."

"I know, but it can wait for a while. You're not doing it, you're hiding behind it. And I think it's time you finally came out."

"Well, thank you very much, but…"

"But nothing, Reanne, How long are you planning on keeping this desk job? You resigned from your morning show, you haven't done any on-air stints since you got back from Hawaii. That's no way to live. Look I know, Colton Wright and you were pretty involved—there's all kinds of rumors around—but that was a while ago, Reanne, try to move on. I mean the guy went back to his wife for crying out loud, he's a jerk."

Reanne toyed with her pen, not looking at Sasha directly. "Sash, there's a lot of stuff you don't know, and I can't really explain it either. Suffice it to say that he's not as much of a jerk as you think. Maybe some…hey most guys are, but Sasha—I love him and no matter what happens, I think I always will."

She looked up at Sasha, her green eyes wide, almost pleading, "But every time someone requested one of his songs or I had to read some bit of gossip about him on the air—every single time—it just hurt so much. That's why I asked for this transfer for a while, all right."

"Reanne, you used to be in love with him, used to be—past tense. It is time to move on."

Reanne had a faraway look. "Yeah, and I will, someday. But not today, and not tomorrow, and not the day after. Right now I feel like I lost everything and everyone I ever cared about, and I can't ever imagine feeling any other way."

"But you know you will."

Reanne turned away and busied herself in her desk drawer. She didn't want Sasha to see the sudden tears pooling in her eyes. Tears that had been too close to the surface for too long a time.

"You're wasting your lunch hour Sasha. Thanks for trying, but why don't you head out now."

"OK, if that's what you want. But I won't let up, and you know that."

Reanne watched Sasha leave silently. *You will feel better—some day.*

Easier said than done. Every song on the radio reminded her of Cole. Every time she went out she found herself looking for an old Cadillac Fleetwood in the parking lots around town. Every morning brought just another day where she still loved Cole but wouldn't see him again; his new wife had taken care of that.

She took another swig of ice-cold coffee and turned back to her paperwork. Resolutely she tore her mind away from Cole and back onto her work. A little piece of notepaper reminded her of her voice lessons that afternoon. They were rather expensive, she mused, and these days every dollar counted, so why was she still going? She had signed up on impulse after coming back from Hawaii, as a tribute to Cole perhaps? After all, music had brought them together in the first place. Or maybe it was just a way to occupy her time.

She was well into her work and getting ready to finish for the day when a knock on the door interrupted her again.

Turning around, she froze. There in the doorway stood Colton, looking so handsome, so wonderful that he took her breath away. Her heart did that little leap that told her she still did, and probably always would, love him. Where had he come from, how had he escaped from his wife, what did he want? So many questions, and still her heart would not let her say or do anything except stare at him open mouthed.

He carried his hat in one hand and kept running the other through his hair. He only did that when he was nervous, she remembered.

"Reanne, I had to see you, hoping you wouldn't throw me out."

"I should, Colton, if I knew what was good for me. I shouldn't even be talking to you. How? Why are you here?"

Colton shrugged. "Ken. I don't know how much it cost but he convinced my *guards*—Ambhara's spies—to look the other way. My God Reanne, I haven't talked to you in weeks, why are we talking about Ambhara? I don't even know where to start. I am so sorry, so sorry for everything that happened. Did Ken talk to you, did he tell you anything?"

"He told me some things, that she had some sort of hold over you."

"You've got to believe me, if it wasn't for that…"

"Then what Cole? Then it would be something else. It always seems to be something. You don't really want to be with me."

"That's not true."

Reanne turned away, knowing that if she looked at him any longer she wouldn't be able to say what she had to say.

"Cole, I don't know what your wife is holding over you to make you stay with her. I would like to believe that it would have to be pretty big to make you just toss me aside…"

"I didn't…"

"But the truth is Colton, she's everything you need. She fits your image to a T. She's beautiful, famous and classy. She looks amazing standing there beside you."

"That's just another show, like those dates I went on for years. I don't love her, and that's the God's honest truth!"

"I can't see how that makes much of a difference right now. Let's face it, this situation is not going to change any time soon and I won't sit here waiting. Waiting for the odd day when Ken bribes your guards so you can come see me. Do you know how ridiculous that is?"

"If I loved her Reanne, would she need detectives tailing me twenty four hours a day to keep me away from you?"

And if you loved me, Reanne thought, wouldn't you at least tell me, wouldn't you say so? But she only shook her head.

"Reanne, don't do this to me—to us, there's so much I want to say to you."

"I know you do. But there is no us Cole, is there? And even if there was it wouldn't change anything, would it?"

"If I could…" Colton started, a helpless rage building inside him. "Dammit Reanne I would do anything to stop this from hurting you."

"Then just leave Cole, just leave. Seeing you here, right in front of me and not being able to have you, that just hurts worse than anything. There's nothing you can do at this point. And that's just exactly what is hurting so much."

"Reanne, I wish things were different, and I know some day…"

Colton faltered and she turned away from him. It broke her heart to see him standing there, lost, alone. "Wishing won't make it so Cole."

"I still wish it didn't have to be this way—with all my heart," he said but when she remained silent he walked to the door.

"Good bye Reanne," he said quietly. "I have no right to ask you to wait for something that might never happen. I guess I thought you might—I don't know—give us some hope. But…"

Still she remained bent over some papers at her desk, seemingly unconcerned. He jammed his hat back on his head and left.

"I want to—oh how I want to—but I can't allow myself that hope. Good bye Cole, my love," Reanne said softly to herself after she heard the door click into its lock.

"Good bye forever." She walked to the window and looked out at the late afternoon traffic moving steadily out of the parking lot. Quitting time for most KSOM employees. For a moment she thought she saw a beige Stetson, but no, it couldn't be. A lot of men wore Stetsons in Nashville. She scanned the lineup of cars for the old Cadillac, all the while telling herself not to be foolish. There was nothing down in that parking lot for her but heartbreak.

There were no tears left inside her no matter how badly she hurt. One last look out the window for a glimpse of the familiar car, but nothing.

"Guitars, Cadillacs…Hillbilly Music," she heard. The hidden speakers in her office played a constant background of the current KSOM program and as she returned to her desk, contemplating the next mountain of paperwork waiting for her, she found herself humming along. *"It's the only thing that keeps me hangin' on."*

How true, she thought, and touched the spot on the wall behind her desk, where the KSOM advertising poster featuring Colton still taunted her daily.

Chapter Seventeen

"And just where have you been all day?" Ambhara fumed.

"Working."

"Working? What do you mean working? The album is done, the tour is moving along well—I don't see why you have to be at that studio all day long. You could put a little more effort into our social life."

Colton stopped rifling through the mail and various messages long enough to cock an eyebrow at her. "And why, pray tell, should you care?"

"There's a grand opening at the theater tonight. I think it's about time we were seen in public together on an ongoing basis Colton."

"Unfortunately I don't have the time to spare tonight Ambhara. There are a million insignificant yet nagging details that require my prompt attention if my albums are to continue to sell adequately—and to provide you with the lifestyle you so enjoy. I'm afraid you'll have to enjoy the theater on your own."

"That would look stupid, and you know it."

For good reason, Colton thought, but aloud he said, "Well I am certain there is no lack of people willing to accompany you, if it means that much to you. As it stands, I'm afraid I shall be buried in menial paperwork for the rest of the night."

"That's all you ever do, work in that silly studio of yours all hours of the day or night. I don't see why a star of your prominence has to concern himself with all those minor details."

Colton went to the built in bar and poured himself a drink. "It was your choice, Ambhara, to marry a musician. All those minor details are what make my fans happy. My fans—they're the ones who decide to spend their hard earned money on my albums and concerts, providing you with a quite comfortable living. I'm sure you do remember how much work goes into the creation of an album, you were there when I brought out the first one."

He sipped his drink, enjoying the early evening view of Nashville and tried not to think about the expensive gowns and jewelry and the charge accounts at various trendy Nashville boutiques that had shown up lately. To mention them would only have caused another argument, and money was the least of his concerns right now— although now and then he couldn't resist a little barb about her sudden rise in lifestyle. Ken was right, he thought, Amber's sudden isolation in this palatial condo was starting to get on her nerves. She was used to being entertained, to being the center of attention and it just wasn't happening.

"I don't have to put up with this," she hissed.

She seemed in quite a state and Colton counted to twenty carefully before he answered. *Just don't start a major fight now*, Ken had lectured him, *let her burn herself out—as she will, in time.*

"Are you threatening me again, Ambhara? Because they're starting to wear a little. I've done everything you asked of me, I…"

"You've done nothing!" she spat. "You've simply dropped me into this penthouse and left it at that. You're gone most of the day. What do you expect me to do?"

Colton could see himself gaining just a little upper ground. "If it was your acting career you wanted to further then you should have considered that Nashville isn't exactly Hollywood. I'm not in the movie business; I don't have any connections there. Now what I do have is plenty of work running the business I am part of, if you don't mind. Aside from that, perhaps you remember from our early years, I do lead a fairly quiet life, I guess that's just the guy you married."

He took his drink and went into the study he had added by having split the larger guestroom in two. Thank you Ken, he thought. Maybe Ambhara was starting to be bored enough. In that case, if he could wait her out, then perhaps, just perhaps, they could strike a deal with her.

He sat down at the piano and absentmindedly struck a few keys. Reanne—the hurt in her eyes had cut him deeply this afternoon. After being put through so much pain ten years ago it tore his heart out to be doing the same thing to her. Amber had up and left him for another man who had more to offer and here he was doing the same thing to Reanne. He certainly knew how she must feel, he did know with all his heart.

His fingers followed a sad little tune on the piano, a sort of inner musical dialogue that seemed to be going on in his head at all times. He was aware that the material he had written lately was not exactly top-drawer stuff. Most of it was sounded rather sad and depressing and, if it went on too long, Amber would destroy his career whether she made good on her threats or not. He had seen the doubts in Ken's eyes lately when he dropped his compositions at the studio, he had seen the faces of the guys in the band, it was a miracle nobody had said anything to him yet. Sooner or later they would. Sooner or later his fans would have something to say about his *depressing* phase.

These days it was the live concerts that kept him hanging on, made him feel connected, like he was doing something worthwhile. His fingers continued tapping out a rhythm on the piano. *Oh Reanne*, he really shouldn't have gone to see her today, he should have told Ken to save his money.

"You don't want me."

Her words still echoed in his mind. *You don't want me.* "Reanne you don't know how wrong you are," he muttered. "You don't know how much I want you, how much I love you."

He had to laugh at the irony of it all. He couldn't get his mind off Reanne. Every time he thought of her and the pain in her eyes his heart clenched painfully. After years of searching, of vowing never to give his heart away again, he had finally found the woman he wanted to spend the rest of his life with. He had fallen in love with her, heart and soul, and still he could not tell her. He couldn't tell her, didn't dare tell her. What good would it do—if Amber were to find out, there would be hell to pay.

Reanne was certainly no match for his spirited ex wife. Gentle, loving Reanne, who could be naïve at times when it came to the things people would and could do to each other. She called herself a wimp because she shied away from the things that hurt. He remembered her gentle hands on him, her passionate kisses and the way she held nothing back, gave all of herself when she made love.

He wanted to write a song for her he decided suddenly, a song that was as gentle caring and loving as she was. That song required the haunting melody of a lone guitar he decided but, when he sat down with his trusted stratocaster, the semi-hollow fender e-guitar, the only song that would come to him was *Paradise*. He played the chorus over and over, remembering how the words had sounded coming from her. How she had taken the lyrics and put her own inimitable style on them, reached deep inside of herself and used the love and the passion she found there to make the song come to life.

Not a day went by that he didn't play that tape at the studio at least once. It had become almost a ritual for him to start and end his day. Whenever he played it he remembered the first afternoon they had spent together, remembered that first shy kiss and the wonder and joy in her eyes when he made her his totally and completely.

Every day when he left he carefully hid the tape again. If Amber was ever to find it…

Fortunately, so far at least, she had shown little to no interest in his music and his studio, which suited him just fine. At least it gave him a place where he could be completely and totally himself.

He flung the guitar aside angrily and began pacing his small study. A man didn't get a chance to find love for the second time in his life only to have it yanked away from him—again. Amber had left and destroyed the first great love of his life, but there had to be a way to be with Reanne, there had to be.

You and I, we are one, one in creation and one in life, the little voice in his head said, and he quickly wrote in his notebook:

> Let our love a lantern be,
> That lights the way between you and me
> Let our hearts carry a flame so bright,
> It turns this darkness into light.
> Let our souls be open to receive
> This love in which I still believe.

On and on he went until he had a complete song. It had gone so fast—the song wrote itself. He brought the guitar out again and began a soft melody that had been cruising through his head for the last few days. When he looked up from his sheaf of note pages, two hours had gone by, but he had a song.

Light of Our Love he put down as the title, but he knew that forever it would be *Reanne's Song* to him. One day she would hear it and she would know he had written these words only for her. Somehow it would speak to her. She would know that he loved her, she would know how he loved her strength, her tears and her laughter—even if she didn't believe it right now.

He laid his pen down and stared at the many awards that lined the bookcase in front of him. Ambhara could force him to stay married to him, she could take away his freedom to a certain point, but there was one thing she could never take away from him, his art, his music. She could never make him stop loving Reanne and turn to her again. No matter what threats Ambhara came up with; she could never change the way he felt. That thought gave him strength and hope for the future. As long as one heart believed in the future there would always be hope.

Austin Taggart leaned back in the chair in Ken's office and studied the other man carefully. In his dark fringed leather jacket and faded jeans he could have been a singer himself instead of a private investigator. He had the rugged good looks and the charm for it. But complicated puzzles and old secrets were his specialty. He had a way of digging and never giving up until he found just the grain of information he needed. It usually didn't pay to try and keep something from him for too long.

He folded his hands behind his head and focused his intense gaze on Ken. For all intents and purposes he looked relaxed, but there was a wariness just below the surface that kept him alert.

"I wasn't expecting you to call me again, Ken," he finally said. "Usually when you do it means major trouble somewhere."

"Trouble is your specialty, isn't it?"

Austin chuckled. "Still the same old Ken. Fortunately your cases tend to be—interesting."

"Do you think you can help us?"

"It's quite the story you told me there Ken. You know, proving somebody innocent is notoriously harder than the opposite. And the case is old. After ten years? Who'll remember anything?"

"Neither Colton nor I had anything to with it, Austin, I give you my word on that. Clay Fender might have committed suicide, or it might have been an accidental overdose, but we were not involved with this."

"I gather there's a lot riding on conclusive evidence of Colton's innocence."

"Yes, and I don't have to tell you that discretion is of the utmost importance. Colton is not only one of my major clients, he's also one of the very few personal friends I have."

"All right, so we start with the assumption that you two are indeed innocent, or let's call it not guilty. Somehow I can't think of you and innocence in the same sentence. How do you expect me to prove this?"

"There must be people around who knew all of us back then, people who knew what was going on, what kind of a snake Amber was..."

"Whoa, you don't think she did it, do you?"

Ken hesitated for just a moment. It wasn't like he hadn't considered the possibility himself. It would be an easy vindication if Amber was the guilty party, but somehow, as much as he wanted to, he just couldn't picture her doing something like that. She was manipulative, cunning, conniving, and treacherous even—but she would stop short of violence, wouldn't she?

"Don't hesitate Ken, I need to know where we stand. I need a clear yes or no, so I know what direction to start digging in. If you're not sure, we won't rule her out."

"I want to say no, I really do, but I also know that she is sleazy enough to have...I don't really know I guess."

"All right, we won't rule her out then. Who else, who else might have had it in for him?"

"Nobody had it in for him. I'm still going on the assumption that Clay's death was an accident, not foul play. The complication is that the whole thing is somehow tied in to the almost missed recording session."

"I'm getting to that. My feeling is that if we unravel what truly happened that night, we might hold the keys to Clay Fender's death right in our hands. Let's start with Wright. Why on earth would he get that drunk if he knew what was riding on that recording session?"

Ken shrugged. "Amber I presume. She might have got him started. You ask him, he doesn't even remember drinking that much, although in those days that type of fun was a major part of the business."

"Think she might have done it on purpose? Getting your boy drunk—to sabotage the recording? I mean, even if he didn't pass out, he would have shown up totally wasted, that might have done the trick already."

"Yeah," Ken said carefully, "but then what?"

"Clay shows up at the door, sees what's going on and decides to save the recording session, the band if nothing else. You could replace him with a session player."

"Which we did, but if Colton had been missing…"

"The whole thing would have gone down the toilet. So Clay somehow messed up Amber's plan."

Ken sighed. "But that still doesn't get us any closer to how he died."

"Sit tight Kenny boy, I'm getting there. What about the drugs, did you guys know about it, where did he get them from?"

"I guess we all knew, we just didn't want to. I don't know Austin, it was a long time ago, there were things going on back then that today… Well let's just say it was different back then."

Austin Taggart stared at a spot on the wall behind Ken, thinking. "Did he have anybody—a girlfriend, a buddy who might have known something?"

"Clay? Let me think…let me think. Yeah, he went with a gal who was a waitress at one of the honky tonks they played at night. All the guys envied him—she was there quite a bit when they rehearsed. Cute thing too, Shelley I think her name was."

"Shelley what?"

"Heck I don't remember."

"Well think. Your boy's career might depend on it, ok."

Ken rubbed his head with his forefingers. Dredging up things from that long ago wasn't a thing he particularly relished, but he had promised Cole. And anyway, their continued success might depend on it.

"The paper," he finally said. "They were all in the paper at one point—with all their girls. I remember, even Amber showed up for the photo. She was real proud to be in the paper. It was a Christmas show at the *Barn Door*. Some charitable thing I think. All their names were under the photo. Does that help?"

A lazy grin spread over Austin Taggart's face. "I'll say. If you have a good computer nowadays, it's amazing the things you can find…"

Austin rose from his chair and stretched slowly, as a cat might, getting ready to stalk its prey. Ken found himself wondering if he carried a gun somewhere on that long, rangy body of his.

Taggart was successful enough he didn't need to advertise—he didn't even have a phone listing. Those who required his services knew how to find him. The way he figured it, if you were good enough to find him, you deserved his services. A bit arrogant, but he was good.

"Well, I reckon I'll go do some digging," he said with a smile. "And no Ken, I'm not carrying any guns or knives…not anymore."

Reanne had dawdled long enough at the office, clearing her own desk and most of Jack's. He would be eternally grateful tomorrow, although he would probably acknowledge all of her hard work with just one raised eyebrow. He still hadn't forgiven her for abandoning him and the morning show to the questionable talents of Marilyn Matters. He kept mentioning how her chatter that early in the morning gave him a headache. He wanted Reanne to come back, but right now on air just wasn't the right place for her. This was a time to come to terms with events. So she had decided to hide behind a desk for a while and give herself the chance to make the right decisions. Sending away Cole today had been one of them, perhaps the worst one.

There did come a point, however, when it was time to go home, but she didn't feel like facing the empty rooms of her apartment yet. The sun shone brightly out of a blue, clear sky, and downtown Nashville seemed to be full of couples strolling hand in hand along the streets and through the parks, enjoying the late September sun. Why was the city always full of couples when you were single?

She couldn't help but envy what she would never have with Colton. Whether he believed it or not, life had reunited him with his long lost first love and one had only to look at them together to see that they were perfect for each other, that they belonged together.

Two beautiful, glamorous people—media sweethearts both of them. The papers had been full of gossip about them for the last few weeks, how they had lost and found each other again, how true love could not be kept in the shadows forever. One tabloid even went so far as to say that he had only had brief, meaningless, superficial flings all these years—holding on to the one true love of his life. No one mentioned how Ambhara had betrayed him with a Hollywood producer for a chance at a movie role and left him without a backward glance. That wasn't the stuff of fairy tales and Nashville, like Hollywood, loved fairy tales.

Reanne pulled into the grocery store parking lot. There were only a few things she needed, shopping for one didn't take all that long. Aimlessly she pushed the cart around the aisles.

If only Cole hadn't come to the station today. Seeing him again, seeing that handsome face her fingers had touched, hearing the voice that had whispered sweet love into her ear—it had almost been too much to handle. To watch him standing there when all she wanted to do was throw herself into his arms and be safe, be held and be loved again. She shook her head, but still the memories stayed with her. Cole listening to her singing in the car, Cole singing *Paradise* with her. She smiled, remembering how patient he had been teaching her to ride a horse again on the day of the surprise picnic, or the passionate way he had made love to her high above Honolulu with the lights at her feet and the stars above. For the rest of her life, that moment would remain the one happiest moment of her entire being.

Forever after Cole had given her a treasure to lock away in her heart and take out and cherish every day, even if he could never be hers again. Even considering all the heartache she couldn't regret the time she had spent with him—the joy loving him had brought to her life and still would in years to come.

Frowning, she contemplated her half empty grocery cart and her single life. How could anyone ever measure up to Cole? How could anything compare to the delicious little shiver that ran through her every time she heard his voice on the radio. Cole was a star, yes, but he had a fire inside him that made everyone else look pale by comparison. Perhaps it would fade over the years, as her friends told her. Perhaps, but Reanne didn't think so, Cole would always be the most wonderful man she had ever known.

Perhaps, she thought, it was in honor of this love that she had signed up for music lessons again, One day she would stand in front of an audience again, just as he had said she would, and one day maybe he would hear her on the radio and think of their brief time together. They might never be together, but they would always have that connection. Music would always be a thread running between their hearts, stretching taut at times, but never tearing.

Reanne paid for her groceries and loaded them into her car. She deliberately tortured herself, playing Cole's latest album on the cassette deck on the way home, pretending he sang every word just for her.

"Your magic makes my world go round, you are my true Paradise found," she sang along. Would one day come when her eyes weren't blurred with tears when she sang this particular song?

She wiped them away with the back of her hand and tried to grab her purse and all the grocery bags at once, trying to avoid making more than one trip from the underground garage up to the third floor. Perhaps it was all the packages in her arms or the tears in her eyes but she didn't noticed the 'Please use the stairs' sign by the elevator.

She pushed the button and tapped her foot impatiently while she waited. "Your magic makes the world go round." *Oh Cole*, with the mischievous smile and those blazing blue eyes that could turn so dark in a moment of passion. She got on the elevator and pushed the button for her floor. The cables groaned and creaked and once again she contemplated moving out of this dump to somewhere better. Unfortunately her music lessons ate up any extra cash she might have at the moment so she would have to stay here for the time being.

Suddenly the elevator came to a screeching halt. Reanne lost her balance and dropped most of her groceries. "Damn!" she cursed and bent to pick up her bags when the lights flickered and then went out completely. Reanne tried to stay calm and wait out the power failure, certain that was all it was. But the lights failed to return and the elevator cables were making terrible noises—at least she thought they were the cables. Something sounded as if it was ripping. Ripping??!

Reanne started to get very scared, crouching in the dark and feeling for her purse. There had to be an old lighter in there somewhere. If she could have a little light she would calm down, everything would be all right. If she just had a little light…

Somewhere in the elevator shaft something metallic screeched and clanged again and Reanne froze, trying to keep as still as possible. Whatever was happening to this elevator, her movements seemed to be making it worse.

Music lessons or not, she insisted, this time she would finally move out of here. Tomorrow morning first thing she would start looking. Even if she had to move into a basement somewhere. Gingerly she began to search for the lighter again. Then, again, she heard the horrible screeching sound this time longer and more drawn out. She clapped her hands over her ears.

"Oh God, just let me get out of here," she knelt on the floor trying to make herself as tiny as possible. She had never been this scared before. Time seemed to stand still, every thought, every emotion centered on getting out of there in one piece.

Carefully she tried to stand up, just as the ground dropped out from underneath her. For a moment she had the sensation of free falling, of flying into space on and on.

'Cole," she screamed, "Cole." Her last thought was of him, just before she heard an immense crash, and every sensation, every motion stopped just as suddenly as it had begun and everything around her went mercifully black.

Chapter Eighteen

Colton awoke on the couch in his study where he had fallen asleep after last night's marathon writing session. He stood to stretch the kinks out of his back and considered going back to the guestroom for another few hours sleep. These were the times he truly missed his own huge bedroom suite. He had never been an early riser but, of late, discomfort made him miss a lot of hours of sleep. After Ambhara's frequent attempts at seduction he tried to put as much space as possible between them. He had gone as far as hiring a housekeeper to do the daily chores and basically run errands between them. He didn't want Ambhara delivering meals or drinks in his study. This room was his and his alone. Ambhara might be married to him, but her daily life was more like that of a disliked houseguest.

Colton spent most of his time in here when he was at the penthouse. He ate his meals here, he had all his clothes, his papers and the piano moved into the adjoining guestroom as well as, of course, his beloved collection of guitars.

Between the study and his studio downtown, he managed to get away from her well enough. Of course there were still her hired detectives who made no attempts at hiding from him. He knew they were there to keep an eye on him—keep him in line, as Ambhara called it. He had fought Ken for years on the issue of security guards, he couldn't stand to have someone around him twenty-four hours a day, his concerts were the only time he put up with them, but now—now his own wife had him under surveillance. Every time he stepped out of a room, there they were, consequently he tried to stay inside his studios as much as possible.

His current situation was cramped as hell, but worth the anger in her eyes when he saw her. His fury had given way to an icy politeness, and every move he made said, 'I know I have to put up with you but I don't have to like it.'

He decided it was too late to go to bed again and went to the guest suite for a shower and shave. He dressed in comfortable jeans and a T-shirt, and paged the housekeeper to bring him breakfast while he called up the last sales reports for the new CD on his new computer.

They were holding steady at number two on the country charts and at eight on the billboard charts, both gave him a bullet, meaning the CD was not finished rising yet—it still had a lot of power left. The whole affair with Ambhara had indeed not hurt sales, proving once again that there is no bad publicity, just as long as they spell your name right.

For the hundredth time he wondered just how much damage Amber could do going public with her little secret. True, it would hurt his reputation as a singer, but he had done that same song a hundred times in concert and on numerous compilations, he had proved himself as an artist with each subsequent hit and concert. His label, SoundMaster, might have a few problems with it—was there such a thing as fraud if someone else sang on your supposed recording?

On the other hand, what were they going to do, fire their best selling artist? Ten years ago, he had pulled SoundMaster out of a slump with *Always You,* steadily increasing their profits, so that now he was responsible for some sixty percent of their sales. They would not like it, no they would not like it one bit, but Colton had a feeling that if push came to shove they would close ranks and back him up as necessary.

That only left Ambhara's ludicrous accusation that Clay Fender's death was a suicide or, worse, somehow arranged by the CW organization to keep him quiet. Somehow, if they could prove he had nothing to do with Clay's death he might have enough leverage with Ambhara to get her to sign the divorce papers.

"How," he mused, "how...how to prove that.' Ken came to mind suddenly. Ken knew the type of people who could possibly be helpful. Ken worked with a lot of characters who preferred working in the shadows of the night. His own past was perhaps not exactly shady but there were areas that remained mercifully blank. Ken would probably know who to hire to get into the details of Clay's death. He was just about to pick up the phone when the housekeeper arrived with his breakfast and informed him that Mrs. Wright would be out at her dressmakers for most of the morning.

Dressmakers! Spending money again, Cole sighed, his money. It had become a sport with her.

He decided to move his breakfast and his papers into the main living room for the morning and take advantage of her absence. At least the view was better there. He poured his coffee and, for good measure turned on KSOM on the radio. Ambhara would have an absolute fit if she came in and heard it, even though Reanne was no longer on air. For some reason she sensed that Reanne posed a threat to her that had nothing to do with looks or fame. If her wrath was ever unleashed on Reanne—heaven help us.

In a way he felt guilty at having torpedoed Reanne's radio career, but then he remembered hearing that she had come away with a nice little promotion, thanks to interference from her mentor, Jack, who at times seemed strangely buddy-buddy with Ken.

Ken! He had been about to call him he remembered. He dialed the numbers automatically and doodled on a scratch pad while Ken's secretary put him on hold. On hold! Funny how one could own the place and still be put on hold. With half an ear he listened to the news on the radio, most of it passing him by until a particular name caught his attention, he stretched the phone cord to the max to reach the stereo to turn up the sound.

"—and for news on our own KSOM employee, Reanne Parker, who was involved in a serious accident last night and is at the moment at Nashville General Hospital with unspecified injuries, please stay tuned to KSOM. Our prayers and best wishes are with Reanne."

Colton felt a cold fist in his stomach. Reanne— serious accident—unspecified injuries. The words kept repeating themselves in his head and an icy fear went through him. A tiny voice reminded him of his phone call and automatically he picked up the receiver.

"Hello?"

"Hello, Cole, are you there, hello?"

"Ken, oh yes."

"Cole, what's the matter? You sound awful."

"Ken, something's happened to Reanne. I just heard it on the news, I have to get to her."

"The news? What on earth happened? How bad is it?"

"I don't know, but I have to get to her, she's at General. Cancel all my appointments and rehearsals. I don't know how long I'll be."

"I'll take care of everything at this end, don't worry, go—go. Call me if you need anything."

"Thanks Ken."

Colton had already hung up and grabbed his keys without waiting for a reply. He didn't realize that he had automatically taken the keys to the Cadillac when he thought of Reanne and he had to race back up to the penthouse and get his other set.

He raced his truck through the streets of Nashville, so frantically it bordered on a miracle he didn't get into an accident himself. He made Nashville General in record time and wasted no time finding a parking spot. He left the truck in front of the main entrance, barely taking the time to take the keys out, not caring that it would most likely get towed and ran through the automatic doors.

"Reanne Parker, where is she, I need to see her," he barked at the receptionist, breathlessly. "I need to know how she is."

The nurse behind the desk leaned away from him automatically and he realized that he must look crazed and out of his mind. He took a deep breath and repeated a little more calmly. "Please, can you tell me what room Ms. Reanne Parker is in?"

"Are you a relative, sir?"

"No, I'm not—we're—she is—I mean she's one of my best friends."

"I'm sorry sir, that information is only available to relatives."

"You don't understand, I'm the only one she has," he said frustrated. "I'm one of her best and closest friends." Right now Reanne herself might not agree with that statement one hundred percent, but it would have to do. Unfortunately it didn't seem to impress the duty nurse.

"I am sorry sir, but the answer is still no."

"Listen Ma'am I know you might not believe me, but I'm Colton Wright—the Colton Wright—and I need to see Ms. Parker." He had never been one to trade on his fame after it came to him and he despised stars who did so. Too often he had heard someone say "Do you have any idea who I am?" hoping to trade their fame for some favor they would not otherwise receive. He had sworn he would never do that, but right now he would say or do anything.

The nurse looked at the disheveled man in jeans and a rumpled T-shirt before her. "Yeah, and I'm Whitney Houston. What you are is a nuisance. Now please stop blocking the reception area. Oh, and I do believe that's your truck that's being towed away out front."

Colton struck the counter top with his fist. Corporal Nurse here was about to call security and have him thrown out, so he withdrew and headed for the nearest payphone—his cell phone had just disappeared with his truck.

This time he reached Ken on the first try.

"What's going on, have you heard anything?"

"No, they won't give me any information—family members only. Do you know anyone at Nashville General who could bend the rules for us? Any favors you could call in?"

"Colton, are you implying I would do anything improper?"

"Just give it a try will you?"

"Stand by, I'll see what I can do. Anything else?"

"Yeah, I think my truck just got towed."

"Again?"

"I was in a rush, ok? Now will you please see what you can do?"

"I'll take care of it Cole, just cool your heels for a while and try not to antagonize them too much ok?"

Colton began to pace in the reception area under the watchful eye of the sour faced nurse. Short of opening every door in the damned hospital until he found Reanne there was little he could do and in a little while he was prepared to try even that. After about twenty minutes a nervous young doctor came into the lobby.

"Ah—Mr. Wright?" he asked carefully.

"Yes, I'm Colton Wright, what can you tell me?" Apparently Ken had worked the Taylor magic and found this young man, apparently willing to at least partially overlook the rules.

"You are a friend of Ms. Parker?"

"Yes, what's going on? What happened? I heard she had been in an accident?"

"Well, we don't usually give this information to anyone who is not family, but…"

"Listen to me Doctor! Do you see any of her family here? Does anyone care? Ms. Parker—Reanne—is one of my closest friends and I need to know what is going on now! I'm the closest thing she has to family right now and I'm getting a little tired of this runaround."

"Well..." still the young doctor hesitated and Colton wondered idly just what his connection to Ken was. He seemed extremely uncomfortable with what he was doing.

"Your friend was in an elevator in her apartment building when the cables snapped. The elevator plunged three stories to the ground Mr. Wright."

"Oh my God! How bad is it?"

"Well, she suffered multiple factures, lacerations, bruises—those we have under control, but I'm afraid that we're also dealing with severe head trauma."

"What does that mean, severe head trauma, plain English, please."

"It's impossible to tell at this point, she's still unconscious, we're hoping that she'll regain consciousness as fast as possible, or..."

"Or what?"

"Let's just hope for the best Mr. Wright. Every day she spends unconscious increases the chances of...permanent damage."

"Thank you for your honesty, can I see her?"

"Well..." again the young doctor hesitated.

"I don't see anyone else here, do you?" Colton pressed. "What possible harm could a few minutes do?"

"All right, follow me. But only for a few minutes." the doctor relented and led the way through the entrance down a long set of corridors.

The walls were a sickening beige, marked 'Trauma Unit' in large, black block letters. The words themselves made Colton sick to his stomach, but he carried on to the room at the end of the hall.

Chapter Nineteen

Ken turned around, smiling, enjoying the sight of Ambhara sulking on the sumptuous leather couch in the Wright's elegant living room.

"Would you like me to help you pack, dear?" he asked cheerfully, but his offer was met with a stream of expletives. He shook his head. "Tsk Tsk, you know Ambhara, all those years ago, when you were still plain old Amber, I could see the guttersnipe in you. I should have told Colton then, but you managed to hide it from almost everyone. Still, I have to tell you," he lowered his voice to a stage whisper, "it's showing now."

He poured himself a generous drink at the bar and joined her on the couch. She moved away from him as if he were something disgusting, something she wouldn't want to touch under any circumstances. Ken pretended not to notice and sipped his drink with great relish.

"I knew you were insanely jealous of his success, but Cole loved you more than anything. He wouldn't have listened to a band of angels if they said something bad about you. You know I talked my tongue into ribbons to get him to see reason, but he insisted you would eventually come around, make it on your own, share gracefully in his success. So I kept my mouth shut and my fingers crossed, and I hoped for the best."

Ambhara made a rude noise, but Ken went on regardless.

"All right, so I didn't keep my mouth all that shut. I love Cole like a brother, what else could I do? If I had known, even suspected, you would be capable of doing something like this, believe me I would have dragged both of you to divorce court kicking and screaming. What on earth were you thinking? If you could make him look like a loser, that would make you a winner? Well honey, it don't work that way."

"Ken? Why don't you just go and…"

"You know," Ken said, laying his finger on the side of his nose and thinking. "I don't think it's anatomically possible for the average human to do what you're thinking—but you, you just might have managed here. Back to your story, what did you think? You'd just go and ruin him, and then wander off into the sunset—revenge achieved, movie over, the end? Just because he hit the big time before you, and without you?"

"I did no such thing, and anyway where is your proof? You think Cole is just going to believe you, just because you say that's the way it was? Don't try it, I can still convince him you're lying, you know. You said yourself he loved me, more than anything. Maybe I'll just get him to fire you. What you've got is a big fat nothing!"

"Oh but that's where you are wrong Ambhara. Did I not introduce this young woman with me to you? Oh I see, you thought she was just another one of my girlfriends did you? Your memory failing you? Well let me correct my mistake right now. Ambhara, meet Shelly Reynolds. Of course, when you knew her, her last name wasn't Reynolds, it was Bartell—soon to have been Fender. Ah well, you meet so many people as a movie star you probably forgot all about her."

Ambhara went deathly pale and looked like she was going to be sick. Ken laughed, reveling in her discomfort. "Are you still wondering my dear, just how much I know? Well let me tell you—I know everything. And as soon as Colton gets here, so will he"

"You have no idea." Amber tried desperately, but Ken just continued to pour drinks for himself and Shelley, smiling that amused little smile of his. He hadn't looked forward to anything this much in a long, long time.

Shelly was trying to take the grand penthouse and the magnificent view of Nashville all in, her eyes huge and unbelieving. Austin Taggert had dragged her to Nashville against her will, but now that she had heard Amber's story she was enjoying herself immensely.

"Who would have thought he would make it this far," she said, shaking her head. "Back when we were all struggling musicians—never knew where our next meal was coming from. We were all out on the road together, just hoping the next gig would be the big one. Next time a record label exec would hear us." She paused for a second. "I remember you Amber, you were the lucky one, you had Colton. Once he saw you, none of us had a chance. The other guys might have had girls on the road but not Colton, never him. How you could ever…"

"Oh cut the crap," Amber said rudely. "You're going to make me cry with your sob story. He was a bastard and he was holding me back. I could have made it if he hadn't been hogging the spotlight all those times. Well it doesn't change anything. I can still ruin him just like that," she snapped her fingers. "And don't think I won't just because you've dug up some old skeletons in closets that don't even interest anyone any more."

"You can try Amber, you can certainly try. But I believe that when Colton hears the whole story he'll simply take his chances with his fans, and all your stories be damned. After this, I do believe he'd rather start over than live with you for another day."

"Nobody would work with him again, certainly not at the level he's used to."

"Do you really think so? Maybe you should be in management instead of me. Amber wake up! If it hits the fan, we'll simply announce a creative break for a year or so, go touring in Europe, they go just as nuts for him over there. He'll come back bigger than ever—and you…" he pointed straight at Ambhara with his outstretched forefinger, "will be yesterday's news. You see," he smiled his satisfied little smile again, "the difference between Colton and you is that he has talent, major talent. And talent will always win out Amber, remember that."

Amber hauled out with her right hand to strike Ken, but she froze with her hand in the air. The front door to the penthouse flew open with such force that it hit the wall with a crash, and Colton stormed into the room—all coiled nerves, pent up energy and anger. He stopped short in the middle of the living room when he saw the girl standing with Ken.

"Shelley?" he asked. "Shelley is that really you?"

Shelley looked up and smiled at him. "Colton, look at you. You're still the same as you were ten years ago. Always in a hurry, always barging into every situation headfirst. How the hell are you?"

Colton hugged Shelley tightly to himself. "Just an aging honky tonker, honey, that's all. Do you have anything to do with this…?" he indicated Ken and Ambhara with a sweep of his hand, "this situation?"

"You bet she does," Ken said, clearly relishing the moment he had orchestrated. He turned to Amber. "Would you like to tell him dear or should I?"

"Suit yourself!"

"Oh I do so enjoy this. You see Cole, the reason Shelley is here is really simple. You remember she was engaged to Clay way back when you and the Blonde Strangers just signed your first recording contract?"

"I remember, you used to hang out at rehearsal with us and all the guys thought Clay was the luckiest SOB there was until…"

"Until Clay died you mean?" Shelley asked. "You can say it now, it was a long time ago Cole and I would have told you the truth long ago if I had any idea someone would go and accuse you of his murder."

"What truth, Shelley, what are you talking about?"

"The night of that final recording session Cole," Ken said. "Do you remember telling me you couldn't imagine drinking so much it would make you pass out? That's because you didn't. It was all a setup. Amber slipped Roofies into your drink."

"She did what?"

"Rohypnol Colton, it's guaranteed to make you pass out, it's tasteless and odorless."

"I know what it is Ken, they call it the date rape drug, but—but why?" He turned to Amber who was still trying, unsuccessfully, to look as if none of what was going on in the room had anything at all to do with her.

"Why?" he asked again, and the single word hung in the room for a long moment.

"She wanted the label to drop you Cole, she was convinced being with you was holding her back," Shelly finally said quietly. "And when Clay stepped in to take your place…" Shelley looked away and stared at the Nashville skyline, wrestling with the painful memory. "She seduced him Cole, and tried to get him to reveal the truth to SoundMaster. He confessed to me and I forgave him Cole, but he couldn't handle it—he couldn't handle betraying me, betraying you. That's when he started to take more and more drugs."

"And the accident?"

Shelley shook her head, her eyes glittering with unshed tears for the fiancé who had died so long ago. "I know he was in enough pain to have done it on purpose, but I don't think so. He wanted to tell you, he wanted to tell you what happened, make things right. But your wife here just kept supplying him with drugs, telling him to stay quiet or something bad would happen. And in the end it did. That's the God's honest truth Cole, she was the one who gave him the drugs, and if there is any guilt to be placed…"

Colton joined her at the great picture window and put his hand on her shoulder. "I'm sorry for making you remember Shelley, but thank you for telling me, I know it must still hurt." He shook his head, "Yeah, I know it can hurt for a long long time. Both of you, thanks for being here, for helping to clear up this whole sordid story. Would you both mind leaving us alone for the moment?"

Ken took Shelley's Arm. "I've checked her into the Plaza, that's where we'll both be. Call me with the news about Reanne."

Colton nodded and when the door closed behind them he turned back to Amber. The despair of the last few weeks had been replaced by sheer anger blazing from his cold blue eyes. He stared at her a long time until, finally, she had to look away.

"I loved you," he said simply. "I loved you with all my heart and soul, and I would have done anything for you. When you left me something inside me died. Everything that was good and kind and loving inside me died, and I thought I would never find it again. For years I thought it was my fault, that I had failed you in some way, that I had failed to make you happy, to give you what you needed. But now…First tell me why Amber. Just make me understand how you could do such a thing."

"Oh get off your high and mighty horse Colton Wright. How do you think I felt? You were going to be a star. People were starting to ask for your autograph, you were the one who was invited to all the happening parties. I was just the hanger on, the backup singer. You even had the gall to ask me to cut background vocals for you. Do you have any idea how humiliating that was for me?"

"Humiliating? Amber we swore to each other that whoever made it to the top first would bring the other one with him. That was the only thing I was doing. I thought that you would be happy for me, for us."

"But it wasn't supposed to be you Cole!" she cried. "It wasn't supposed to be you who got to the top first, it should have been me."

"Did it matter that much who got there first?"

"It mattered to me Cole, it mattered a lot. I wanted you to be successful, I wanted to you to be a singer, but you were about to outshine me. Your star was getting to be so bright no one would have noticed me any more. I would have been stuck in the background for the rest of my life."

"So you decided to destroy my life and got Clay Fender killed in the process?"

"Nothing was ever supposed to happen to Clay, I swear to you. Something must have got mixed up with the drugs. I don't know, but I had nothing to do with that."

Colton waved her away like an annoying insect. "It doesn't matter any more, it's over now. It's over Amber and I want you out of my house and out of my life right now. I just hope you'll find a way to deal with everything you've done."

"I could still go public with what I know," she said in a last ditch effort, but the fire in Colton's eyes told her she had lost before he even answered.

"Go ahead," he said coldly. "I will deal with it, somehow I'll deal with it, but there is no way I will ever—do you hear—ever, have anything to do with the likes of you. It took me ten years to get over what you had done to me, ten years to find someone again who thought there was something worth loving, worth saving inside me. Me, Cole, not the glittering image of *Mr. Right* that everyone adores, including you. I will not have you screw this up Amber, no matter what the cost."

He paused for a moment and shook his head. "You see Amber, I don't know if it's within your grasp to understand this, but I didn't realize I loved Reanne until it was almost too late, and now I'll do anything to see that she does not have to suffer the way you made me suffer. Understand, Amber, that if you want a fight you can have one, but let me tell you right now that there is no way you are going to win this one, is that clear? If I have to lay down every last thing I own I will make certain that you do not win this one."

Amber nodded, she had lost, and she finally understood that. For a moment Colton felt almost sorry for her, the dejected slump in her shoulders, the realization that everything she had done to get ahead had finally caught up with her. All her moves, all her schemes upon schemes had finally come tumbling down like so many children's building blocks. She had lost and, he was almost certain, she had nothing to go back to in Hollywood either. Too many bridges had been burned.

Yes, he felt sorry for her, but then he saw the defiant gleam in her eyes, and in the toss of her hair he remembered everything she had done to Clay and Reanne—and to him, to all those he loved. He remembered all the lives that had been affected or destroyed, for nothing but pure petty jealousy, and he knew there was no need to feel sorry for her. Somehow, like the cat she was, she would land on her feet and keep on scheming and manipulating until she finally hit bottom, but God willing that would be a long time and a long way away from here.

"Go," he said tightly. "Go now, and don't ever come back. Ken will wire you some money and send whatever in this penthouse belongs to you along with the divorce papers—and I can assure you this time everything is going to be legal."

Ambhara nodded. "I'll survive," she said contemptuously. "I've done it before and I'll do it again. Unlike you, I don't wear my so called suffering on my sleeve. I don't write songs about it and I don't let all my fans know. Oh no Cole, I will be back on top again, one day, but I will never stop hating you!"

Colton looked at her and beneath the glamorous, polished and glittering beauty he saw hardness, an edge he should have seen ten years ago. Then love had made him blind to her willingness to do anything to get ahead, now he was free to see. No, there was no doubt in his mind that she would survive. Before long her name would show up in show business again, linked to the newest, hottest young producer no doubt.

He nodded slowly. "I'm going back to the hospital now, I'd appreciate it if you were gone by the time I get back."

"Cole?"

"What?"

"For all that it's worth, I really didn't mean for any of this to happen, you know. I never thought anyone would get hurt. And I think, in the beginning, I loved you too, before…"

"Yeah," he said, "for all that's worth Amber." And he quickly left the penthouse, closing the door behind him and taking the stairs down, too anxious to get away.

Reanne was tired, she was so tired all she wanted was to lie down and go to sleep. Her mind was weary, her bones were weary. She had been walking through this forest forever, trying to find her way out. She had no idea where she was or where she was going, her only clear goal was to find the source of that beautiful voice again and to join it in its song. All around her there was silence, an eerie, complete silence, she could not even hear the sounds of nature like she should have if this was any kind of forest she knew.

Desperate, she sank down on a clump of moss in a small clearing. She was too tired to go on, every step and movement hurt. She would just lie down here for a moment and rest. Somehow, she had a nagging fear, though, that if she lay down and closed her eyes she would not get up again, but she could not go any further. She buried her head in her arms when suddenly she heard it again. It was there—the guitar, the song, that voice! She didn't recognize the song but the voice was familiar, it spoke of love and of a light and suddenly she saw it, the faint light of a lantern in the distance. Like a lighthouse, like a travelers' lantern, it drew her to it, beckoning with a promise of safety and home.

Tired as she was, she made herself get up and put one foot in front of the other, faster and faster until she finally ran toward the lantern, reaching out with her hands, trying to reach the light, trying to get closer to it, to pull the light to herself, inside herself. She would be safe and she would be home if she could just reach the lantern in time, before the weariness in her body made her stop and lie down forever.

Colton had gone back to the hospital immediately after his confrontation with Amber. Elated, every step carried by the knowledge that everything would be all right now, he arrived in a joyous mood. The hospital staff were by now aware of his identity and treated him with a certain kind of deference. All he had to do was open his mouth and anything would be brought to him. Every five minutes it seemed, somebody wanted to know if he needed something. It had become bothersome quickly but he held his annoyance in check, hoping that some of it would spill over on to Reanne and give her the best possible care there was.

For want of anything else to do he picked up his guitar and began strumming it quietly, without really playing any particular song. Music had failed to work a miracle the last time, was there even any point in playing anymore? He had overcome his own fears, he had overcome Amber and her schemes, was he only to fail now, faced with Reanne's unconsciousness?

"I love you my darling," he said quietly and picked at the strings. He watched her lying in the white hospital bed, her hands folded on top of the covers. Hands that just a few weeks ago had torn the buttons off his shirt in their haste to get it off him, hands that could roam gently over his body exploring, stroking, gentling in ways that made him shake with desire. Hands that had held him, giving him strength he didn't know he needed. He picked up one of her hands and kissed every fingertip in turn, resting his lips in her palm.

"Come back to me. I promise from now on everything is going to be all right. Nothing is going to come between us, ever again."

Carefully he put her hand back onto the covers, picked up the guitar again and started playing. He wanted to play *Light of Our Life, Reanne's Song*, but his fingers and his guitar wanted to go somewhere else and, as always, he followed his own musical instinct and realized he was working out another song in head. Gingerly he tried out a few phrases and chords.

> Let our love a lantern be,
> That lights the way between you and me.
> Let our hearts carry a flame so bright,
> It turns the darkness into light.
> Let our souls be open to receive,
> This love in which we still believe.

He plucked the strings of his guitar, humming the melody, lost in his thoughts and his inner musical dialogue when, suddenly, the monitors around him seemed to erupt in noise and lights—a shrill alarm went off somewhere above his head and Reanne's hand seemed to be twitching, reaching out for him.

"Reanne? Sweetheart?" he asked and laid the guitar away.

"Cole—is that you?" her voice sounded strained and hoarse, unused to speaking, and clouded in pain.

"You're awake, oh my God. Doctor, Doctor, Nurse…somebody!!!"

He opened the door and hollered down the hallway at the top of his lungs. "Get the Doctor in here right now!"

He returned to her bedside and took hold of both of her hands. Reanne blinked, trying to focus tired bloodshot eyes, trying to make sense of her surroundings. How did she get here, why was she lying in bed with Cole standing beside her looking like he'd slept in his clothes?

"What—where?" she tried to ask, but Colton stilled her.

"Sssh, don't try to talk yet. Do you remember the elevator?"

She nodded.

"It crashed, and you got yourself banged up pretty good, but I think you'll be just as right rain in no time. Now that you're awake, and I tossed Amber out. You'll see, we'll have you up and out of here before you can even think. Oh my God, I'm babbling, I'm sorry, I'm just so glad you're finally awake—love."

There was so much he wanted, needed to tell her but the doctors and nurses had arrived and politely but firmly ejected him from the room.

"Go home, sleep," they told him. "We'll be working on her for a while now, and after that she needs to rest, come back tomorrow morning."

"I don't want to leave her, I just got her back again!"

Around all the bodies crowded around her bed he could see Reanne's face, smiling, her fingers waggling a tired, exhausted hello to him.

A couple of nurses politely, but firmly, ejected him from the room. How could he sleep now, after the day he had had?

It was the middle of the night, in a few hours the sun would rise and Nashville would begin another day.

He sat in the cab of his truck, staring out at the city, unseeing. The sounds of the highway had already started to increase, despite the early hour of the morning. He listened to the traffic rushing down interstate forty, remembering it carrying him into the city so many years ago. How many hopefuls would it bring to Nashville today, with all their dreams and worldly possessions packed into old, beat up cars—thinking that because they had arrived Nashville would be waiting for them? It would only take a few days for most of them to find out that hundreds of others were thinking the same thing.

He had been one of the lucky few who had made it, through talent, luck and a fortunate accident. So many others had all their dreams destroyed, like Reanne, like Ambhara maybe? And still they kept coming, thinking—knowing—that for them it would be different. Tonight again, so many would climb up on some stage. Some would make it, most would fail and some would hang on for years, hoping and dreaming, And, through all of it, Country Music and Nashville would go on.

Sometime during the night he fell asleep, and when he awoke the sun had started its ascent. He felt as if he had been tortured all night, every single muscle in his body was stiff and sore from sleeping in the truck. Cursing quietly he tried to make himself at least halfway presentable in the rearview mirror. A day's worth of beard growth gave him a roguish appearance and his clothes looked—well, as if he had slept in them—none of that could be helped now.

He turned back into the direction of the hospital and bought himself two strong cups of coffee on the way. By the time he hit the lobby he had halfway recovered and bought a huge bunch of roses from the florist.

All of a sudden he felt as nervous as a sixteen-year-old going on his first date. The nurses gave him coy little smiles and he tried to be his usual charming and debonair self, but inside, his heart beat a mile a minute as he opened the door to Reanne's room.

She was sitting up in bed finishing the rest of her breakfast. "Hi," he said. "How do you feel?"

"It only hurts me when I cry," she said wryly, quoting another famous country song. "Sorry, that's not one of yours. I'm sore all over, I think I broke or bruised every single bone in my body. Plus a few I didn't even know I had."

With her good right arm she pointed to a cast on her leg and another on her arm. "Look at all this hardware on me! Disgusting!" she looked up and smiled. "I didn't dream then, you were here yesterday when I woke up. You were singing!"

"I've been here since I heard what happened. They had to throw me out physically last night or I wouldn't have gone. If I could have I would have camped out here in the room all night. As it was, I spent the night in the parking lot."

He set the roses aside and sat down. All of a sudden he didn't have the words to say what he needed to say, to tell her what was on his mind and in his heart.

"So I heard," Reanne said. "I think all the nurses are half in love with you, anyway, *Mr. Wright this Mr. Wright that,* it's all I've heard all morning. I think they're volunteering for extra shifts. Plus I must have been asked about a thousand times what you're really like." She smiled, laid her head back in the pillows and then looked directly at Colton. "Where's your wife?" She sounded bitter and a little anxious, she really did not want to risk a showdown with the formidable Ambhara.

Cole only shook his head. "She's gone, gone forever sweetheart, I sent her packing forever, she won't come between us any more."

And then piece-by-piece the whole sordid story came out. From the time he and Amber had been married, to her jealousies, to his getting drunk and missing the recording session. To the time Clay stepped in on his behalf, Amber trying to seduce him, and Clay's eventual death, Colton left nothing out. Reanne listened silently, one part of her was happy that Amber was gone and nothing could stand between Cole and her anymore, but another part frighteningly understood what Ambhara had been going through, feeling she couldn't measure up to the talent, the success, the fame that was Colton Wright.

She stayed silent for a long time remembering how she had felt that afternoon in Hawaii and every time they had gone out secretly. Insignificant, unworthy and definitely not good enough, not good enough to bee seen in public with the great *Mr. Right*. Perhaps Amber had felt the very same thing and, in the end, it was that which had destroyed their love. And if she let it, it would do the same thing to her and Cole. She must not allow it to happen.

"Did you hear me?" Cole asked. "Amber is gone, and as soon as you're better you can come home—with me. Move out of that dump you were living in." He took her hand. "Did you hear what I said, we can be together now."

Reanne pulled her hand back and looked at Colton, wishing she didn't have to say what she was feeling now. Her next words would bring his world down and there was nothing she could do about it.

"Cole—it's not going to happen."

"Oh sure, you'll need some time to recover I realize that, perhaps I can move a nurse into the penthouse for a while, but I've got it all planned out, love and later…"

"Cole, I said it's not going to happen—ever."

"What are you talking about? I told you Amber is gone—forever—finished, nothing can stand between us now, Reanne we can get…"

"Cole," she hurried before he could finish his sentence. "It has nothing to do with Amber don't you see? I've felt what she felt. Never being good enough, never measuring up, always being in second place, Cole if I stood beside you I would always stand in your shadow, I would always feel like I had to fight to deserve to be there, to justify my existence and eventually I would grow to hate you. I could never do that to you or to me Cole, please you have to understand. It only makes me sad that Amber felt the same thing. I'm not angry at her, not the way you are, I'm just afraid I might…end up the same way."

"You can't really mean that. That would never happen, you're a totally different person. Your mind—the fall—it will just take a little time."

"The fall has nothing to do with it Colton, I mean every word I say."

"But Reanne, how could you feel that you're not good enough? You've got talent, you've got—everything. Reanne I love you—I love you. Did you hear me? I couldn't say it for such a long time, but now…" He stopped and she saw the confusion in his eyes, the despair and worst of all the loneliness.

"I am sorry, Cole, for everything, but that's the way I feel, I can't do it. I don't want to end up like Amber."

Colton smoothed the sheets around her needlessly, turning his head so she couldn't see his face. "Then this is good bye? It can't be, it can't be good bye," he asked softly, still hoping for a last minute reprieve.

"Yes Cole, this is good bye." She fought to keep her voice steady, fought to keep her hands under the blankets instead of hugging him to her fiercely. She tried not to see how he wiped his face surreptitiously and how he looked so lost and lonely all of a sudden. He was not a superstar any more, just someone who had bet everything on his heart and lost on a single roll of the dice.

"I don't know what to say, I don't..." He choked, and the sorrow in his eyes and the deep lines around his mouth almost made her relent. She touched the little dimple on his chin, remembering how it had always made him laugh when she did that.

"Thank you Cole, thank you for everything. You've done so much for me and I will never forget you, never. You've been so wonderful and you've taught me— a lot, I wish we could stay friends."

He squeezed her hand so hard she grimaced. "I love you," he said. "I love you. If you remember anything, remember this, always and ever. I've been friends with so many people over the years, but there's been only one that I love."

He got up took his guitar by the neck and walked out of the room without another word. For a moment he was silhouetted against the white wall, a solitary man with his guitar. It was a picture that broke her heart, again it was just Cole and his music. Because he was that good and that talented, was he forever destined to have nothing but his music in his life? She almost called out to him but he moved and the door closed and he was gone—from the room and from her life.

"What have I done?" she whispered, "Oh what have I done?" But the room was empty, save for a remembered echo of his song, and there was no one to hear her.

Chapter Twenty

It was front-page news in all the gossip papers, but it came as no surprise to Nashville society when Mr. and Mrs. Colton Wright announced their divorce a few days later. Thanks to some vicious rumors that had circulated concerning Amber, she had not made too many friends here. She was a newcomer, she had muscled in and she hadn't managed to garner any supporters. Amber could never figure out where those rumors came from, but Colton thought he had to look no further than Ken—who understood, arranged, and fixed.

There were some things even Ken couldn't fix, though, and when he found Colton holed up in his studio for three days in a row instead of being out celebrating, he knew they were in trouble. He listened to Colton, tried to help, to understand, but he had no magic for this, nothing that could fix a broken heart. Just like the last time around work would have to do the trick. Intense, constant, ongoing work that brought Cole the one balm for his heart—live appearances, standing in front of a cheering crowd.

So it came as even less of a surprise when Colton Wright announced a massive ten state, twenty-five date tour a few days later—everyone assumed he was healing a broken heart after the divorce, which was quite close to the truth.

Ken worked faster than he ever had. In a hurry, he put together a road crew and tour band, expanded their stage show, improvised fudged, faked—Colton wanted to be gone, play any venue that was large enough and would have him.

His stage antics became bolder and more risky every single time. The whole *Paradise Right Here* tour traveled in twelve semis and five buses and they garnered rave reviews everywhere they went. No wonder, Cole poured his heart and soul into every single show. Daily, the concert reviews poured in and there wasn't one that wasn't singing his praises to the heavens. Everybody loved him. The more his heart was broken, the more his emotions were hurt and wounded, the better his music seemed to get. Night after night he got up on that stage and offered himself to the crowds in exchange for their cheers, their appreciation, and their love.

With the help of a generous insurance settlement from the building owner's policy, Reanne finally managed to move into a quiet little townhouse that she shared with two other girls, both hoping to get their singing careers started while they worked as waitresses in dingy bars.

Reanne had redoubled her efforts in her music lessons and, after a brief period of recovery and some intense physical therapy, she could do almost everything she had before. She was as good as new again—physically anyway.

She continued to work at KSOM although she tried to stay off the air as much as possible. There had been a brief news flurry when Colton spent so much time at the hospital with her, and rumors continued to fly every now and then, but Reanne mostly stayed mum. There were several rumors about their brief time together and about their breakup, Reanne didn't care to deny or acknowledge any of them. Her brief time with Colton was a precious memory to her, to love and cherish in the privacy of her own mind, not to be tarnished by the prying eyes of strangers.

She continued to collect and save pictures of Colton as they appeared in the trade magazines. She had a scrapbook of interviews, reviews and official photos which she took out at night, when she was alone, remembering and loving every moment they had had together. Carefully and gently she would touch his face in a picture, trace the strong outline of his jaw or the sensual line of his lips, but she could never go as far as to imagine herself in those pictures there beside him. He looked just as he always had, just as he did in her memories, even though he stood alone in each and every picture.

She followed his tour closely and scanned the reviews as soon as they came out, but even in the lowest gossip rags he was never linked amorously with anyone, and pretty soon even the gossips gave up looking for dirt where there was none.

I have well and truly broken your heart, she thought, adding his latest clipping to her growing pile. "Cole, if only I wasn't afraid of what would happen, how I would feel, if things were different—if only."

She swept the clippings into thick file with an angry swipe. What was the point? There was no future for her and Colton, not in this life. She was too afraid of ending up like Amber, resentful, jealous. She picked up her pen and continued to work. One day, perhaps, it would hurt less and one day she would meet someone who was as perfect in every way as Colton was. As funny and as loving and as sweet, just not as famous, and then she would finally be able to put this memory to rest. But until then, it would continue to hurt.

"Thanks for coming everyone, be safe going home, bye bye!" Colton gave one last wave with his guitar, tossed his guitar pick into the front rows and turned to leave the stage. He was dripping with sweat, temporarily blinded from the stage lights and the last fading cheers of the crowd were still in his ears. The backstage area was crowded with people who had managed to score the coveted passes and he greeted and hugged his way through a throng of fans.

"Let me clean up guys," he called to them, "You don't want to touch me now. I'll be right back out."

Three of his security guards in red and black satin shirts and black cowboy hats flanked him, always keeping an eye out for anything suspicious. It was hard to control a crowd of this size and there had been a few incidents before. Folks had managed to get into his dressing room somehow and left odd notes and gifts. His security people constantly complained that he had gotten careless lately. Well perhaps he didn't care, not about security and safety anyway, he reveled in the appreciation and adoration of his fans when he waded into the crowd and accepted their homage.

The noise back here was deafening but tolerable after the pandemonium of the stage and he still had to do a Meet and Greet with a group of fans.

"Let's just get this done. I'm tired as a dog," he grumbled when he had finally made his way to his dressing room and managed to sit down.

"Don't let your Atlanta fan club hear that." someone said behind him.

Colton spun around and saw Lee, one of his media relations people, his *handlers* as he called them.

"Oh, it's you. Who's not supposed to hear me?"

"The folks from the local fan club you're about to meet? Atlanta...Georgia?"

"Man, I've been on the road too long Lee, I start forgetting where I am. One hotel room looks like the next after three months."

"I don't know why you're killing yourself like this Cole, all these concert dates? The album is selling like crazy. The original tour schedule didn't have half these dates on it," he handed Colton a fresh shirt. "There are rumors going around of course, but..."

"But I'm telling you the same thing you've hopefully been telling the fans out there...?"

"No questions about your private life, specifically the divorce, I know, I know," Lee said. "And they know, so no worries, ok? You ready?"

"Ready to go," Colton said, stretching and practicing a smile then he ran his hands through his damp hair to give it that roguish disheveled look. When he stepped out of his dressing room he was *Mr. Right* personified, sparkling, charming and handsome as usual.

He shook hands with the fans, gave hugs, answered questions and gave autographs—all the while flashbulbs popped away like fireworks.

He smiled and joked through all of it, never showing the strain of just having finished a strenuous ninety minute performance on stage. He gave them what they wanted, a few minutes with their hero, and no one noticed the shadow of loneliness behind his eyes—popular opinion being that he had gotten over his broken heart faster than expected.

"Cole, I should never have left you, I love you with all my heart, can you ever forgive me?" Reanne said. "I made a terrible mistake leaving you, please say you'll forgive me."

He put his hand to her chin, losing himself in the bottomless depth of her eyes. He saw his own longing and desire reflected there. "Sweetheart, there is nothing to forgive," he said. "I've been waiting for you for so long, I'm just glad you came back to me."

The moonlight put red flames into her hair and she tilted her head ever so lightly. Slowly, tenderly he kissed the lush red lips she offered to him.

"I've missed this so much," he said, slanting his lips over hers again and again and drawing her lower lip between his teeth. "I love you." And with his kisses he tried to communicate everything he felt, the shattered wreck she had made out of the walls around his heart.

"So do I Cole, so do I, more than you'll ever know."

He drew her close until there was nothing between them, their bodies molded to each other as if they were cast from one mold. He knew she had to feel how much he wanted her, needed her right then and there.

"So you have missed me," she whispered and ran her hand gently over the evidence of his desire. Cole groaned hoarsely.

"Sweetheart, you're killing me."

"Only with love," she said, taking her time unbuttoning his jeans, kissing every inch of the flesh she exposed with every new button. "Only with love my darling. You really should wear jeans with zippers, you know."

"Ah, my love, come here," he said and pulled her long red gown over her head with one smooth stroke, ignoring the silver buttons and hooks that strained and broke away finally. When she was wearing nothing but her long double strand pearl necklace, his hands roamed over her body freely, stroking and loving, delighting in every little shiver they caused. He kissed and tasted, teased and enjoyed, reveling in her little moans of pleasure. But her revenge was sweet and swift, her own hands taking him to dizzying heights until he could wait no longer.

Their bodies had known each other and they recognized the need in the other. There was no time for waiting today, they were drawn to one another by a flame inside them that threatened to consume them with its fire. Their joining was swift and hard, fed by their hunger for one another. Their bodies knew what they wanted and slaked their thirst for one another, faster, higher, deeper, until they both burst from the joy of belonging and joining. Their joy washed over them in huge waves, filling them as they filled each other, one giving where the other took, and finally they touched a star in the dark night together—they were one.

"My love, I will never let you go again," he said, when he could finally breathe evenly again. "Never again, you hear."

"I'm not going anywhere, Cole, my heart would break."

"I love you, I love you with all my heart."

"For always and ever," she answered and kissed him gently. "For always and ever my love and we will never be alone again."

Reanne woke with a start and clutched the damp sheets to herself. The house was completely still. Her roommates were away for the weekend. There wasn't even so much as a creak in the new town house.

"It was just a dream, Reanne," she said to herself. "Don't be silly, it was just a dream. But what a dream, oh my, Cole, what a dream!"

He had been so real she was sure she could reach out and touch his warmth on the sheets beside her, somewhere on the air there was still that scent that mixture of his cologne and pure maleness that was so uniquely Cole, but when she turned she knew that she was completely alone. She hugged her pillow tightly, shutting her cry of loneliness inside her.

"Just a dream, just a dream," she told herself over and over. There was no one in the house with her. Cole was a thousand miles away and he would never be here beside her again. Her own decision had driven him away, why then did she still think about him every day. If in her heart she knew she had made the right choice, why would dreams of him not let her go? Despite everything, he haunted her days and nights and it took all her strength to get through one night at a time. One night at a time she told herself and, when she finally fell back asleep, her face and her pillow were wet with tears. Tears for a lost love and a broken heart.

"Yo, Colton—Colton, wake up, 'less you want to spend the night in this here dressing room."

"What? Oh!" Colton stared at Lee standing beside the couch he had fallen asleep on.

"Oh, it was just a dream."

"Not likely," Lee said. "You just gave one of the best performances of this tour and sent a whole bunch of fans home deliriously happy. If it was about bein' a star, you sure ain't dreamin'."

"Just a dream," Colton repeated and ran his hands through his hair. "Jeez' the stuff being on the road does to you," he laughed nervously. "I've never fallen asleep in the dressing room before, let's get the heck out of here."

He found his hat, turned out the lights and left the dressing room, but not before casting one quick glance back over his shoulder. The room was empty, save for his guitars, clothes and various and sundry paraphernalia of getting ready for a major concert. The stage crew was packing up for tomorrow's concert, his road manager was waiting.

Reanne, he thought, *I could have sworn you were here with me.*

He closed the door with a hard shove, wishing that the dark lonely feeling in his heart would finally go away, and that he could pack up and stow away his emotions as easily as the road crew were moving all the equipment around him, getting ready for another move, another day, another venue and another concert. But despite all the work he piled on himself, despite the hundreds of distractions he provided himself with, not a day went by when he didn't think of her and wonder what might have been—what could have been.

He would look out into the crowd and see a face like hers—red hair like hers. He would sign autographs and suddenly someone would smile like her. Now she had started to invade his dreams too, with her quick smile and her bright green eyes. One day at a time he thought, what he had to do was just fill every single day so full that he didn't have the time to think and dream of her. One day at a time, and one step at a time away from the memories and the what might have beens.

His security people took charge and transferred him to a waiting limo and the hotel in town. They escorted him to a room he hadn't bothered familiarizing himself with. He simply fell into the bed and went to sleep, hoping the dream wouldn't come back again to haunt him. Tomorrow would bring a new city and new faces, but inside he would still be the same. Tomorrow would bring just another day to get through again.

The next morning both Colton and Reanne woke up groggy and tired, the remainder of their dreams clinging to their mind. *It was just a dream*, they both told themselves.

Colton stared at the unfamiliar generic artwork in yet another hotel room that was modern, sleek, yet completely impersonal, trying to remember which stop of the tour this was and what city was next. For the hundredth time he wondered why he had thrown all these extra dates into the tour. The answer was obvious, if not one he wanted known. Right now he couldn't be in Nashville, couldn't be near Reanne without phoning her several times a day, trying to change her mind. He couldn't drive the streets they drove, couldn't go to the clubs they had gone to together—taking a chance on turning a corner somewhere and running into her.

He knew he couldn't do any of these things without taking a chance on breaking his heart over and over, tearing open a wound that was stubbornly refusing to heal. He had taken the only way out he knew, he had buried himself in his work and in his music. The last time it had worked and it had made him a star in the eyes of his fans, so why would it not work this time? Sooner or later, he knew, he would have to return to Nashville, he couldn't spend the next ten years on the road—but for now this was as good as it got. Ken kept him apprised of things in Nashville. The business side of things seemed to be running splendidly, so he kept going, from one place to the next, one performance to the next, without knowing where he was headed.

He should have known that all the rumors, innuendos and speculations would entice just that many more people to buy the album, to come to his concerts. So he had yet another possible platinum selling album, a sold out tour, a huge loyal fan community, and more ideas for new songs than he could ever hope to write. Songs and melodies seemed to flow from his guitar, from his heart as if driven by magic. Then why, pray tell, was it that he was feeling so empty inside? Here he was, one of the top grossing entertainers in the business, people lining up night after a night for a chance to see him, and yet none of it meant anything. He turned on the TV and listened to the news. Atlanta, right. They were still in Atlanta.

Reanne took one look at the alarm clock and hit the ground running. She had to put in a few hours at the radio station before heading for the music studio for her daily lessons. At the station she would probably spend most of her day in planning sessions. This was the day when they decided how many spins they would allocate to each artist—in essence, how often they would play his newest release or some of his old stuff. As soon as those numbers were published on the Internet the artists' publicity companies would respond with enticing giveaways, offers at interviews etc., just to increase their number of spins. Some weeks there were regular bidding wars going on via e-mail, competing over the limited number of airplay spots that were actually available. It got hot and heavy, and sometimes quite exiting until the final numbers had been settled.

Reanne went through some brief calisthenics and grabbed her own music sheets on her way out. Her eyes fell on a yellow stick-on note her teacher had attached to it: 'You know that there is not much more I can teach you' it said, 'go out in front of an audience again!'

"Yeah," Reanne said. "Easier said than done. We've been there before and if I had his confidence in my voice I would never have taken lessons. If I was ready I wouldn't go through all this."

Resolutely she tore the note off and finally left for work. Rumor had it she was about to be promoted to assistant program director—she couldn't be late.

Meanwhile it was better to work hard, work some more and then take music lessons in her spare time. In time she would be able to figure out what she really wanted to do with her life. Until then, she intended to fill every moment of every day with some task or another. Nothing was worse than having time on her hands. Time to think, time to doubt, time to wonder if she had done the right thing, sending Cole packing. Or perhaps the worst thing of all, time to mourn what could have been. Finally, she thought, it was time not to be a wimp any more, to take charge of her own life, to do what she really wanted to do.

Ken Taylor stopped pacing his office long enough to fix his assistant with an iron glare. "Something has got to be done before that boy of ours either works himself to death or sinks into a constant depression."

"Colton?"

"Of course Colton. Who else would I be talking about? Haven't you been following along. Get me Jack Daniels' phone number at KSOM and then take a good long break."

"Sure thing Mr. Taylor."

Ken sat down and thought for a good long while. Then he picked up the phone and dialed the number Sheila had written down for him.

"Jack? Ken Taylor here. I think we have a problem in common. You and I have got to have ourselves a good long talk buddy."

Chapter Twenty-One

Colton shifted uneasily in his first class airline seat. It had been months since he had set foot in Nashville. If it weren't for Ken and his crazy ideas he wouldn't be doing so now. He wasn't quite sure how he felt about returning and, instead of enjoying the in-flight entertainment and meal, he had spent most of the flight trying to figure out whether he loathed the idea of coming back to Nashville or looked forward to it. So far, an answer was elusive.

Fame had its privileges. He was ushered out of the aircraft and through the terminal building ahead of everyone else by special escort. Lately, through the tour and all of his other business interests, it seemed he had been spending most of his life in airports, in constant transit. Always going somewhere, always leaving something behind, past experiences to future experiences, never staying anywhere long enough to make anything memorable.

Ken had even had someone bring the Cadillac around, knowing how much he would enjoy driving himself. It awaited him in front of the terminal building, freshly washed and gleaming in the hazy sunshine. Colton threw himself behind the wheel and ran an appreciative hand over the rounded wood grain dashboard. He had missed this car and his long drives in the country—amongst other things. Time to leave another airport behind.

The streets, the buildings, they still looked much the same as they had when he left, but traffic, he had forgotten about the traffic. Nashville traffic had a nasty yet well-deserved reputation as being among the worst in the country. Of course he managed to get stuck right in the thick of it.

Sighing, he got comfortable in the deep leather and looked over at the passenger seat, imagining Reanne there, remembering her delight at the car, the way her long fingers had traced the Cadillac insignia on the dash, the way she had stretched her arms overhead out through the open roof and enjoyed the breeze in her red hair. He heard her singing the song again, *Forever love...*

Running away for three months hadn't changed a single thing. He still missed her every single day. Every heartbeat reminded him of the one he was missing, the one his heart was beating for.

"How did I ever come to need you this much? If you had just given me—us—another chance Reanne."

Impatiently he tried to tear his thoughts away. There was no point in wishing for what might have been, he reminded himself again, Reanne had made her choice and they would all have to live with it, going on, transiting, past existence to future existence.

He saw that Ken had also thought about recharging his cell phone and placing it into the car. That was probably a subtle hint—he expected him to call. Why disappoint him, Colton thought and reached for the little cell.

"So what's this award ceremony I'm supposed to be at tonight?" he asked without preamble when Ken answered the phone.

"Hello Colton," Ken said cheerfully. "Nice to hear from you too. Yes, I'm fine, thanks for asking!"

"Okay, sorry. It was a lousy flight and I'm tired, dirty, hungry, and stuck in traffic. Welcome to Nashville all right. So tell me again, what did you call me here for?"

"Artists against poverty, it's a TV show, it's a lot like one of these pledge shows for public TV. We have a few big name artists like you performing, a lot of lesser knowns. We put on a good show, ask for donations, viewers phone in with their pledges. It'll be a good little publicity thing, good for your image."

"Never heard of it."

"No reason you should have. It was created just recently. We decided big time charity contributions would be good for …"

"We, Ken?"

"All right, all right, I took the liberty of acting on your behalf. Look you've been out of town for a long time now. A lot of big names are in on this. Rumor has it Alan Jackson and Reba McEntire are going to be there, Vince Gill, Tracy Lawrence…"

"Ok, ok," Colton muttered, "I guess I'm in, but I'm still not too thrilled having to be back in Nashville."

"Colton, if it's good enough for the President of the United States, I don't think it's beneath you."

"The President is coming?"

"You bet, also several senators, congressmen and other assorted politicians."

"I guess that's big time, wow."

"That's right, wow. Now quit complaining. You're booked for a fifteen minute slot. That gives you time for maybe three songs, a little bit of talk, that's it. You also get to assign your favorite charity for a portion of the proceeds. So, are you still cussing?"

"Sorry if I'm having a hard time getting excited. I guess its being back in this city."

There was a long pause on Ken's end. "Believe it or not Colton, I actually understand better than you think I do. Thus I took the liberty of having your penthouse scrubbed, repainted and redecorated top to bottom. There isn't even a whiff of Amber left."

"Have you heard anything else from her?"

"Since she cashed her cheque? Not a word. But I assume it won't be long until her name pops up somewhere in the Hollywood society pages."

"I don't doubt it, thanks Ken, I owe you one."

"You had better remember that. Also, Reanne Parker is still with KSOM. She's assistant programming director now."

"There's a reason you are telling me this?"

"I thought you might want to know, that's all."

"Reanne made her feelings for me quite clear before I left Nashville, so I don't think we should even go there."

"Suit yourself Cole, suit yourself."

"Yeah—I guess I'll see you tonight then. The traffic is starting to move again. Have everything ready for me at the auditorium."

Ken stared at the phone for a moment after he hung up and then dialed another number quickly.

"Target one is ready," he said in an amused tone of voice when the other party answered. "Time to get target two into place."

Reanne's phone shrilled incessantly. "KSOM RAD," the call display window read. "Oh, leave me alone," she muttered, "It's my day off." The phone, however, would not quit ringing.

"All right already, what is it that's this urgent?"

"Reanne, is that you?"

"Jack? You sound awful. What's wrong?"

"My temperature for one thing. I'm awfully sorry to do this to you, but could you fill in for me at the charity concert tonight? I'm feeling completely and utterly awful."

"Jack!"

"I know, I know, it's your day off and all that."

"I'm rally not into these publicity things. I don't come across as—approachable as you do."

"I know, and I wouldn't ask this of you if it wasn't terribly important, and if I wasn't feeling so horrible—but could you, would you?"

"Jack!"

"Nobody has been as involved in this thing as you have. You know all the little minutiae, there is no one else who could fill in at such short notice and…"

"All right already, Jack, but you owe me, big time! Now fill me in quickly, what do I have to do?"

"Not much, really, pitch the cause between acts once or twice, mention our station a couple of times, introduce the next act, that's all. You can probably read most of your lines straight off the TelePromptR."

"That's all?"

"That's all, it'll be a piece of cake."

"OK, now who's going to be there?"

Time to tread very, very carefully. "Oh, I don't know if I remember them all." He mentioned a few big stars, a few lesser known names. Names Reanne would probably recognize without getting suspicious.

"You get the drift Reanne, a good mix of people."

At least Cole hadn't come back to Nashville for this thing, she thought. Jack would surely have mentioned it if he had. The less she saw of him right now, the better it was.

"Please, Reanne, my notes are on my desk."

"Alright already. Don't worry, I'll pick them up on my way over there, but this is awfully short notice I'll have you know and you…"

"Owe you big, huge—massive. You're a doll."

"Yea, yeah, I've heard it before. Now you get your butt back into bed and get better soon so I can collect on that debt."

Reanne hung up feeling excited and miserable at the same time. Even though she had made it to assistant programming director she still couldn't shake that awful stage fright that overcame her every time she had to speak, let alone perform, in public. No amount of courses or seminars on the topic had helped, not even imagining the entire audience naked, she could never stop worrying long enough to concentrate on and deliver a good performance, no matter how hard she tried. The moment she hit the stage with a microphone in front of her, her palms turned clammy and her mind turned into a huge black cloud, devoid of all the facts and information she had crammed carefully into it.

On the other hand a big schmooze event like this was a good way to get out of the house again. The evenings at home were starting to get unbearably boring and a large part of her promotion was due to the long hours she put into her work.

Colton wandered through the studio restlessly, picking up things just to discard them again few moments later. Ken might have had the penthouse and studio cleaned, repainted and rearranged but there was nothing he could do about the memories. Nothing would ever erase those he thought, as he replayed the tape of their duet again and again, just to torture himself. Every time he sat down to study sales reports, expense reports or critiques, every time he sat still, the memories came flooding back. He and Reanne in the studio, he and Reanne out for an afternoon ride—he shouldn't have come back to Nashville this soon.

Impatiently he swept all the reports off the desk. Stuff for the accountants, that's all they were. Numbers, figures, dollars, what did he care how much money he made? It didn't make one iota of difference.

"You look like hell, buddy," he said to his own reflection in the window in front of him. He picked up his guitar and started on a song only to discard it after a few lines and resume his restless pacing.

Finally he picked up the phone and dialed her number. He let it ring a few times, listened to the announcement on Reanne's answering machine and hung up again. There was nothing he could have said anyway.

I've got to get out of here, this is driving me nuts. He phoned a few of his band members and had them meet him at the auditorium for an early rehearsal. Perhaps work, as always, would help keep the ghosts of old memories at bay, or at least it would keep his mind off things for a little while. He had learned to think in terms like that. Any little moment he could spend thinking about something else was a moment earned. A step toward sanity again.

Who knew, perhaps he would relocate to California or New York after this tour. Someplace that wasn't tainted by old memories and old ghosts. At this point in his career it didn't really matter where he lived. The more he worked the idea around in his mind, the more he liked it, and he resolved to talk to Ken about it tomorrow, after the charity benefit.

Reanne arrived at the auditorium late. She hadn't been able to find Jack's notes and, when she finally did, there was barely time to glance at them en route. Consequently she was in a bad mood, she didn't like public performances like this to start with and to walk in unprepared felt like facing an enemy without a weapon.

When she got to the auditorium however, she was immediately caught up and swept away by the huge machinery driving the charity concert. She had barely walked into the building when one of the organizers took over. He talked non stop and Reanne had to hurry to keep up with him, not only physically but with his dozens of hints and instructions. She was whisked to a table in a huge communal dressing room and a makeup and hair girl started to work on her. The kid kept chatting merrily while Reanne tried to glance through Jack's notes, and to remember everything the event organizer had told her. Of course there was no pen to be had, she was supposed to sit still, never mind making notes, and her evening seemed to be going downhill from here.

"What?" she said as her eyes fell on a familiar name on the lineup of performers. She sat up so straight the girl almost stabbed her with a hairpin.

"What? What's the matter?"

"Colton Wright?" she pointed to his name in the pamphlet.

"Oh yes, he came on board last minute. Isn't it neat? Me and the girls, we're all hoping to meet him. They say he's absolutely gorgeous."

Reanne started to get off the makeup chair and take off the protective cape around her shoulders.

"If he's in this show, I can't be," she said resolutely.

""Oh, but you can't, I mean—you can't just walk out of here—Mr. Masters, Mr. Masters!"

A tall, dark haired young man, himself in a state of being made up came over to their table.

"I'm Richard Masters, one of the organizers of this benefit. Is there a problem?"

"You bet there is," Reanne said furiously and handed him her cape. "If *Mr. Right* is in this show, I definitely won't be…"

"Oh…" Richard Masters said, and looked at her name badge. "Miss Parker, KSOM Radio, yes, you're one of our announcers. Mr. Daniels assured me there would not be a problem. We are quite grateful Mr. Wright has agreed to perform tonight. It should increase our donations tremendously. But…" he paused for a moment to let his words sink in dramatically. "If Mr. Wright's being here tonight offends you this much then…" he let the rest of the sentence trail off.

"I'm not offended as such." Reanne said, embarrassed because of the scene she was causing and because she recognized Richard Masters, one of the eminent figures of Nashville society. She could feel her cheeks turn flame red as she realized that every last person in the room was staring at her.

"It's just that Mr. Wright and I don't—I mean we are—Well. It's complicated…Oh never mind I'll do it."

She took her cape back and slung it around her shoulders.

"Splendid Miss Parker, splendid." Richard Masters said, though it was evident he thought no such thing.

There was no way to get out of the situation anymore without causing more embarrassment and looking like a spoiled brat or a diva or possibly both.

She returned to her makeup chair muttering under her breath. "Jack Daniels you owe me so big you won't be able to pay this one off in a lifetime. I can't believe he knew and didn't tell me."

The young makeup artist continued to work on her hair popping her gum every now and then. Her opinion of Reanne had just sunk to an all time low.

"So you don't like Colton Wright," she asked. "Don't think I've ever met a woman who didn't. I think he's—like, the absolute hunk."

Reanne made a disparaging sound. "Yeah, if you go for that type."

"Don't you? Well I tell you I wouldn't throw him out of bed at three in the morning, if you know what I mean."

Reanne shook her head. "Just fix my hair, will you."

The girl rolled her eyes. Divas! And this one wasn't even famous. Reanne practically read it on her face, but at least she did the rest of her job in silence and left Reanne to stew in her own thoughts.

Colton was here, in this very building. That was the first and foremost thought in her mind and she kept worrying over it. How would she deal with him, could she avoid running into him, what would she say to him. Perhaps, if she hung out in here until just before she had to go on, she wouldn't have to meet him and, even if he saw her on stage, what would he do, cause a scene? Not likely, there had been too many of those lately. This was probably a safe spot. Surely he had his own dressing room.

She didn't want to meet Cole tonight—did she? Her heart was saying one thing while her mind was demanding quite another. If she saw Cole tonight, would he even talk to her? Did he still have feelings for her? Too many questions, too many unanswered questions. *Concentrate* she reprimanded herself *Concentrate so you won't screw up tonight.*

Quickly she scanned the list of acts she was to introduce. Lone Star, The Rodeo Riders, Jennifer Jones,— no Colton Wright here, at least she was spared that humiliation. She studied the provided notes of the acts she was introducing, so she would have something to say about them.

Meanwhile the atmosphere in Colton Wright's private dressing room was a lot less hectic. He was listening to music and enjoying a drink, his eyes half closed while his own assistant, Eric, worked on him. His trademark, skintight jeans and denim jacket were already laid out for him. His white Stetson was being brushed and steamed into perfect shape—someone was probably polishing his white boots—and all he really had to do was wait for his cue to go on.

He would just perform, attend the party afterwards, shake a few hands, make a few appropriate comments and then get the hell out of Dodge—or Nashville as it were. There was no reason to run into Reanne, no reason at all. No reason to even think about her. Then why was that all he was doing?

"What's the time look like?" he asked Eric, opening his eyes just a little. It was still hard to sit still and let another guy brush his hair even after all these years. It felt wrong somehow, even if it was necessary. He shook his head briefly, of course messing up all of Eric's beautiful work.

"Thirty minutes to show time. And hold still. They're cutting a live album out there, you don't want your hair to look like a dust mop on the album liner, do you?"

"My hair is not one of the things I'm worried about right now Eric, and it's under the hat anyway, who would know. Ouch, do you have to do that?"

"I would know Cole, so hold still. Bitch bitch bitch, you know what you need?"

"No, I don't, but I'm sure you're about to enlighten me."

"What you need is another girlfriend."

Colton looked at Eric in the mirror from under raised eyebrows. "I don't even want to know where that came from. And what would you know about that anyway?"

"Hey!" Eric pulled a little harder with his brush. "I might be a hairdresser, but I definitely know. Now hold still or you're going to lose a lot more hair."

"Why, oh why do I put up with you?"

Eric leaned a little closer and smiled at Colton in the mirror. "Because I make you look mah-velous for the ladies, that's why."

"One more comment like that and I'm taking your brush away and burning it!"

"Oh, could I watch that?" Both of them turned around. Ken had come into the dressing room during their little exchange.

"Colton, small change of plans," he said.

"How small?"

"Just in the order of songs, nothing major. They want you to do *Paradise* last, seeing as it's the lead off single of the new album—some guy will do a special intro for you. Apparently it'll look better on the live album that way."

"I don't see why..."

"Neither do I," Ken hurried to say. "But that's what they want so, hey, let's give it to them."

If Colton suspected anything he didn't show it. He merely shrugged his shoulders. "All right. *Honky Tonk Hardware, Always You,* special intro, *Paradise.* Sounds ok to me. Did you let the band know?"

Ken nodded. "Everything's ok out there."

"Well then," Colton rose from his chair and dusted himself off. "It's time for you gentlemen—and I use the term loosely—to leave me to get into my work uniform. Enjoy the show you two."

"Sure you don't need any more help?" Eric asked innocently.

"Out, both of you!"

He contemplated his stage outfit and checked his watch. Fifteen minutes—plenty of time. Truth be told, this skintight denim outfit was darned uncomfortable at times, until he got on stage that was, then everything but the music had a habit of just fading into the background. Sighing, he got dressed and strummed his guitar while he waited.

A stagehand came to collect him and led him to an area just behind the stage where he waited for his cue to go on. Amazing how backstage always seemed to look the same no matter where he went, no matter what type of venue he was playing. The area was busy with stagehands carrying props and instruments, people going on and off stage, cameramen checking angles, carrying and laying cable. The air was abuzz with shouted commands, cautions and the friendly ribaldry of the stage workers.

A monitor off to the side showed him the action as it would show up on millions of TV sets. A petite brunette in a long gold lamé gown smiled prettily at the camera. Where did he know her from, a TV show? Country music television perhaps? He didn't have time to think about, as someone signaled him.

"Thank you all for coming here tonight, your contributions will make a difference to charities all over America. Now join me in a hearty welcome for that hunk in denim, that gorgeous sexy heart breaker, that *Mr. Right*, Colton Wright and his band, the Blonde Strangers!"

The applause was thunderous, cheers and whistles from all sides. Colton loped out onto the stage waving and bowing. The cheers and whistles got louder and louder and just would not end. The stage lights came up and his band was ready with their instruments. The spotlight hit him, he gave them their cue and from then the music took over.

Colton was determined to give the show of his life. Nashville was still his city, his turf—if not for long anymore. He knew he was giving the TV crew a hard time running from one end of the stage to the other, into and out of the first rows of seating. At one point he took a flying leap and slid right over the top of the highly polished black grand piano, stretching long and hopping off the other end. He climbed up in the rigging, hopped up on a speaker—in short he was the Colton they all knew and loved.

He knew he had his audience right where he wanted them, the noise was deafening and even in the last rows they were on their feet, singing and screaming. At the end of the second number, when he did his customary hat toss into the audience, they almost came to blows in rows seven and eight. This was his crowd, his audience, and he belonged to them for this night. He spread his arms wide and let their applause and cheers wash over him, his eyes were closed and he absorbed their energy like the warmth from a sun.

The stage lights dimmed to a single spot focused on him and then wandered away to the stage entrance. Skip Jones on keyboard plinked away at a quiet little tune that would eventually become the intro to *Paradise*.

Colton stood in the shadows, waiting for his special introduction. This was the part they hadn't been able to rehearse, they would have to pretty much wing it. The TelePrompTr at his feet had gone strangely dark and the audience hushed, waiting.

Then, into the spotlight stepped Robert Masters and his beautiful wife, introducing themselves and thanking everyone for coming. Colton still waited, reaching for his spare hat that someone was handing him through the shadows. The spotlights glittered and winked blindingly off Stephanie Masters' diamonds, all real no doubt.

"Miss Parker, Miss Parker they need you on the stage right now!"

"Now? I'm not supposed to be on until…"

"Never mind that, someone got sick and had to go throw up, you're a pro aren't you? Just come on out and wing it, you're our only available host right now.

"Wait, what am I going to…"

"Just read it off the TelePrompTr—quick. You only have a few seconds, follow me."

Reanne hurried to follow the retreating stagehand. Something was wrong here, desperately wrong. These things didn't happen at well-planned events like this, but for the moment she had no choice but to go along or embarrass herself.

On the stage Stephanie Masters turned to her famous husband.

"You know Robert, I really have to thank you for bringing Colton Wright here tonight. I have to admit I have a special fondness for him."

"Oh do you now? So what's your favorite song?"

"Right now, I would have to say his new song, the lead off single of the new album, that would be *Paradise*. There's just one thing I've always wondered about, Robert."

"How he gets into those pants?"

Laughter and cheers in the audience.

"Well, yes, that too. But what I always wondered was what *Paradise* would sound like as a duet between a man and a woman."

"Well that's an interesting question Stephanie, but I think I can help you there."

"You can?"

"I think so. You see, very few people know that *Paradise* had been recorded as a duet before, but it's never been released in public. So tonight, for the very first time, here it is. Especially for you Stephanie and, of course, for all of our guests tonight, Mr. Colton Wright and the lovely Miss Reanne Parker, doubling up on *Paradise Found*."

Colton froze where he stood as the spotlight captured him in its magic circle, then split in two and picked out the stage entrance. Someone gave Reanne a little shove and she followed the beam of light as if mesmerized. They both ended up face to face in a golden circle, they both heard Skip Jones segue into the song intro, signal them and start over. The professional entertainer in Colton took over. They had missed their first cue, it was not going to happen again.

On the second cue he was ready, he raised the microphone and his voice found the words to the song he had performed a hundred times live. His mind, his thoughts, his emotions in turmoil, he still sang, his eyes never leaving Reanne's.

She heard her own voice harmonize with his as if they had practiced it like this all along. None of her thoughts were making any sense, there was just Colton— his eyes on hers, his mouth singing the words she had heard in her heart so often. And here she was beside him.

Their voices combined and, as she sang, something inside her unfolded, a passion, an emotion that had been vibrating on the inside for so long finally broke free. It was like an unfolding of wings, a spreading, a soaring.

"Your magic makes my word go round,
You are my only paradise found."

Suddenly a power she had never felt before went through her, shot from her to Colton and back. It hummed and resonated between and around them. She looked up and she saw the same feeling reflected in the blue depths of his eyes.

Her arms reached out for him at the same time as his did—their voices caressed and loved each other. Their hands touched and held, and they finished the last verse holding on to each other. Her voice almost broke on that last high note, from the intense emotion of the moment, but they both knew in their hearts that this song never had and never would be performed with more passion than here tonight.

For a moment the entire auditorium was silent. Five thousand people held their collective breath and not a sound was heard. Then someone started clapping and another pair of hands joined in and another and another and then everyone in the great hall stood applauding, whistling, screaming—the noise was thunderous.

Someone started it and, like flames in the darkness, people started pulling out their lighters and holding them aloft like candles. It was a sea of cheering and light out there.

Colton saw nothing but a pair of green eyes looking into his, vulnerable and scared—and without thinking he bent to kiss Reanne.

The applause that had just started to taper off built again to a thundering crescendo. Reanne felt like she was in a dream. Only this time it was no dream. She had performed again, in front of a crowd. She had stepped out there without thinking about what she was doing and it had worked, it had worked! She had given one of the grandest performances with Colton, and she felt drunk with the success of it. They were applauding. An auditorium full of people applauding for them—and Colton kissing her—she felt like a world had suddenly opened, like the clouds had drifted away and it was sunshine that was shining down on her instead of the hot glare of the spotlights.

She threw her arms around Colton and hugged him as fiercely as she could, she never wanted to let go of this magician who had surely made all of this possible. Colton straightened and waved at the cheering crowd, there was just no stopping them so he took of his hat and threw it into the crowd for the second time tonight.

"Thank you," he heard Reanne whisper, "Thank you for making all this come true, thank you for giving this to me."

He shook his head almost imperceptibly, still waving at the crowd. "It wasn't me, sweetheart, it was all you, believe me. You did it all yourself, it was inside you all along, all you had to do was let it come out."

He bent until his lips nearly touched her ear. "Don't ever leave me again," he said fiercely, and she shook her head.

"I won't, I promise."

Colton bowed and waved a few more times and then took Reanne by the hand and led her backstage, they could still hear Stephanie and Robert Masters talking about romance and fairy tales coming true.

"Ken will have a lot to answer for," Colton said, but without malice, "So does Jack."

"Cole?"

"Reanne?"

"I'm so sorry I made this so hard on us, that it took me so long to figure out where I belong. Cole, don't ever, ever even think about leaving me again. I've been so miserable without you."

"I won't, I've played every honky tonk that would have me just to forget about you—and it hasn't worked."

He hugged her so tightly she could hardly breathe. "You absolutely knocked them dead out there sweetheart. I knew you could do it. I knew you belonged in the spotlights."

"I belong with you. I could only sing because you were there, I would have died out there by myself."

"Reanne? Would you like to try singing duets for a while?"

"With you? Yeah, I think I could handle that. I could do anything with you."

"How about forever?"

Reanne looked at him, thunderstruck. Here was everything she had ever wanted, wrapped up in one question, all she had to do was trust fate and take that one giant leap. *Do it'* a little voice in her said, but that other little voice doubted, *what if you don't measure up, what if you still aren't good enough?*

She saw Cole and the question in his eyes—she knew that he had overcome ten long years of doubts and a broken heart to find love with her again, She knew that he had swept away all of his own doubts and fears and broken his own vow to never love again. He offered her himself and only himself.

Suddenly she knew that the road ahead would not always be as smooth and as glamorous as it had been tonight, there might be tough times ahead and, once in a while, they both might feel like giving up, but they would be together. In the short time that they had known each other they had overcome so many obstacles, so many stones placed in their way, she knew that if she didn't take this chance she would regret it for a lifetime.

With the cheers of the crowd still ringing in her ears she smiled her brightest smile at him.

"Yes, Colton David Wright," she said. "I might be breaking thousands of women's hearts, but I'll sing duets with you—forever. For the rest of our lives if you'll forgive me and if you'll have me."

Ten months later a story appeared in The Nashville Courier, Entertainment section.

'After much speculation and expectation Colton and Reanne Wright released their first album of duets together today. *So Good Together* is a beautiful collection of upbeat dance songs and soulful ballads that celebrate life and its journey. The two voices are a rare match together and this album is a treat for every country music fan. The newlyweds are celebrating their album release in Hawaii, which is said to hold special memories for both of them. One can only hope that *So Good Together* is only the first of many such releases.

Watch out Colton, if you can't find your duet partner, it might be because she's a little busy with her first solo release, due out in December of this year, *My Own Road*. Congratulations Colton and Reanne.'

Coming soon in the *SoundMaster Romance Series*

Long Way Home

Sometimes you have to be careful what you wish for. In a moment of temporary abandon Victoria Masters, heir to the vast Masters Enterprises conglomerate, and Calder Knight, the mysterious lead singer of *Knight Rider*, meet innocently in a Nashville park—where both of them impetuously decide to make a break from their pasts and, suddenly, Vicky Masterson and Cal Duncan are born. Not realizing each has done the same, their lives quickly become very, very complicated.

A Broken Wing

Rena Shayne has a solid spot at the top of the charts as a country music star. She should be able to sit back and enjoy everything her fame has to offer, but a celebrity stalker is driving her into a gilded prison. The one person who manages to bring her out of the constant hiding is the handsome stranger she meets on a plane—despite the warnings from her managers and friends that Austin Taggert may in fact be the stalker.

As time goes on all the signs begin to point towards Austin. Why is he always there when the stalker strikes, why is he caught with the stalker's trademark flower in his hand and why is it his gun that was used in an attempt on Rena's life? When Rena gets kidnapped everyone has to work together to find her...before it's too late!

How Do I Live

Lynne Wells seems to have it all. An enviable job in music management—the glittering world of Nashville literally lies at her feet. Behind the façade, however, her life is crumbling, as her husband, Wayne, turns abusive and starts systematically ruining everything she has worked for. The only constant in her life remains Brady, the charismatic musician who wandered into her life one day.

The attraction between them is undeniable, but can it overcome the memories from the past?

Fool Hearted Memory

Raylon Carter has just made the biggest mistake of his life, he has gambled away his band, his best friend and the woman he loves.

Kendra Waters has a fair idea of the man she will one day commit herself to, and Raylon Carter is definitely nothing like the image in her mind.

But life is precious and fragile. Through a near tragedy, Kendra and Raylon come to realize that some things are more important than fame, success or a career. If they have the courage to forgive each other, then perhaps love has the power to undo what they have done and to heal their hearts.

All Access **Registration Form**

If you would like to receive a free copy of the first chapter of the next book in the SoundMaster Series, **Long Way Home**, and other freebies, please register your email address at this link:

SoundMaster *All Access*-Sign-up.

Playlist for the music from Guitars & Cadillacs
https://open.spotify.com/playlist/71ymCTx5YJP
zroWBg4gWHF?si=6ba9447454a64aa7

We hope you have enjoyed this story, and thank you for your purchase.

Dedicated to my dog angels, Worf, Midnight, Dakota and Harley. They'll always live in my heart.
Thanks to Dwight Yoakam for the words and music that inspired the characters who live on these pages and for his best quote:
"Listen to the voices in your head"
I'm still listening!

www.ingramcontent.com/pod-product-compliance
Lightning Source LLC
Chambersburg PA
CBHW070112120726
47909CB00002B/580